The
Enchanted Opal

By Alan R. Smith

Adapted from
Enchantments of the Haglady: Ancient Lands, Wonders.
By Alan R. Smith

ISBN
978-1-954932-05-0 (Hardcover)
978-1-954932-04-3 (Paperback)
978-1-954932-03-6 (eBook)

To Aya and Simone
Seek challenges, and you will be rewarded
with a life of enchantments.

Acknowledgements

To Kathryn Hagmann for inspiration, and her compelling request for me to put pen to paper.

My sincere APPRECIATION goes to Irene Wiener who began as a "beta" and gave more than I asked for giving clarity to my words.

Also, a special THANKS to Leigh Fisher for "smoothing out" my rough edges.

And of course, to the LOVE OF MY LIFE, my extraordinary wife, Hunya, for without her continued support throughout our five decades together, my life would have been empty.

Part One

Kathryn, Teresa, and Abbadon

Chapter 1

New York City

A Ninth Birthday, the Watch, and the Perfume

A figure dressed in a red tunic, his face shadowed under a hood, watched from a city park as an SUV slowed to a stop in front of a New York City residence.

Kathryn opened the car door, her sneakers finding a city sidewalk, began to run, paused. She shivered, glanced at the park as if she expected to see someone. The red figure was shielded from her sight by a stand of oaks and maples.

As quickly as she had stopped, Kathryn once again dashed ahead of her parents, Amelia and Greg Pangburn, unlatching the wrought iron gate to the grey slate walkway leading to her grandparents' brownstone home.

Greg was taking packages out of the back seat when he heard Amelia gasp.

He looked up; she was rubbing her arms, "Amelia, you okay?"

"Fine, just felt a chill," her eyes turned to the other side of the street.

Greg, amusingly questioned, "A chill? It must be 80 degrees."

Amelia turning back, "Let's catch up with Kathryn." Again, Amelia looked to the park.

The short path led to the front porch. Draped above the arched entrance was a bright multi-color rainbow banner: *"Happy Birthday Kathryn and Grandma!"* Every event at the Hastings' house involved a ceremony of some sort—her grandmother loved merrymaking.

Kathryn's grandfather had guided her hand when she scratched a heart and her initials "KIP" for **K**athryn **I**sabella **P**angburn into the pathway's wet cement. Her mom had chosen Kathryn saying, "it easily rolls off the tongue" with the rest of her name. Isabella was Grandma's first name and her maiden name was Cappelli. The Cappelli family left their home in 1884 from Villetta Barrea, Italy and arrived in New York

City two weeks later to establish a new life in America.

Grandma Hastings always called the three cement steps rising from the walkway to the porch, "the stoop." Most folks on the block went to Grandma Hastings for advice on all sorts of subjects: recipes, clothing, raising their children, and gardening. Grandma was famous for her honeysuckle vines and garden vegetables.

Grandma told Kathryn, "In my day, all you needed to do was sit on the stoop each night for an hour or so, and you could know everything about everybody; all you had to do was listen." Kathryn spent a lot of time sitting with her grandparents on the front stoop during school vacations. Visiting New York City was a sensory adventure. Around every corner one could find new sights, sounds, smells, and tastes. New York was the home to every culture on earth since New York is the center of international trade—and sometimes, it seemed there were "visitors from outer space" on the streets of the greatest city in the world.

Oh, it was a glorious day for a party, one of those days everyone would remember for years to come; the sun shone in a cloudless sky heating the mid-June air. The trees, whose late-spring buds had just turned from flowers to tender leaves, were showing off their many shades of green to shoppers scurrying to complete their morning tasks. Tourists enjoying the city's museums and shows, as well as artists, musicians, and other New Yorkers, maybe out for an afternoon stroll in Central Park—a day of fresh air mixed with the anticipation of surprise.

Bounding up the steps, Kathryn lingered before the open, carved wooden entrance doors, momentarily captivated—the chiseled panels now in shapes she had never noticed before, yet, familiar, though not knowing why.

The Pangburns gave Kathryn a guided nudge through the doorway breaking her ponderings. The townhouse was filled with relatives and friends for the grandest party since Kathryn's parents' wedding reception. This party was a combination birthday celebration for Kathryn and Grandma Hastings; their birthdays fell on the same day. Kathryn often wondered why Grandma's age was never discussed; she seemed much younger than her stories would suggest.

Grandma Hastings stood just inside the room anticipating their arrival. Kathryn and Grandma not only shared a passion for baseball, they loved royal blue, anything to do with plants, shopping for clothes, pepperoni, peanut butter and strawberry jelly on rye bread, the smell of honeysuckle, and along with Kathryn's mother, they shared the same color eyes, the bright brown of ground cinnamon—a neighbor thought their eyes were like a dark shade of amber—Kathryn had a touch of green surrounding her brown eyes. The three of them had curly hair the color of milk chocolate fudge. The generational resemblance of Kathryn, Amelia, and Grandma was uncanny. Most of all, they loved to spend time together, just to laugh at each other's silly jokes.

Wrapping her arms around Kathryn, Grandma asked, "How is my Kathryn today?"

"Grandma, your house smells delicious!"

"Great neighbors who are great cooks."

Hugs and kisses for Amelia and Greg. "Amelia, I love your dress. The vines with their soft yellow flowers are enchanting."

"Amelia said you would," interjected Greg, "since you have them covering your back fence."

"I do love those vines."

"Grandma, my dad can't figure out how they grow all winter?"

"I have special honeysuckle food, an old family secret," looking up at Amelia, "Someday, which may be soon, I'll pass the formula to you." Amelia responded with a hidden scowl only her mother understood.

Taking Kathryn's hand, Grandma led the way to the back yard passing through the bustling kitchen of friends filling dishes and arranging platters.

As they stepped onto the patio, Grandpa Hastings greeted them with a wide, welcoming smile. His first duty was to embrace Kathryn who stepped ahead of the others to squeeze him. "At last, the birthday girl has arrived."

The excited Kathryn observed, "Grandpa, I think most of New York City is in your backyard."

Grandpa pointed to the long and wide backyard table, "Hungry?"

The aroma of roasted turkey (both Grandma and Kathryn's favorite meal) followed the tray carried past them. All was ready for the afternoon banquet. Mrs. Mizzy brought her famous macaroni and meatballs; Mr. Zell, who owned an Italian grocery, provided a large variety of yellow and white cheeses, black and green olives, sweet and sour pickles, and roasted red and orange peppers. Other visitors had prepared scrumptious specialties and drinks for the bash.

Kathryn ran down onto the grass and wiggled her way to the table; she studied the options before her.

In the middle of the cloth covered plywood table, a magnificent centerpiece captured everyone's attention; without a doubt, it was the grandest cake anyone had ever seen. Grandpa Hastings stood with a big smile, proud of his creation—the cameras did not stop flashing as he described his sugar and flour masterpiece. Grandpa's bakery had been opened by his grandfather 72 years ago, and despite that long-standing history, he admitted that this was the "cake of cakes."

The cake was over two feet tall. Grandpa Hastings had worked hours on this special-order wedding cake. The reason the cake was in the Hastings' home and not at the wedding reception, was that the bride, dressed in her beautiful white wedding gown, had changed her mind halfway down the church aisle—most of the guests in the church pews agreed with the bride.

The cake was a replica of Yankee Stadium. It had the well-known stadium façade, a mint green baseball diamond with root beer candy bases, chocolate base paths, and with blue pinstripes framing the outside edges. Grandpa went so far as to put the numbers of the Yankees' starting lineup in their positions on the field—even the Mets fans had to admit the cake was a work of art.

With a bit of work before the party, Grandpa Hastings replaced the names of the wedding couple on the scroll in center field and replaced them with Grandma's and Kathryn's names.

Grandma stood alongside Kathryn who had just stuffed her mouth with a pignoli cookie.

"Kathryn, your mother is concerned your dreams often interrupt your sleep. Is that true?"

Greg and Amelia walk up behind Grandma and Kathryn. Amelia listens intently.

"Grandma, sometimes I wake up scared, thinking the people and places in my dreams are real"

"My dear, there are many mysteries to uncover in **our** world."

Amelia abruptly positions herself and Greg between grandma and granddaughter, taking Grandma to the side. "This is not the time."

"Okay. When?"

"She's too young," Amelia, intent on making her point, "She is Not ready for this."

"Amelia, she dreams. You understand what is happening. She must know."

"Why?"

Grandpa's voice interrupts Amelia and Grandma. "Amelia, bring your mom over here. Kathryn, where are you? Oh, okay. Greg, please lead my granddaughter over to the cake."

The many visitors surround the birthday girls.

To make it special, nine candles were placed as flagpoles for Kathryn to blow out when making her wish, and for Grandma Hastings, there was a single candle which looked like a golden flagpole. One of the visitors called Grandpa the "Michelangelo of baking," and everyone agreed.

With a match in hand, Grandpa was ready to light the candles, "Ladies, make a wish!"

Kathryn grabs Grandma's sleeve, tugs down and whispers, "I wish to go to the life of my dreams."

Grandma returns the whisper, "My dear, I am certain your wish will come true."

"How can you know?"

"A grandmother knows there are many unanswered questions for you to experience."

Amelia breaks up the conversation, "The candles are waiting for you to stop talking." Amelia raises her hand for the crowd to count, "Ready! Three, two, one!"

Kathryn and Grandma blow out the candles. Everyone cheers. Grandma winks at Kathryn, looks up seeing Amelia watching, gives her a wink.

Greg takes center stage, announces, "Let's open presents!"

The party was a huge success. Everyone participated doing silly party dances, sang with Grandpa's band—he played the accordion—and all agreed Grandma Hastings threw the best parties.

Of the many gifts Kathryn and Grandma Hastings received, Kathryn got four tickets to Yankee Stadium and a book about the life of a real princess who lived in a faraway land over 900 years ago, while Grandma unwrapped a box filled with garden tools and seeds, and a bowl overflowing with wooden kitchen utensils, spices, and jams.

Grandma was overcome by another gift; she could not stop crying. It was a cruise to Alaska from Grandpa Hastings. She would often say it was the only place on earth she had not seen—which everyone assumed was an exaggeration, but Kathryn thought differently. She had heard her mom, grandmother, and a special visitor tell very amazing stories.

Kathryn's favorite gift was the box with a delicate red bow from her parents. Inside was a Minnie Mouse watch. She had seen the perfect watch, this watch, New Year's Eve on Main Street, Disney World while on vacation months earlier. At the time, her parents had said they wished they could buy it for her, but it was not in their budget. They somehow bought it without her knowing and saved it as a surprise for this very day. Just like her grandmother, tears rolled down her face.

But even the greatest of parties must end, so, after dessert was served, Grandpa Hastings' cake, along with ice cream, coffee and tea, folks headed for home as the sun began to set.

Amelia interrupted a story Grandpa was telling about the day he met Grandma, "Kathryn, time to head home. Your father is concerned about the weekend traffic."

Grandpa Hastings added, "Even the greatest of parties must end. Your parents have work and our customers will be at the bakery door early."

No one knew what was to come. Grandma and Grandpa Hastings would need to leave their brownstone apartment on New York's Westside, just off 79th and Broadway, to live in their daughter and son-in-law's house in Toms River, New Jersey. They would move into Kathryn's home one month after her ninth birthday party.

Chapter 2

The Accident

Sadly, Kathryn and her parents began to say their goodbyes to Grandma and Grandpa Hastings shortly after the last guest closed the entrance gate behind them.

The Pangburns and grandparents walked to the car.

"Wait a moment," blurted out Grandma Hastings, "just wait one moment, I will be right back."

They waited, knowing what was going to happen before they could get on the road. Grandma Hastings always had food for them to take home. A minute was all it took for her to run into the house and return with a large Macy's shopping bag in one hand and balancing a box with the other. Grandma rested the bakery box containing part of the Yankee dugout on the seat next to Kathryn.

She handed the bag to Amelia. Grandma not wanting to be heard, walked Amelia to the other side of the car. "You must be watchful. I sense the past is upon us, upon Kathryn."

Amelia's voice reveals her concern, "I felt it too."

"Does Greg know?"

"No."

Grandma forced the discussion, "You must!" Taking a moment to decide what to say next, "I told your father just after we were married. Of course, he thought I was taking my dreams too seriously, but he grew to understand."

Firm in her decision, Amelia answered, "I can't bring myself to tell him. Especially after all these years."

A gold chain around her neck draped low under her blouse. Amelia's hand pressed against an object in the center of her chest, said, "This will keep us safe. And with **her** close by, **he** will keep his distance."

Amelia embraced her mother, confidently smiled. "It will be okay." She hugged her father and got in the car.

When Greg started the engine, Kathryn, with half her body

extended out the back window, yelled, "Hope to see you in two weeks." She waved goodbye and blew a kiss to her grandparents—it was caught by her grandfather's extended hand and placed on his cheek. Grandma walked to Kathryn.

"Grandma, I have a question to ask about my birthday wish."

Grandma responds, "Try to understand your dreams. You can't run away from them."

Amelia turns around in her seat, "Kathryn, we're leaving."

Kathryn continues, "I'll call when I get home." She drops in her sleep.

Amelia looks from Kathryn to Grandma with a nod of agreement.

The Pangburns drive down the street to their New Jersey home.

The trip home usually took about an hour and a half, and as Kathryn's father often said, "Sometimes two hours, depending on tunnel traffic."

On the New Jersey Turnpike, Mrs. Pangburn always wanted to take the car lanes, while Mr. Pangburn was sure the truck lanes were faster. He had driven a truck for a couple of years before he and Amelia "got hitched." He always felt a certain kinship with the road warriors behind the big steering wheels.

Enjoying the ride home, Kathryn could not stop talking about the special day's activities: all the people at the party, and she could not stop looking at the watch on her wrist or the cake box at her side.

"Can you believe how beautiful Grandpa's cake was?" She giggled to herself, "I ate second base."

Amelia began to look pale. Her hands felt clammy and her forehead sweaty. She moved her fingers to tightly surround the necklace under her blouse. In a weak voice, asked, "Greg, I'm not feeling well. Can we stop at the next rest area?"

Greg looks over at Amelia who is breathing heavily, asks, "What is it?"

"I'm not sure, but we need to stop."

"Okay, I'll slip over, the rest area is just ahead."

Greg pressed his blinker to change lanes. From seemingly nowhere, a dark grey tractor-trailer comes within inches alongside the Pangburn's car.

Kathryn and Amelia sensing peril look out the window, the truck now dangerously close. Amelia fearfully warns, "Greg! The truck!"

Greg accelerates to avoid a collision. The truck keeps pace. Greg glances up at the truck.

In the truck's passenger seat sat a red-hooded passenger. His yellow eyes and brown smile peered down at the alarmed Greg.

The truck slammed into the side of the Pangburn's car forcing it off the road, tumbling over and over down a grassy embankment—in an instant, Kathryn's life changed.

The Pangburn's car rested on its roof, all three passengers strapped in their seats—not one of them moved.

Approaching the car is the red-hooded passenger from the truck which forced the Pangburns off the road.

It is Abbadon the Assassin!

He is centuries old, a time-traveler, who was once the influential vizier of Egypt to Queen Cleopatra. She banished him from her kingdom when she learned of his evil plan against her. Abbadon knowing the magic of her enchanted opal has journeyed though time waiting for the moment it could be his, to change history, and become Pharaoh of Egypt and the world.

His yellow pupils are aglow, and his yellow-brown teeth exposed as his cruel smile widens. The gem which Amelia held safely in her grip was just steps away from his possession. Suddenly, he stops, vexed, furious, his plan failed.

A lady with curly brown hair, soft brown eyes, in a long purple dress fringed with yellow flower petals, a purple cape, and matching wide-brimmed hat, comes between the car and Abbadon. She faces him. He steps back.

She whirls, kneels next to the car, pulls Kathryn from the wreckage. The lady next stretches her arm through the broken window releasing Amelia's fingers still firmly wrapped around the pendant dangling on the golden chain. She gently lifts the chain over Amelia's neck, easing her hand back through the shattered window. Holding it over Kathryn for Abbadon to see, the lady rebuking him, commands, "BE GONE!"

His smile becomes an evil scowl, but he turns away.

The lady breathes, "You are safe."

Kathryn's eyes open momentarily to a blurred vision of a woman's figure at her side. Her nose inhales, wiggles at the scent.

Sirens are blaring. Police and First Aid responders pour over and down the green landscape.

At the Hospital

As Kathryn begins to come out of her sleep, her body hurts. She remembers tumbling in the car; her father and mother calling out her name, blackness—then a woman at her side. The woman from her dreams.

Her eyes blurry, her mind perplexed. Kathryn begins to understand, and her confusion elevates. The first sound to alert her of calamity is a voice over the call system. Kathryn realizes she is in a hospital.

The previous year, when her mom was diagnosed with a kidney problem the family spent many hours in and out of the hospital. Kathryn had been to other hospitals, and each shared the similar sounds and smells of routine and emergency medicine. Kathryn had visited her friend Nick who had an operation when he was four, and then again when his sister Nelly fell ill with Rocky Mountain Spotted Fever the year after that. She wondered why it was so hard to invent an air freshener for hospitals. This might be a subject to share with her best friend Samantha—they had been in the same classes since kindergarten, and always shared new ideas.

As all the clues came together, she understood her situation. Kathryn's eyes darted around the room; it was a pale blue box. She saw sun-bleached blue and gold curtains, and on the walls were wide white stripes painted to resemble foamy ocean waves breaking at odd intervals around the room. There was a very oddly shaped chair with sports logos in gold and silver against a worn green background. The elongated "S" chair must have been made to accommodate sleeping guests or a comfortable way for patients to relax, and hangers in an open closet. Nothing in the room seemed to match.

Her alarm surfaced when she thought, "I'm the patient."

"Mom! Dad!

Now fully awake, she became scared as pain intensified in her right arm. She reached for the pain with her left hand and touched the intervenes line crossing her body.

Suddenly panicked, she blurted out, "Somebody, come here, there is something stuck in my arm!"

She heard two voices outside her door. Recognizing one as her grandmother's, she yelled, "Grandma!"

Pain immediately followed her cry.

When her grandmother came into the room from the hallway, tears of relief clouded Kathryn's vision, making the situation even more frightening. She reached out and cried, "Grandma!"

Grandma Hastings moved very quickly to her side, reaching over Kathryn to push the red button on the rail of the bed. Kathryn looked at her grandmother's eyes, which were normally incredibly beautiful, but now, they were very red—red and burning from salty tears.

Kathryn promptly figured out that her grandmother had pressed the emergency call button to the nurse's station, which made her more petrified because she knew **she was the emergency**.

She looked down and began checking her body from toes to head— she didn't get very far. She was tired, her body hurt in more than one place, it seemed each minute brought more pain, and she was unsure of her situation.

She was becoming groggy. As she began to move, she screamed out in distress, and reached for the two broken ribs on her right side. The quick motion forced the intravenous tube move again, causing more burning. Luckily, the tape holding the tube in place was doing its job. Kathryn jerked her arm and the metal stand holding a clear plastic bag, containing whatever it was the doctors wanted to go into her body, fell against her legs.

Kathryn alternated between crying, fear and unknowing. The throbbing from her ribs, shoulder, and hand, and the general confusion of the moment, was more than she could stand.

"Kathryn, dear," Grandma pleaded, "wait until the nurse gets here before you move. Honey, please, the nurse will be here soon."

At that moment, a nurse and an assistant came into the room, followed closely by Grandpa Hastings. The lead nurse went right to Kathryn. "Missy, you have yourself all tangled. You can help by relaxing and leaving it all up to me." Kathryn's grandmother moved away from the bed as the nurses began untangling the tubes.

"Relax," Kathryn thought, what a stupid word. She sobbed, "Relax. Why are you using that word? Where is my mom? And where's dad?" It was impossible for her to relax considering the pain, the surprise of waking up in the hospital, and her memory of what had happened the night before becoming clear.

"Where's Mom, where's Dad?" Kathryn was shivering in fear.

The nurse and her grandparents exchanged heart-wrenching glances in a very strange way.

Chapter 3

"Two Years Later" Grandparents

It had been a couple of years, almost to the day since Kathryn lost her parents. The ache in her heart and the painful memory of her ninth birthday remained in her thoughts every day. It was a wound, a weight on her heart, with which Kathryn learned to live, and over time, she had been able to manage the sense of loneliness and loss of her parents by keeping busy with her friends, activities at school, Girl Scouts, and soccer. She was coping with her loss by having Samantha at her side and with the love of her adoring grandparents.

Since the accident, her grandparents had been with Kathryn every day. Three busy weeks had been spent in the Hastings' apartment preparing to leave. Kathryn could tell moving was difficult for them. They had grown up in that neighborhood and had lived together in same house for the past forty-two years. The Hastings had a life filled with many friends, family, and a business that added to the fabric of the neighborhood. Grandpa Hastings' nephew, ZiZi, ran the day-to-day operations, and his sister's husband, George, had been doing most of the baking for the past six years.

Grandpa and Grandma met in the bakery. Grandma said she would go to the *Hastings Bakery* every Sunday morning before church to buy Kathryn's great-grandpa's world-famous dark pumpernickel bread. Important people from New York were customers at the store. In fact, some folks recalled that Marilyn Monroe and Joe DiMaggio had been regular customers. Their picture, taken with Kathryn's great-grandfather, Harold Hastings, along with other NYC celebrities who stopped by the store, still hung on the wall. They wrote on the photo: "To Harold H. Our Favorite Baker," and under their signatures, Joe wrote, "September 15, 1954." Grandpa Hastings said they had been in the store many times while Marilyn was filming her most famous movie, *The Seven Year Itch.*

Grandma Hastings had been going to the store since she was

fourteen, and she said Grandpa never noticed her until she was seventeen. He always delivered his version of the story a bit differently than Grandma's account, telling, "I was just waiting for her to grow up and notice me. I used to go out of my way to wait on her." Grandpa recalled the only words she would say to him were, "Cappelli's order please." Continuing, after a pause, and a smile at Grandma Hastings, he said, "Then, after paying for the order, she would run out of the store before I could even start a conversation. I knew she was interested in me, but she was very shy," with a confident smirk, " It was only a matter of time."

Grandma interrupted Grandpa and continued the story with a different twist on the facts, began, "There was only one counter-person in the store when I came in, late the day of my seventeenth birthday. The bakery was empty of customers, a rare occasion, and he, your grandpa, totally ignored me. I said, 'Excuse me, can you help me?' Your grandfather looked around, as if he heard something, but looked right past me. I repeated my question in a louder voice, thinking he was as deaf as he was blind. 'I would like to pick up my order if it is not too much trouble?' He looked me straight in the eye with a very mischievous grin, and somewhat of an uppity tone in his voice, and being the smart aleck he was, inquired, 'I'm sorry, did you say something?'"

Grandma Hastings, trying to make an angry face at Grandpa, but failing, described the rest of the story. "Now I am sure my face was getting red. So I looked him square in the eye and said, 'Yes, I want to pick up the Cappelli order, the order we, I mean I, pick up every Sunday, the order I have been getting every Sunday for the past three years.'"

"He looked at me with a giant smile and whispered, 'You, can have your order, I mean the Cappelli order, and in fact you can have your order at no charge, and I will throw in an almond ring, if you let me take you to Sandy's Sweet Shoppe across the street as soon as I get off work. And, I'll pay for any sweetie dessert you like.'"

"I told him he could 'keep his order and he could throw it and the almond ring in the garbage can!' His face went pale—the boy who seconds before was so sure of himself! I walked out of the store.

But I gave a quick glance back through the window just to see his disappointed face one more time."

Grandma continued the story after an affectionate wink at Grandpa, "Well, when I returned to our apartment without the order, and was made to describe the incident in detail, Great-Grandma Cappelli took hold of my arm, walked me down the stairs of the apartment, and made me go with her back to the bakery. Great-Grandma went through the front door of the bakery alone, while I stood outside looking through the plate glass window. I was sure she was going to take his head off."

Kathryn could tell Grandma loved telling this story. Through her teasing smile, Grandma resumed, "I peeked through the corner of the window, hoping to see her give him 'a talking to,' but at the same time began to feel a little uneasy. I had to admit to myself, he was cute, and I started to feel sorry that I got him in trouble. But Great-Grandma Cappelli wanted to show him he could not flirt with me like that, probably the way he did with all the girls coming into the bakery." Grandma's story took a twist. "Anyway, my eyes could not believe what I saw. Your grandfather and Great-Grandma Cappelli were having a much-too-friendly conversation. He was flashing that big smile of his, and Great-Grandma laughed. All I could determine was she believed whatever lie he was telling her. I felt like running in and throwing something at him."

With a bit of attitude in her voice, and pointing at the former counter clerk, she made the story sound as if she were double-crossed by her mother. "Your future Grandpa Hastings and his future mother-in-law were gabbing for about five minutes. When she left the store, I figured they must have had some sort of agreement. So, out comes your Great-Grandma Cappelli with her order and an extra-large almond ring on top. I could not believe she listened to him—he talked his way out of trouble with a smile and a breakfast pastry! She walked over to me with the beginning of a grin taking shape on her lips and said, 'Isabella, go in and talk to that nice boy, and try using the manners you were taught, but somehow seem to have lost.'

"Well, I can tell you, I planned on going in, not with manners a young lady should have, but with an attitude. When I walked in, I looked for something to throw at him. The first things I saw were long loaves of Italian bread in a wicker basket in front of the counter. I walked over to the counter and wrapped my hand around one of those loaves, and the moment he smiled, as if he had just won a prize, I took a swing."

Laughing, Grandma Hastings finished the story by saying, "The bread broke in half when it hit his hard head, and all he could do was smile, and he has smiled at me every day since."

Grandpa stood and moved alongside Grandma Hastings to tell his favorite part of their encounter. "Well, she helped me close the store that afternoon, and off to the Sweet Shoppe we went."

Grandma added the last loving note, said, "We talked for two hours, and from that day on, except for Grandpa's service in the Marines during Vietnam, we have never been apart."

Chapter 4

Saturday: Just before Noon

"Three Hours Earlier"

The buzzing alarm clock awakened Kathryn. Knowing Saturday chores had to be accomplished and leaving herself plenty of time for the day's important meeting, she had set the alarm thirty minutes earlier than usual. Kathryn rolled out of bed and put on the clothes she readied the night before, then quickly brushed her teeth, washed her face, combed her hair, and headed downstairs, stepping over Chubby her black and rust striped cat.

As she entered the kitchen, a chorus of three singers greeted Kathryn with birthday wishes, "Happy Birthday to you…!" followed with hugs and kisses from her grandparents, Grandpa and Grandma Hastings, and a hug by her best friend Samantha, who was a regular visitor at the house every Sunday morning.

"Kathryn, I didn't want to miss your silly Hastings' birthday sing-along, so I told my mom I would run home right away after seeing you." Tapping her palm against her brain, "Oh yeah, both my parents wish you a great day. Okay, I'm going home." And with a roll of her eyes and a sing-song voice, "You know my mom is a clean freak, so I have to clean my room before I do anything else. So, I run the vacuum, take a couple of swipes with the dust cloth, and she's happy." Before she walked out the door, Samantha inquired, "Did Nelly and Nick tell you they saw the Haglady only four blocks from here yesterday afternoon?"

Grandma Hastings twisted on her seat to listen to the conversation.

Kathryn answered with a note of disappointment in her voice, "Am I the only kid who has not seen her?" Taking a moment, she continued, "I know you saw her two weeks ago, and a lot of kids have seen her on this side of the street. Why do you think she's been around here so often?"

Acting like a detective trying to connect clues of a puzzling case,

Samantha lifted her hand and stroked her chin, and after a moment of deep thought stated, "My friend, something is brewing, and we need to investigate."

"How can we search for someone we know nothing about?"

"That is a project we need to develop." Now remembering she had to go home, Samantha headed toward the screen door, waved, and with a quirky smile and a giggle looked to Kathryn, "See you at **high noon!**"

Kathryn was extremely excited, more energized about what was planned for the day with Samantha and her pals, than about her birthday. In fact, she had completely forgotten about turning eleven.

Grandma and Grandpa Hastings watched their granddaughter eat a larger than usual breakfast and listened as she gave them, what Samantha called, the "run-down" of her plans for the day. Kathryn felt pangs of uneasiness about not being forthcoming with all the details. She had never been untruthful with her grandparents, but she was going to stick to the plan. She assured them, "I'll be home way before dinner."

After completing her Saturday to-do list faster than expected, Kathryn ran upstairs—she always ran, almost never walked—gave Chubby, positioned at his favorite place outside Kathryn's bedroom door, a quick rub on the belly, just before stepping through her glass-beaded door. To pass the time before the adventure, she grabbed, *Anna of Byzantium,* a book about a princess in Constantinople she had had for some time but never got around to reading it until now. As Samantha, Kathryn's best friend, would say, it was almost "*Show Time.*"

Samantha always said, "Everyone needs to be ready for everything, because you never know what will happen, until it happens!"

Having three hours until *Show Time* on this first day of summer vacation, Kathryn flopped onto her beanbag chair, pulled the bookmarker back and began to read about Princess Anna and the Palace of Blachernae. She dozed off, her book resting on her lap.

Kathryn always dreamed. Her dreams were always of far-off places and people she could not have known—they were of places that once existed, persons of long ago.

A slight breeze through the open widow caused the curtains to ruffle. Kathryn sucked in a breath; her body stiffened in fear. Abbadon is standing before her. Despite her fear, she faces him. A lady's voice, "There is danger. Abbadon is near."

Kathryn shouts out from her dream, "Who are you?"

"You know who I am."

Terrified, Kathryn awakes, sits up expecting to see the figures of her dream. She is alone in her room and reaches for her phone, dials her best friend and classmate Samantha. Samantha is the smartest kid in her school—in fact, the teachers know she's smarter than them.

Samantha answers, "Hey lady!"

"Sam, I'm scared. I had another dream. It was him! And her again! Can you meet me?"

"Sure. Don't you know what time it is?"

Kathryn looked up at the Goofy clock on her wall.

"Oh my gosh. On my way."

She exploded off the chair, her body flying across the room as if shot from a cannon instantly realizing the special plan for this long-awaited day was in danger of failure, and worst of all, the possibility she might disappoint her friends, something she would not let happen. Those few seconds of sleep had become minutes—she must make her meeting—she bolted toward the door as a cheetah accelerates to catch its prey.

There was a sudden clamor of clinking purple and pink glass beads—some long and thin, others round, several with fascinating irregular shapes, a few smooth, while many had intricate designs fashioned into sparkling jewels to capture the sun's rays, propelling slivers of light in every direction. The beaded cords formed crystal columns, held in place by knotted yellow-gold colored threads. The glimmering strands were attached so tightly together at the top of the door each crystal was forced against the other. It was almost as if they were a single sheet of glass, but they were filaments of glass columns closely hanging side by side, a shimmering curtain alive with the sun's late morning rays. The sparkle of lights filled the bedroom and hallway with twinkling stars as Kathryn's hands cut a path in front of her when she bolted from her upstairs bedroom. She could still hear the beads colliding when she turned down the hallway.

Kathryn's feet began to give way as the hallway rug moved under her feet when she sidestepped over Chubby, the rust and black family cat sleeping on the hallway rug outside her bedroom. She caught her balance when, along with the rug and Chubby, slid to an abrupt stop as they crashed against the lavender and crème striped wallpaper.

She instantly determined there were far too many purple-carpeted steps to take if she was going to get out the door on time. She stretched her legs, taking two steps at a time, and then in a practiced airborne move, planted her left hand, then her right, firmly on the gleaming varnished wooden banister assisting the vault over the long descending oaken handrail avoiding the final three steps. For a moment, Kathryn was suspended in mid-air, her head only an inch away from touching the intricately crafted brass hallway chandelier. Gravity taking over, she began to drop, her arms out to her sides as a swan readies itself to land, and like that elegant bird, she prepared to make contact with the floor.

Her perfect vault ended in a flawless touchdown, one-foot landing next to the other, her bright red canvas and yellow-laced sneakers each making a high-pitched squeak upon impact when they touched on the black and white checkered linoleum floor. She was now perfectly positioned to continue her quest to meet her pals.

With shoulders squared—her feet and legs in the squatting position of an Olympic broad jumper—Kathryn let out a groan as her body lifted from the floor. She had practiced this maneuver many times before, but this time, she was determined to surpass her previous mark. She simultaneously thrust her arms from behind her back to the front of her body, aiding the forward explosion from both legs, and leaving her hands ready to open the front screen door exiting her grandparents' house on Audubon Drive.

She burst through the door, then speedily accelerated from the porch, down the newly paved driveway, and then she turned sharply onto the sidewalk maneuvering over and around all its familiar cracks and bumps. Her two-tone colored sneakers barely touched the ground as she picked up speed.

Chapter 5

The Friday Night Before: Samantha's Plan

Samantha had summoned the group of classmates to schedule a special meeting to take place Friday after dinner at their secret tree behind the school bus stop. She called it her "Tactical Meeting" to be sure everyone knew each step of the next day's event. Their planning session ran longer than any of them expected, mostly because Samantha made each person tell how they had prepared for the adventure. Samantha was quite a stickler for details.

Samantha always talked more like her engineer father than a kid. She always lectured her friends using a deeper voice, and her chin sticking out: "Attention to details is the difference between experiencing success and the other option, failure, which is not acceptable."

The classmates were familiar with Samantha giving orders. She was called "T2" in class by their teacher, Mrs. Burke, who considered Samantha the "second" teacher in the room.

With her usual authoritative manner, Samantha took charge of the Friday meeting. "We have one mission and one mission only—to be the first kids in our town on the circus grounds. We are going to do it before the circus opens." Pacing back and forth holding up a circus advertisement for the gang to see, and at the same time pointing to the gate time on the top of the brightly detailed cardboard, she proceeded with her directions. "We know the gates don't open until 5:00 PM tomorrow night, but we will be inside by1:00 PM and out by 2:00 PM."

Each of the schemers began to show some nervous energy about the plan now that the day they would sneak into the circus was just hours away.

The idea had jumped into Samantha's head the moment she saw the first advertisement two months earlier. She immediately tore down the cardboard poster, put it on the seat of her bike, rode home and wrote out a plan. The group's philosopher told Kathryn a week later,

"You must write down what you want to do, so you can *see* the plan as well as *think* the plan."

Samantha looked up and down the street to be sure no one was coming, giving a sense of danger to the collection of collaborators. Once she determined all was clear, Samantha continued with her strategy discussion. "Kathryn, tomorrow's birthday girl, who will finally be eleven years old, and I, as you know, have gone to inspect the circus grounds every day after school this week. We walked around the entire fenced-in area, and just as we suspected, the same access spot we found on Monday was still not gated this afternoon. That'll be our entryway to the circus backlot where the circus workers park their personal trailers, so a small section is left open for them to drive in and out."

Samantha looked at each of the conspirators. Once certain everyone was set for the adventure, she continued, "Now here is how we will do it. We meet at the bus stop at noon tomorrow to make sure there are no changes to the plan. At that point, we ride to the construction site next to Nick and Nelly's house because it is closest to the sneak-in location on the other side of the woods, drop our bikes there, and without stopping, quickly cut through the woods to the fence opening. Everyone at the circus will be busy getting ready for opening day. We will walk through without being noticed. If we are stopped, we act as if we are visiting Mrs. Jolly. She was in the ticket booth when Kathryn and I met her on Wednesday, and she said, 'Make sure you visit me on Saturday, I'll be working cotton candy.'"

Making sure everyone understood, she emphasized the last instructions: "**If questioned**, you say, 'We are friends of Mrs. Jolly, who told us to meet her at the cotton candy stand.'" She hesitated, made eye contact with the plotters, and then asked, "Everyone understand?"

Nick eagerly chimed in, "Sounds to me like we have a personal invitation to visit her."

With the beginning of a smile coming to her lips, Nelly kicked in, "It would be rude of us to ignore Mrs. Jolly's friendly invitation, especially since she is new to town."

Not one of the crew was going to change their mind; this was going to be the most fun any of them had ever had, EVER!

At the end of the meeting, each of the friends joined hands, placing one over the other in a solemn pledge to be on time. The meeting ended as Samantha said, "Get ready to synchronize," she paused, looking to see that everyone had their watches or cell phones in hand. "In ten seconds, it will be 5:00 PM," she started the countdown: "Five, Four, Three, Two, One, 5:00 PM!"

Samantha looked at everyone, and said, "Remember, it is always better to be a lot early than a little late—see you tomorrow."

As if on order, the group stood, jumped on their bikes, and headed home. Kathryn, Samantha, Nick, and Nelly rode in the direction of their houses, none of them sure they would be able to sleep that night.

Chapter 6

How to Get Your Parents to Say, "YES!"

They had been scheming for three weeks to make "Circus Saturday" a special day. It was the perfect way to begin summer vacation--have a **kids only** trip. They left no part of their day unplanned, discussing every possible option that could cause the plan to fail. They considered younger and older brothers and sisters, their morning chores, what their parents had scheduled, and in Kathryn's case, her grandparents' daily routines.

The first part of the undertaking was to casually mention the subject a day or two earlier to parents. Samantha called it "floating the idea."

Kathryn's best friend, Samantha, had many ideas on many subjects, and spent a lot of time thinking, not just for herself, but for her friends. A result of one such discussion with Kathryn was about a person's first name. Samantha could not understand why parents gave their child a name, and then chose to use a shortened version or some nickname. This applied to her as well as others. For some reason, her parents only wanted to use the first three letters of her name and called her "Sam." Did they think this saved them time? Did they consider someone listening to them might think she was a boy? A few months ago, Samantha called her parents to have a meeting after dinner—her family had meetings after dinner. She presented her argument on names, and her parents said they would try to use "Samantha" in the future. It took time, but Samantha's family followed her request.

Each of the single-minded plotters was to introduce the idea at home to determine if their always-inquisitive parents would object to a vacation day with friends to start the summer. Samantha was perplexed why parents had so many questions about subjects that are not important. Why couldn't they accept that eleven-year-olds are just about *grownups* and needed to think on their own and make decisions?

Samantha expressed her frustration at the meeting, saying, "Heck, we will be twelve next year, and twelve is almost a teenager, and a thirteen-year-old is almost an adult." All of them wholeheartedly agreed with Samantha's point of view.

The group thought of Samantha as its philosopher, probably because Samantha told them she was their philosopher. She was always concocting some situation or pondering an idea. She explained the point of introducing the concept without really asking their parents for permission was to make sure they did not get a "No" answer. Samantha constantly advised the group on how to talk to parents. She reminded her friends, "Always be sure you control the question and answer situation, otherwise, you are almost certain to get the exact opposite of what you want."

Samantha educated the group about the perfect circumstances when asking permission for any special situation. If it appeared that their parents were positive, that would be great. If not, one of Samantha's techniques to be employed was the use of tears. They would need to determine the degree of real or fake tears, depending on their acting skills, to get what they wanted. "Tears are important," she instructed. She coached them on how to "tear up" if necessary, to help sell their parents on the adventure.

Samantha wanted to be sure they understood each important parent point, "Never ask your mothers first. Mothers "actually listen" to every word you say, and sometimes they know what you are not saying. Be sure to ask your father, and the best time to ask him is when he is in the middle of a busy home project. Watch his face. When the project is proving difficult, this is your chance to strike. You walk up and quickly ask your question. Fathers say, 'Yes, of course dear,' because they really don't listen, but do not want to seem uncaring."

Kathryn made a point to check with all the plotters the week before to find out who could take part in the plan.

The *buzz* on Samantha's phone meant Kathryn had just sent a message. The text read: "EVERYBODY is IN!!!!"

Chapter 7

The Circus

It was Saturday, the circus crews were busy early in the day getting ready to open the gates on time. Circus managers had earlier meetings at town hall explaining to the mayor their planned use of the grounds. They identified the best location for the centerpiece of the circus, the Big Top, also, where animals would be housed, fed, and exhibited. Then with the circus's safety officer, reviewed all the procedures from last year's show with the town's Chief of Police, Fire Chief, and Emergency Services Director. The key points of discussion were safety plans for the circus's patrons so they would have a fun and protected experience from the moment they pulled into the parking lots, along the midway, on rides, and viewing the animals until they left that evening.

About five days earlier, the first tractor-trailers with circus hands rolled into town. Their crews immediately got to work, banging different colored fence stakes into the ground, and roping off areas for animal pens. Advance set-up crews of workers arrived daily and positioned rolls of fence around the grounds. In what surely was an all-night project, the circus workers quietly and quickly erected the perimeter fencing, parking signs, ticket booths, and large billboards facing the two entry points to the circus grounds.

Weeks before the circus was to arrive their advertising campaign began when a circus promoter had pasted posters on telephone poles. Before long, the local newspapers were running articles about circus life and the attractions soon to be enjoyed by all who attended, and advertising directed at kids was flashing on cable TV channels. The large roadside billboards were covered with pictures of wild animals, clowns with painted faces, and high wire walkers.

Since the first circus van had parked at the fairgrounds, the preparations by the circus workers for the Saturday spectacle had not stopped. A procession of trucks arrived both day and night at the vendor's parking lot with many contraptions sure to make the circus a success. Each truck and everything they pulled or loaded with was painted in vibrant circus colors, and each picture of the animals or rides elevated the anticipation of every child in town. Kathryn and Samantha knew this year's circus was going to have more visitors than last because the circus was being held just after school let out, and each day the previous week they saw long lines of people standing at the advance ticket booth.

Moms and dads with their children stood outside the fences watching the once empty land become acres of attractions. Little kids looked for clowns and elephants, older kids scoped out rides which would make their heads spin and stomachs turn, older circus-goers reflected on past memories and anticipated a chance to spoil their grandchildren with sticky cotton candy and mustardy corndogs.

Everyone on Main Street stopped to watch the eighteen-wheelers pulling circus rides: the spinning Tea Cups, the speedy Whirl-a-Gig, which was Nick and Nelly's favorite, the twisting Dragon's Tail, and dozens of other circus games.

Everyone marveled at the efficiency of the workers as they unpacked flatbed trucks piled high with giant wooden boxes and bundles to be unwrapped.

On Thursday afternoon, Kathryn and Samantha climbed a tall oak tree just outside the fence to watch one of the trucks unload the biggest tent either of them had ever seen. Men swung heavy mallets pounding long, rusty steel spikes into the ground ready for tent lines. Long ropes with loops at one end were hung on the crane's enormous hook, and the other ends tied to wooden poles were lifted straight up. Workers guided the poles into steel buckets already dug into the ground. In less than 15 minutes a wooden skeleton was ready for its canvas skin.

The girls, becoming more interested, climbed higher in their look-out tree, and slowly slid out on the thinner branches to watch the orange crane extend its arm and drop its hook for workers to attach the tent resting on a trailer. A circus worker wearing a bright red hardhat was yelling commands as he waved two flags, one red, and the other green, guiding the crane operator. As the tent was lifted in the air, workers ran to grab its dangling lines. Once the crane stopped its lift, the man with the flags waved directions and linemen scurried to grab a line ready to tie to an anchor post as the canvas was gently put atop the wooden frame as easily as putting on a glove.

This tent would be the center of the animal and daredevil acts, where the Master of Ceremonies would announce:

**"Ladies and gentlemen, boys and girls…
Welcome to the Big Top!"**

Chapter 8

The Watch and the Coach

Having lost time because of the unplanned nap, Kathryn needed to hurry to be on time at the noon rendezvous point with her pals. While in mid-air after launching herself off the front porch, Kathryn looked down at her watch and happily realized she would make the appointed meeting, but with only a few seconds to spare. The watch was incredibly special to Kathryn, given to her two years ago as a birthday gift from her parents.

The day after **that** birthday, she pledged to wear her watch every day, everywhere—and she had kept her vow. The only time it was not on her left wrist was when she took a shower, at the beach, or swimming in Samantha's pool.

At school Kathryn wore a wide, thick wristband like other kids did; some also wore knee pads or headbands to be like professional athletes. Coaches and teachers did not seem to mind; they occasionally wore them, especially since the Intermediate School PTA sold them during their Annual Spring-Sports Fundraiser. The wristbands were so popular last year that the PTA doubled the order and still could not fill the demand. Samantha's mom, the PTA President, always knew exactly what to sell. Samantha proclaimed, "My mom could sell milk to a cow."

But Kathryn used her wristband to hide the watch. During sports, students were asked to remove watches, necklaces, rings, or belts that could injure other players.

She hadn't protested the rule with Mr. Gepp, both her gym teacher and soccer coach, about his safety rules concerning jewelry. She reasoned there was nothing to gain by giving more information than was necessary.

Her deception had ended one day at soccer. And it was her fault. This season, at one of the final practices before the opening game, Kathryn had arrived later than usual. She was always early for practice—early for everything—because, as Samantha taught, "Early is not just for catching worms, early offers opportunity."

As Grandpa Hastings pulled to a stop at the practice field, Kathryn thanked him for dropping her off, grabbed her soccer bag, ran to the field, tossed her bag and jacket on the bench, and hurried onto the field for warm-ups.

She had forgotten to wrap her wristband over her watch.

A few minutes into practice Coach Gepp noticed. "Kathryn, you forgot to leave your watch in your bag. Run to the sidelines quickly and get back to your position even quicker."

Kathryn, like everyone else in the school and on the team, liked Mr. Gepp. He was one of the nicest adults she had ever met. He always encouraged players and students to do their best. He never made fun of them, always made sure everyone got time to play each game, even the worst players on the team, and he always had encouraging words no matter how bad the team had been **slaughtered**.

So, she was quite sure he would understand why she had to wear her watch despite the rules. She ran over to him. Before she could talk, he said, "Kathryn, get rid of the watch and get back on the field."

She was shocked that he did not have time to listen, since it was only a practice game—he could have taken a minute to listen. So, Kathryn decided to make him understand her situation.

"Mr. Gepp, I need to explain." Pointing to her wrist, sure all would be fine, said, "I have a thick wristband."

"Kathryn, get rid of the watch and get back on the field."

She had formulated a different response.

Turning away from the field, she walked over to the sidelines, and decided to sit there until Mr. Gepp would listen to what she had to say.

Mr. Gepp did not go to the sidelines, did not look at Kathryn, and continued practice. The other players occasionally looked over at her wondering what had happened. About 15 minutes before practice was over, her grandfather arrived.

Noticing she was on the bench and knowing she was one of the best players on the team, and its fastest runner, he rushed over to her figuring she had some sort of injury. "Kathryn, are you okay? Did you hurt yourself?"

She looked up, her eyes glassy and said, "Mr. Gepp just doesn't understand. He has a silly rule that makes no sense."

Before her grandfather could respond, players were coming over to find out what happened.

Mr. Gepp stepped between Kathryn and the concerned teammates. Turning away from Kathryn, he addressed the players, "Folks, pack your gear, go home, eat smart, get some rest, and I'll see you on Tuesday. Be right here on Field Four at the same time for a scrimmage with the Titans. Now please leave Kathryn alone, she is fine. I need to talk to the team captain."

Coach Gepp turned to Kathryn's grandfather, "Hello Mr. Hastings. Your granddaughter and I need to have a player-coach meeting, and I would like you to hear what I have to say."

"Sure Coach. Is she injured?"

"She is okay, but we have had a difference of opinion on rules and who follows them."

Before Coach Gepp could say another word, Kathryn jumped into the conversation, "Mr. Gepp, you are a great coach, but you just don't understand what it means to keep an important vow to yourself. You see, I made a promise two years ago to wear this watch every day, and I have. And since you never noticed it before, and no one was ever hurt, I should be able to wear it under my band."

Her eyes moved from her coach to her grandfather. She was hoping to see faces of approval from them after hearing her point of view. Then she looked back to Mr. Gepp whose face showed disapproval.

She felt she must continue, but demonstrate she could be an adult if he was to listen, "Mr. Gepp, since you appear to be very hard-down on a rule that could not cover every circumstance, I have the perfect answer. I'll wear a heavier rubber guard over my wrist to solve our situation. I get to wear the watch and your safety rule is taken care of."

Mr. Gepp responded in a whisper, "Kathryn, the rule is not open for discussion or compromise. While I admire your negotiation attempt, I never allow players to be in an unsafe situation. We are lucky no one has lost a tooth by getting hit with your watch. The argument you present holds no water with me."

Continuing, Coach Gepp looked at Mr. Hastings, and then back to Kathryn, "You have to make a decision, Kathryn. I will not discuss it further once you have decided on the two choices I am offering. Wear the watch and sit in the stands watching your friends play or follow the rules and play with the team. The same applies in gym class. Wear the watch and fail or do it my way and pass. What is your decision?"

With a steely response, "Mr. Gepp, I'll give you my decision tomorrow."

She grabbed her bag, grabbed her grandfather's hand, and said, "Grandpa, let's go home."

The next day in gym she would not look at Mr. Gepp. While he did not understand why Kathryn had taken such a strong position on something, he thought was so basic, he did admire her commitment. This was probably the same quality that Kathryn's teammates saw in her when they voted for her to be the team's captain.

For a short time, she was not happy with him, but in the end, after talking the situation over with Grandpa Hastings, both in the car and later that night before bed, she really understood it did make sense. So, for the sake of others and because she did not want to be responsible for another player's lost tooth, Kathryn removed the watch for gym and soccer.

She talked to Mr. Gepp a couple of days later as if nothing had ever happened—and he did the same—she knew all was back to normal.

And they still were slaughtered on the soccer field every game that season.

Chapter 9

Getting to the Rendezvous Point

To make up for lost time, Kathryn needed to be swift if she was going to be on time to rendezvous with her pals. Kathryn was breathing quickly, her legs straining as she shortened the distance to the bus stop. She took a millisecond to glance at the big white mouse hands pointing to the large silver number "12." Kathryn quickly computed the time and distance to the bus stop which was three and a half blocks away from her house. Somehow, she was able to run even faster.

Kathryn had covered this same path every day for the previous two years on her way to school. As she glided over each crack in the sidewalk, she knew the distance to the bus stop was closing fast. A few strides more and she would be there.

She was quite sure her fitness accomplishment from house to rally point would make her soccer coach proud. Her voice rose as she triumphantly impersonated a sports announcer at the end of a close race, "Ladies and Gentlemen, with only Minnie Mouse seconds to spare, at 11:59:49, Kathryn the Great has beaten the clock!" As she crossed in front of the bus stop, the excited 11-year-old raised her hands above her head and spun in a circle just like the helmeted football players do on TV to celebrate with a victory dance after scoring a touchdown.

Breathing heavily with one hand still raised, Kathryn continued to twirl in her victory celebration just before entering the familiar school bus stop with its dull-blue tin roof and scratched see-through plastic walls. She was the first to arrive.

Kathryn reached into the yellow pocket of her crimson shorts—she always wore matching colors—grabbed her cell phone and hit the "1" on her speed dial for Samantha. They did everything, well, almost everything together. They studied together, shared clothes, ate dinner at each other's houses (sometimes two dinners a night to keep their parents happy), and usually spent their weekends planning some sort of activity. The only thing they never shared was Kathryn's watch, and that was fine with Samantha. She didn't mind. After all, Samantha was the only person with whom Kathryn shared the complete story of **that** birthday party.

Kathryn was not the only person out of breath. When Samantha's phone rang, she answered the "bubbling water" ring tone with her usual, and this time, breathless, formal deep voice, "Hello, Ka—"

Before Samantha could finish her sentence, Kathryn jumped in, "Where are you?"

Samantha crisply informed her friend she was in view. "I see you're wearing that dorky red shirt again. Who bought that for you? Anyway, we are at the corner." With a giggle, Samantha continued, "Turn around, and you'll see us."

They both laughed to themselves as the dorky tie-dyed red shirt had been a gift from Samantha earlier in the year. In perfect harmony, and without another word, both girls pushed the red "End" button on their matching phones, and just as they always did, each girl slid their phone into the right back pocket: Kathryn into her red shorts, and Samantha into her blue jeans. As Samantha, the future chef, or possibly an engineer, always said, "One must be organized, if one wants to be successful."

The plan was coming together. All her friends were going to make the bus stop rendezvous point right on time. In growing excitement, Kathryn turned to greet her conspirators: Samantha, Nick, and Nelly.

Kathryn's senses were on alert. She quivered as a sour smelling breeze raced over her. Kathryn called Samantha. She knew someone, other than her friends, was watching her from the other side of the street. Kathryn slowly turned to see Abbadon, the frightful figure from her dreams. His red clothes moved with the breeze, otherwise he stood statue still. His yellow stare chilled her body.

He stepped towards Kathryn—her phone at her side, her eyes on Abbadon.

Samantha answers her phone, "Are you there? Hello!"

Kathryn, terrified, lifts her phone: "It's him. Quick, get here. He's after me." Abbadon is now in the middle of the street. Defensively, Kathryn steps backwards.

The phone still in Kathryn's ear, Samantha orders, "Turn around.

The twins are with me. Who's after you?"

Kathryn chances a moment to look down the street, see the bikes approaching. She turns back to her attacker.

But then IT happened!

A whirlwind surrounds Kathryn, a long shadow is cast from behind her. She fearfully turns toward the inevitable.

It is not Abbadon. It is the lady in purple from her dreams. Only a few feet away, close enough that Kathryn could hear the rub of cloth against itself.

Suddenly, she felt as if time had stopped. She glanced to her right. There stood the figure of a woman. Kathryn, petrified from fear, could only stare at the woman. "Is it **her**?" The words passed between her quivering lips, but she knew there was no one to hear them. Her friends were too far away, and no other people were on the street. Kathryn began to feel her body tighten, until she stood motionless, cemented in position. She could not take her eyes from the figure of the lady now moving ever so slowly in her direction. How could the mystery woman seem motionless and still be coming closer?

Chapter 10

The Meeting

There did not seem to be any way out of this perilous situation, a situation she could not control. Her inner voice, one of dread, questioned, "How did this happen…how did I let it happen?"

None, not one, of her friends would go near the strange lady who lately they have seen near Kathryn's house, was walking toward Kathryn. Always seen wearing the same purple dress and purple hat which reminded kids of a Halloween witch, this mysterious lady appeared and disappeared without a sound, and without detection. The neighborhood kids were frightened of her. No one had ever seen her face. No one had ever heard her voice.

There were scary stories about terrible magic the lady practiced on kids, but no one recalled when or who it happened to. Why didn't parents believe their kids when they told them about this unusual woman the kids called the "Haglady." And why hadn't their parents seen this eerie character in the neighborhood, and usually sighted on Audubon Drive?

The neighborhood kids have been seeing the mystery woman much more often during the past month. Thinking about it, Kathryn realized the woman was always just down the street from her home over the past couple of weeks. But today, the lady was not blocks away from her house, she was on the same street, and the same block as Kathryn—she became conscious of the fact that **this was no coincidence.** Kathryn bewilderingly formed a conclusion about this woman, not knowing why, but was absolutely sure she was correct. **This was planned.**

The "Haglady" was directly in front of Kathryn whose mind was turning over every possibility, every idea. Why me? Why is she here? What Kathryn did grasp, and it became scarier the more it made sense, and she could not *think away* her conclusion is the Haglady had intended for this meeting to happen. Why did she think that thought? Kathryn could not scream for help; her body was no longer under her own control.

As always, the Haglady seemed to appear without anyone noticing. No one ever saw her from a distance; she just came upon kids rather suddenly and unexpectedly.

Kathryn thought of Samantha's discussion and investigation of the Haglady.

Samantha had spent some time thinking about the mysterious lady. After all, a year ago, she had been the one who named the oddly dressed woman "Haglady." Samantha considered "the seeing" of the Haglady as an "appearance" because, according to her Third Edition College Dictionary and research, the Haglady was not an apparition, not a spirit, and not a ghost. Samantha asked her science teacher about the woman's ability to appear and disappear in thin air.

Mr. Murdock had laughed and suggested, "Samantha, you are the owner of a gifted and wonderful imagination, but be careful, you want to make sure you keep what is real, and what is make-believe, in separate boxes."

What Samantha knew about Mr. Murdock was that, just like her parents and her friends' parents, he did not take the situation seriously since only students ever reported seeing her. She could not come up with a single logical answer to the three most important questions: How did the Haglady appear and disappear? Was it magic or not? And, where did she live? In fact, not a single kid on the street knew where she lived. Samantha considered it might be like the magician she saw at a show when on vacation with her parents in Myrtle Beach, South Carolina. Samantha could not believe her eyes when he made a tiger appear, then disappear on stage—and she had a great view because they were in the middle of the sixth row. The Haglady wasn't using tricks; she had to have supernatural powers. Samantha told her friends, that the Haglady was "not of this world."

Kathryn's thoughts returned to her immediate situation, and she nervously wondered, "Why didn't I see her?"

But the thought was quickly broken. Kathryn knew contact with the Haglady was imminent, fixed in place, and there was no other alternative. She was without friends, unable to do anything but stare at the woman who would soon be so close they could touch.

"Help," Kathryn shouted to herself. She couldn't even hear herself scream.

She composed her emotions for a second, and then in a hushed voice, "Think. What do I do? Should I run? Yes, start running!"

But Kathryn could not move her legs; they were locked in place. Her feet had lost feeling; it was impossible to even move her toes inside her sneakers. Kathryn's fear grew.

She became oddly and objectively aware of her circumstances. She found herself thinking more clearly after only seconds, which had felt like an eternity.

This frightening, mind boggling situation was happening on a day of great adventure with friends on the first day of summer vacation. Kathryn thought, "My, oh my, a day can change so quickly."

What was it Samantha had said to do if you wanted to stay alive if you met the Haglady? "You must not let the Haglady's eyes look into yours. They will freeze you and you will die."

Testing to see if she was totally immobile, Kathryn closed her hands tightly. Sweat rolled down her arms, making her fists wet and sticky. She shouted orders to herself. "Don't look at her! Don't look at her!" In spite of the self-commands, Kathryn's eyes opened, and she lifted her head. The Haglady was almost upon her.

Again, her brain was shouting inside her head, "DON'T LOOK AT HER! DON'T LOOK AT HER FACE!" But if her eyes were closed, how could she know when to escape.

An idea struck her, she coached herself, "Okay, I have a plan." Kathryn decided to fix her gaze below that of the strange woman's face, looking at the yellow buttons on the purple cloak, while preparing her escape.

Their encounter now inevitable, only seconds away. The Haglady moved closer. Kathryn was sure she could avoid making actual eye contact with the approaching form. She was sure the plan to stare at something else would work. But Kathryn was taller than the force she was about to meet. Her downward focus moved upward from the handmade filigreed buttons, to the yellow lace trimmed on the rounded edge of the dark-purple hat.

"Oh no, what if she lifts her head," was all Kathryn could think as she could not move her eyes to the brim of the magical lady's velvet hat.

Kathryn's neck tightened even more. "Oh no, I can't breathe," she cried to herself.

The frame of the purple hat began to move slowly upward exposing a yellow scarf wrapped loosely around the Haglady's neck. A light gust of wind washed over them, a dust devil swept around the pair, and Kathryn's nose recognized a familiar fragrance. She tried to reflect on the perfume, but another matter was immediate. The unexpected, potential danger was upon her and she did not know what to do.

It took a moment, but Kathryn understood what she was seeing. In thought, "She is floating. Her yellow slippers are not touching the sidewalk. Is it possible the Haglady is floating, not walking?"

The very slightest tip of a chin was now visible as the visitor inched ever closer to Kathryn. The hat continued to lift, soon to expose a face Kathryn refused to gaze upon. She had been warned not to look at those eyes. Kathryn couldn't help wanting to understand the temptation before her. She was going to look at the Haglady's face, but not into her eyes. Was her life almost over?

Again, to reaffirm what she could not do, she announced to herself, "I can't look into her eyes," and repeated the order, "I can't look into her eyes." Samantha always said those eyes could kill you or turn you into a piece of sculptured stone. Samantha had heard of a dog that once tried to attack the Haglady and was turned to rock.

Kathryn was about to explode with fright.

Their eyes met! Kathryn, brave but scared, fixed on the vision facing her.

Kathryn did not die. She did not turn to stone.

Kathryn was surprised to see a much younger face than she had expected. The Haglady's smooth skin, wavy brown hair, and comforting smile warmed Kathryn's body.

Kathryn stared into the softest eyes she had ever seen. They were bronze-brown eyes. They were like sparkling crystals, at the same time brilliant in color and warm. It was as if she had seen those eyes before.

And yes, she had smelled this lady's perfume before.

They had been wrong. Everything her friends and others on the street had reported about this lady was wrong. Kathryn thought to herself, "She's beautiful."

"Thank you for the compliment, Kathryn. I don't think anyone on this street has ever been so kind to me."

Kathryn was certain she had not spoken aloud. She was positive she had not. And that voice, the Haglady's voice was as familiar as her eyes, and her scent, and everything about her.

Kathryn's body at that moment was released from its paralysis. The initial fear was gone; her anxiety melted away as a peaceful glow now wrapped around her body.

Why did she know those eyes? When had she looked upon them before? They not only provided comfort; they were speaking to Kathryn.

When their eyes met, they became fixed, one upon the other. The familiar eyes allowed Kathryn and the Haglady to connect and share each other's thoughts. Kathryn felt as if they were speaking. Yes, their eyes were communicating. She realized the Haglady's bewitching gaze had released her muscles and commanded her emotions. Kathryn felt safe.

Kathryn was certain those eyes had been a part of her life, and for an instant, she tried to remember, but she just could not place the where or when.

The Haglady spoke, "Kathryn my dear, it is good to meet with you today." The voice addressing her was clear, yet without force. Each syllable projected with a measured crispness, and the animated use of her mouth, the formation and enunciation of each word, the pausing between syllables, riveted Kathryn's attention.

When did she first hear that voice? A picture flashed in front of Kathryn, it lasted for a moment's moment. Kathryn saw, more than that, she experienced a moment of her past. It was after she was dragged from her car, lying on the grassy shoulder of a road, with a hand holding hers.

It vanished.

Kathryn's breathing was now perfectly normal. She wiggled her fingers and then raised her hand to wipe the moisture beaded on her forehead. With both hands, Kathryn swept back the sweaty brown hair behind her ears.

A sweet comforting fragrance overtook Kathryn. The two, the

Haglady and Kathryn, began to talk.

Her three pals were huddled on the other side of Harvey Road watching Kathryn who stood no more than a few inches from the Haglady; three sets of eyes intently focused on Kathryn's face.

Nick determined, "She's not moving." He stared at the statue-like Kathryn, and then instantly, using words that quivered when he repeated, "She is NOT moving!"

"Kathryn's not moving. Is she breathing, do you see her breathing?" asked Samantha in a high pitch that scared Nick and Nelly. Samantha, the most talkative person anyone knew, was considered by everyone in their neighborhood to be a 100% certified drama queen.

"Shh, lower your voice! Do you want the Haglady to turn Kathryn to stone?" ordered Nelly, the group's musician, who was always singing, or at piano lessons or dance class.

"I don't think she's a stone, but her muscles have been paralyzed by the Haglady," replied Nick.

Samantha, speaking as if on stage in one of the school's annual theater productions started to give commands, "We should call the police. And we should yell as loud as we can and maybe scare the Haglady away, afraid she will be captured."

Faster and louder Samantha, said, "I think we should yell." Then, raising her voice even higher, she again announced, "I'm gonna yell!"

Nick shot back in panic, "Don't yell until she comes out of the trance. We don't want the Haglady to run and then Kathryn might be a stone figure forever and ever!"

It was unusual for Nick to take a stand. He was the quiet one of the two, Nelly took after their dad and Nick after their mother.

Samantha retorted, "She is not frozen, she is not a stone statue, she's in a trance. Don't you know anything about hypnosis? I watched a show on TV last week—"

"Oh, shut up!" burst Nick, "Nobody cares how much you know. This is serious. Our Kathryn is not moving."

The concerned trio was nervously trying to determine what was next for Kathryn.

For the first time in what felt like hours, Samantha took a deep breath. Just as she began to let her breath out, she noticed Kathryn move.

In a crisp, thrilled voice, Samantha directed the others to notice Kathryn's hands, "Look, look, she just moved her fingers, she's alive. Oh… my… gosh, she's alive!"

Just then, the Haglady moved a step toward Kathryn.

At that instant, Samantha yelled, "Run, Kathryn! Run!"

Kathryn did not hear her best buddy's advice. It was too late for Kathryn to react, even if she had heard Samantha's voice. At the same time the call to run had been yelled, the Haglady touched Kathryn's hand.

Kathryn felt her body begin to flush from the touch by this mysterious new acquaintance.

"Please come to my house, dear, we will have a wonderful visit. You do know where I live?" invited the stranger. Her warm voice, one of softness and familiarity, drew Kathryn to her, to the unexplained.

Kathryn answered without hesitation, "Yes, I will. Yes ma'am. I would like to see you again." Kathryn asked, "Do we know each other?"

"We will talk later, my dear," answered the lady in purple, and turned away. Kathryn now hearing the panicked voices behind her spun around and looked in the direction of her very unnerved friends on the other side of the street who were now running toward her.

Kathryn spun around to look back at the Haglady.

She was not there.

Kathryn was sure she knew where the Haglady lived.

Not one of the kids, not even Samantha, gave a single thought about sneaking into the circus.

Chapter 11

Back to the Haglady Encounter
Confusion, Hurrying Home, Grandma

In an instant, the Haglady had disappeared. Not one of her friends watching the entire encounter saw the lady in purple vanish.

The three friends ran to Kathryn firing questions faster than she could answer. Samantha implored, "Give us every detail of every second of what happened."

Nick desperately wanted answer to his weighty concern. "Did you think you were going to die?"

Nelly spoke so fast, one question began before the previous one ended: "Did her face have warts, and did your eyes burn, and did her touch freeze you? You looked frozen and did your ears hurt from her voice and—"

Samantha cut Nelly's interrogation short, posing the question she thought was most important, and in her drama queen voice, asked, "Did your blood run cold?"

Kathryn could not answer a single question. She was numbed by the encounter. She needed to catch her breath, unsure what had just happened, and she did something totally out of character—she emitted a thunderous response from within, a voice which reverberated her plea, that not only shocked her friends, she shocked herself. "Please STOP! STOP asking me questions! I'm going home and NOBODY follow me!" Kathryn broke into a gallop straight to her house. Her friends stood completely still.

Taking the same route home, she had traveled earlier, Kathryn seemed to run faster than her legs had ever carried her before. Within a few minutes she was three strides from her driveway and computed the transition from the grey and leaf stained concrete sidewalk to her brown and tan stone driveway. On the last step, Kathryn extended her right hand and gripped the smooth round top of the white fencepost as she had so many times before, especially when hurrying home to report exciting news of school or friends to her grandparents.

As expected, the fencepost did its job perfectly, by turning her body in the direction of the house just as her fingertips were losing their grip on the pivot point—due to what her science teacher defined as, "centrifugal force,"—her feet were put on a direct line to house. Now on the driveway, Kathryn ran straight to the house, and without breaking stride, jumped over the two pine steps onto the deck.

Her hand clutched the screen door handle in front of her, and in the same motion, flung it to the side, letting it go with such force, the door slammed back against her grandfather's tool stand, knocking over his garden shovel, rake, and driveway broom, all of which fell against the large dented, galvanized bucket, making a series of clattering noises that startled Grandma Hastings, causing her to drop the plate of warm, peanut covered brownies she had planned for Katherine and her friends to eat at lunch—lucky for her grandmother, she was using her "summer plastic."

When Kathryn spied her grandmother in the kitchen, she breathlessly shouted, "Grandma, you won't believe what happened to me at the bus stop!"

Grandma calmly began to ask, "Are you going t—?" But she never had a chance to complete the question.

Kathryn's excitement continued to burst. "I spoke with the Haglady!" Kathryn could hardly catch her breath to talk, "I mean, I met her on the street," and taking another deep breath, "What happened was I just walked into her. We…we looked at each other."

Grandma Hastings took notice of Kathryn's exhilaration. Her body was visibly shaking, her arms and legs poised to assist in telling her story; her hands and feet could not stop moving.

Grandma was waiting for Kathryn to slow down, to take another breath before she jumped into the conversation. Her controlled voice and deliberate show of concern was comforting to her young granddaughter.

"Kathryn, slow down. Catch a breath. My goodness, you are shaking. What is all the fuss about, dear? Are you OKAY?"

"Yes, Grandma, I am fine. Listen, I met the Haglady." Reading her grandmother's concerned face, she repeated herself, "Really, I am fine, but I talked to the Haglady, or rather, she talked to me, I mean, we talked to each other."

Grandma Hastings' demeanor changed. Her voice was now intensely inquisitive, "My dear, did you say you spoke with the Haglady? The lady who wears all purple?"

"Grandma, I am sure we talked, but I don't remember moving my lips, or hearing her words." Squinting her eyes, and with a twist of her head she asked, "Grandma, I think I spoke to her without really talking. Can a person do that?"

Hesitating, then deliberately speaking very slowly, pacing each word, Grandma Hastings asked, "Was she familiar?"

Kathryn was momentarily distracted and asked, "Grandma, what did you say?"

Grandma Hastings again, with a seriousness Kathryn had not expected, asked the question "My dear, was she familiar to you?"

Kathryn was startled. The words did not make sense to her. She wanted to know why her grandmother asked that question, in that manner, and did Grandma know something about the Haglady that was being held back from Kathryn?

Kathryn could not help herself, "Is there something I should know?"

Grandma took a deep breath. She looked as if she was going to faint. In fact, she sat up straight and took another deep breath—what Grandpa Hastings referred to as, "catching her breath." She looked into Kathryn's impatient eyes. "Have you ever seen her before?" Grandma continued, "Is there anything at all familiar about her?"

Kathryn fired back, "Grandma, what are you talking about? Tell me! You are keeping something from me, aren't you?"

Grandma paused momentarily, then asked, "Kathryn have you ever spoken with that woman before?"

Kathryn was perplexed, but by this time, she needed answers. "No! Well, maybe, I don't know. Somehow, seems like I know her. Do I?" Frustrated by the thought, "Anyway, I spoke to her, somehow I thought I knew her voice, her eyes, and, Grandma, you are going to think this is strange, but I remembered how she smelled."

"My dear, I must know all the details of your time with that lady.

There is a lot we must talk about."

Kathryn did not want to begin the conversation before she had a chance to think about what she needed to know, and to organize her thoughts, because she was still unsure of all that had happened.

"Grandma is it all right if I go to my room. I just need to be by myself."

"Certainly dear, you will need to search for answers to questions you do not understand. You will find that today is going to be what my grandmother called 'a day of consequence.'"

Again, her grandmother was speaking in terms she didn't understand as if there was a hidden story, kept from Kathryn. For sure, her grandmother was not making any sense.

Kathryn headed to her bedroom to sort out her thoughts. And most certainly, she needed to consult with Samantha—who always asked the best questions in class, usually stumping her teachers.

Kathryn began to plan what to do next.

Samantha once said, **"The person with a plan has decided to succeed."**

Chapter 12

Thinking Position and a Best Friend

Kathryn's weary legs carried her body slowly up the stairs. She grabbed the blue glass doorknob, and quietly closed the door behind her. She flopped down on her bright blue beanbag, folded her legs, crossed her arms, drew in a breath, and sighed—this was her thinking position. It was Samantha's thinking position which she shared with Kathryn. Samantha claimed, "Great thoughts come to those thinking in the right spot. Then you must hear what you are thinking, so stand up and listen to yourself."

Samantha recommended to, "Think out loud!" So, Kathryn, taking Samantha's advice, stood up, walked around, listened to her thoughts, sat down, and began again.

Kathryn continued deliberating aloud, but without answers: "What did all this mean? Really, what happened in the last hour? My friends are glad I did not die or become a stone stature. My grandmother is acting very strangely, and I had a conversation with the Haglady; I'm sure I never I opened my mouth."

After an hour of thinking about the experience, Kathryn decided to take a different approach. There was one person who she could talk to and who wouldn't offer an opinion, unless asked. It was time to talk to Grandpa Hastings. He said he had been married for such a long time because he was such a good listener. When he went with Grandma Hastings to Sandy's Sweet Shop for their first date, all he did was listen—which must have been the magic of their conversation.

Of course, Kathryn could also talk to Samantha, but she always had an opinion, and Kathryn didn't need an opinion. What she needed was a sounding board. Talking to herself, Kathryn said, "Yes, I need to talk to Grandpa. Yes, that is what I need to do, and then call Samantha. She will have some ideas."

Kathryn jumped up to see if Grandpa Hastings had returned from his trip to the store. "Darn, the truck was not in the driveway."

She decided on her second option to call Samantha. She reached into her back pocket. It was empty. Then, she heard a familiar ring, as if some strange communication connected her with Samantha. The phone, resting on the floor next to the beanbag, shook with each ring. She picked it up.

"Samantha," her voice burst into the phone, "I have to talk to you. Can you come over?"

Samantha, trying to control her nerves, responded in a firm voice, "Kathryn, my friend, I am on your back porch. Now, get those skinny legs of yours down here!"

Kathryn paused, trying to think how she would begin describing the Haglady to Samantha and then again later to her grandfather. She rose on her tired "skinny" legs and walked down the hallway, stepping over Chubby, and this time touched each step on her way to the porch. She did not want to talk to her grandmother before consulting with Samantha, who was always consulted on most major decisions: clothes, music, school projects, and certainly on the most personal of subjects, boys.

Kathryn was concerned for Grandma Hastings. Her grandmother's behavior on this matter had been quite out of character for a lady known for her strength in times of trouble. In addition, Kathryn's bewilderment at Grandma Hastings' actions told her to be especially attentive. This very peculiar interest in the particulars of the incident immediately following Kathryn's encounter with the Haglady was indeed strange. It certainly seemed as if Grandma Hastings knew something about the woman, but she did not want to give Kathryn any information and was content not to continue the discussion. Shortly after their brief conversation, Grandma Hastings left the house for about thirty minutes, but the thud of the screen door a few minutes ago told Kathryn that her grandmother had returned, and moments later she heard the closing of her grandfather's truck door.

She heard her grandfather's voice on the front porch. He was talking to Grandma. They sounded very serious. Kathryn ran to the back porch.

"Samantha, I am so sorry for not talking to you right after I talked to HER. Samantha, it was so strange, we didn't need to…to talk." Now with a tone in her voice that is shared by best friends, "I'm really sorry for running away from you at the bus stop, but my head was confused, and my body was twitching. I swear, I thought I was going to explode."

Kathryn told her best friend every detail of the encounter.

Samantha was a little confused why this scary situation did not match Kathryn's face—there was no sign of fright.

"Kathryn, weren't you scared? I would think it would've been terrifying! Why are you smiling?"

Kathryn moved her hands to her face, touching the tips of her fingers to her lips, "Am I smiling?"

With a serious voice, Samantha shot back, "Yes, you're smiling. Do you have a fever? Do you think you might be hallucinating? Oh my, do you think you are under a spell?" Now concerned, and wearing a serious expression, Samantha thought an important thought, "Oh… my…gosh, if you are under an enchantment, you would not know it and couldn't answer the question!"

The fingers on Kathryn's hands tapping rapidly against her legs confirmed what her buddy had just speculated.

"Samantha, you should see her face, it is soft, and it makes you relax. She smells like…like honeysuckle, and her eyes are familiar too. I think I met her before, but I don't know where or even when. Is that possible? No, anyone would know if they met her—wouldn't they?"

"That's it!" Kathryn jumped up, then, just as quickly, sat down on her grandfather's favorite back porch chair, the rocker her mother bought for him as a present when she got her first job working on the Seaside Heights boardwalk the summer of her junior year in high school.

Kathryn could not contain the excitement of the moment; the question unlocked.

Jumping up again, Kathryn said, "Samantha, she smells like honeysuckle. That's it, that's the fragrance."

As Kathryn's best friend, Samantha knew every one of her friend's secrets. Over the years, and especially the past two, Kathryn had needed someone to confide in, someone who could keep a secret, and someone who would listen when she was very lonely. As their friendship grew, all was told; they shared every detail of their lives, but Samantha realized there must be one more secret—and this one, not even Kathryn knew about herself.

Samantha listened when told about the death of her friend's parents, everyone knew that, but it was not until they were by themselves, playing scientist in Kathryn's garage, a few months after the accident, when Kathryn broke out in tears and opened her heart to Samantha. Samantha just sat as Kathryn told her story about the birthday party, the watch, and the accident. Samantha held her friend as Kathryn sobbed telling how she missed her parents, how much it hurt every day. Samantha caringly grasped how special and personal the moment was to Kathryn. Samantha knew she was more than a good friend, she had become Kathryn's best friend, and Samantha took that responsibility very seriously

Samantha, absolutely sure she had just connected all the clues realized the moment had arrived for a best friend to ask a question of her best friend on a sacred subject.

With a knowing, inquisitive, caring voice, Samantha asked, "Isn't that the same scent you remembered when you had your accident?"

Kathryn looked straight at Samantha with astonishment. The sun's rays reflected off her now watery green-brown eyes. Samantha could sense Kathryn was weakening and quickly put her arm around her shoulder and grabbed her arm. Kathryn felt herself becoming light-headed, tried to lower herself, but slumped onto Grandpa Hastings' chair.

"Kathryn, are you okay?" Samantha burst out with a concerned shrieking voice, "Mr. and Mrs. Hastings, COME QUICK!"

After a few minutes and a glass of ice-cold Cherry Kool-Aid, Kathryn began to feel better as did everyone else once Kathryn looked up at them and smiled. Kathryn was a bit surprised at the attention she was receiving from her friend and grandparents. She assured everyone that the lightheadedness was because she had not had anything to drink since early that morning. In fact, she wanted everyone to move from the porch to the kitchen for lunch. Her grandmother promised to have lunch on the table in five minutes, and her grandfather went to the garage refrigerator for a watermelon he had picked the day before. No one could figure out how the Hastings had watermelons and other plants growing way before everyone else. Grandpa Hastings never told them about the glass windows in the roof of his garage or the lamps that glowed on his plants at night.

Grandma and Grandpa Hastings had walked onto the back porch just as Samantha shouted in distress. They had been on their way to speak with Kathryn. Grandpa Hastings had convinced his wife that it was time to talk to Kathryn. There were secrets Grandma Hastings had never intended to divulge to Kathryn at the request of Kathryn's mother, but the circumstances of today's meeting altered Kathryn's future—the secrets needed to be revealed.

Before Grandma left to make lunch, she made a point of talking to Kathryn. "We will talk a little later today dear, sometime after our meal. Is that good with you?"

Nodding, "Sure Grandma."

Kathryn's inquisitive nature piqued. She walked over and got close to Samantha, so that her grandmother could not hear and whispered, "This day is turning out to be very freaky. Even my grandmother is acting weird."

The day was turning into night, and the conversation was not to be, at least not this evening, but before bed Grandma told Kathryn, "We should spend some time together tomorrow, maybe putting old pictures into the family album. I promised your mother I would do it with her years ago. It is something we need to do; it would make her happy."

Kathryn had told Samantha her grandparents always talked about her parents, especially her mom. It was probably to make sure she would never forget them. Kathryn knew she would never forget them and would never change her last name. "If I ever get married, I will keep that hyphen thing attached to my name."

Samantha the psychologist gave her analysis, stated, "It probably makes them feel close to their daughter, by talking to their daughter's daughter."

Chapter 13

Sunday Breakfast and Finding the Haglady

Kathryn was awakened by the salty smell of bacon and the accompanying aroma of freshly ground coffee. Blueberry pancakes, topped with soft butter, and smothered in Vermont maple syrup were hers for the asking, and of course, a cold glass of milk to wash it all down. This was her all-time favorite meal, even better than roasted turkey. In fact, if she could have her grandfather's breakfast three times a day, she would.

Grandpa Hastings had cooked breakfast every Sunday for as long as Kathryn could remember—her father had loved pancakes and bacon. The only time Kathryn missed Sunday breakfast had been when her soccer team needed to be on the bus by six o'clock in the morning for a tournament in Delaware which she thought was way too early, and way too far to travel to experience another embarrassing defeat. As usual, they lost all three of their games, scoring only one goal, and that was accidentally kicked in by the other team.

Samantha had arrived in the kitchen at 8:00 AM for the 8:45AM breakfast feast. This was the day Grandma Hastings stayed out of the way sitting at the kitchen table happily observing the cooks. She enjoyed being waited on by Samantha. Grandma Hastings told Samantha, "Give me a couple of minutes notice when you're ready to move in. You can have Kathryn's room. I'll send her to the basement."

Kathryn could never understand why Samantha did not need sleep. She was always telling Kathryn about "the book I read last night," or an interesting TV show she watched, or a project she was working on, or time spent in her Thinking Position.

No matter when Kathryn came down for breakfast, Samantha and the Hastings were always busy cooking, having coffee, or just gabbing away at the kitchen table.

Kathryn's watch read 8:45 AM. Samantha was right on schedule, belting out a call up the stairs. "Kathryn, get down here! Your grandfather has our breakfast ready. Kathryn! Kathryn! Are you awake? I hope so. If not, that means I get your pancakes."

Kathryn followed the aromas of the breakfast feast, which had awakened her from the fantastic land of her dream, to the kitchen. She really enjoyed their regular guest, her best friend Samantha. Kathryn once asked Samantha if she only spent time with her to get Grandpa Hastings' recipes. Samantha, like Kathryn, called Grandpa Hastings' pancakes "the best food on earth."

Samantha wasn't fooling her best buddy about her reason for being in the kitchen; Kathryn figured Samantha was a secret agent sent by the CIA to uncover the pancake recipe. Samantha was doing her best to trick the architect of the breakfast menu by acting as a loyal assistant chef to prepare the breakfast, but really wanted to learn what ingredients made the pancakes so special. Grandpa Hastings would not give in to Samantha's request, no matter how many times she asked. In fact, Grandpa Hastings often intentionally left the wrong recipe on the counter, knowing Samantha would commit it to memory.

When Kathryn came into the kitchen, she gave her grandparents a kiss, and then to her Grandpa said, "Grandpa, remember, I'm your granddaughter, not that imposter, Samantha. Are you ever going to give her your pancake recipe?"

"Kathryn, my girl," Grandpa responded, pausing between each of his next words to be sure to get Samantha's interest, "Yes… I… am."

Samantha almost jumped out of her apron thinking she was about to be the first to see the secret recipe. She blurted out, "When, Mr. Hastings?"

Answering Samantha immediately, and with a smile on his face, he said, "When I go to your wedding!"

Of course, the fast-thinking Samantha, who was always ready with a quick answer, realized she had been pranked by Grandpa Hastings. She countered, "Mr. Hastings, I will begin the search for a husband this afternoon, the wedding will be next Saturday, right here in your kitchen, and immediately following the wedding, and after I have the recipe in my hands, I will get divorced."

Everyone had a good laugh, and then sat down to eat the "Best Pancakes on Earth."

Kathryn and Samantha usually had Saturday dinner at Samantha's house and Sunday morning breakfast in the Hastings' kitchen. Kathryn liked the dinner arrangement with Samantha. It gave her grandparents a chance to be together for their "Saturday date." They were avid moviegoers and always went to the Crystal Diner for coffee and dessert after the show. The movie and dessert tradition had begun during the first months of their courtship.

But this Sunday morning was unlike any other. Kathryn had resolved this was to be the day she would find the Haglady. She consulted with Samantha. The two girls were sure if Nick and Nelly could get free, the four friends could bike around the neighborhood, asking all the kids they saw about the lady in purple. A Haglady spotting was bound to happen. Samantha had a colored coded chart of the streets each biker was to cover and a worksheet for the four friends, so that no time period or road went uncovered for more than 15 minutes from 10:00 AM to 3:00 PM—Samantha's parents were taking the four friends to the circus at 5:00 PM.

Samantha's best idea was to enhance their surveillance capability using the United States Postal Service during the week if their Sunday plan had no results. She asked Mr. Keenan, the mailman, to keep an eye open for any lady wearing a purple dress. And like everyone else, he had only heard about the lady, but never encountered her on his route.

Samantha tried to greet Mr. Keenan each day to get the mail, give him any outgoing letters, and asked questions about the post office. Mr. Keenan seemed to enjoy answering her questions. When she considered asking him to help look for the Haglady, she told Kathryn she had "a hook,"—meaning the same as having a winning card up your sleeve. Since Samantha was the most interesting person on his route, Mr. Keenan would happily offer any information wanted by his pal.

Samantha and Kathryn had finished breakfast and going into the garage to get Kathryn's bike, then to assemble the search team. The night before, Kathryn had shared with Samantha what she thought was the location of the Haglady's house and suggested they keep that house under observation from the other side of the street.

Samantha knew it was not possible, but again asked about the location. Confused by Kathryn's response, Samantha began to wonder if the Haglady's magical powers were more than just a creepy rumor. Had she done something to Kathryn's brain?

Leaving her house early, before going to Kathryn's, Samantha did some investigative work on Kathryn's behalf. Samantha was quite confident there wasn't a building on the lot her friend identified as the location of the Haglady's house. Kathryn, on the other hand, had somehow become aware of the location of the house, and was bewildered when Samantha could not find it. Kathryn was very specific about the location, but it wasn't where Kathryn said it was supposed to be.

Trying to ask again about the house location, without challenging her best friend, Samantha began to talk around the subject rather than using a forward approach. "I turned at the corner of Audubon and Harvey this morning, right past the lot where you think the Haglady's house is. You said it was next door to Joey Layton's house, opposite Harvey Road. There is nothing there but dirt and boys."

"Yes, Samantha, next to Joey's house," Kathryn responded in a questioning tone. "You know his big sister, Sarah—she always gives us the best Halloween candy?"

Samantha looked at her friend. "Yes, Joey's house is white with green shutters."

By now, Kathryn detected the intent of Samantha's curious questions. "Samantha, why are you asking these questions?" She paused, and then continued, "Did you really go to the house?"

Samantha was becoming a bit curious and confused, worried about the spell. Kathryn, likewise, was looking at her friend quizzically and obviously waiting for an answer Samantha was not able to give.

"Kathryn, you're my best friend, right?" Kathryn nodded, giving Samantha the opening, she needed. "The Simons are three houses left of the lot, and then comes the Smiths, and then Joey's house, correct?" Again, Kathryn offered an affirmative headshake, but this time with a sarcastic half-smile. Samantha felt in control after having Kathryn give her the correct addresses. She then said, "That leaves the vacant lot to the right of Joey's, which has always been vacant. I think Joey's parents own it." Samantha waited for a response.

With an edge to her voice, Kathryn asked, "My dear Samantha, you must need glasses, or was it very foggy when you went by the house?" Kathryn paused and apologized for her tone of voice. "Sorry for being snippy. But I 'm bewildered by your questions and why you can't see a house."

Samantha took a breath, looked straight at her best friend, and calmly said, "Kathryn, there is no house next to Joey's, only the empty lot Joey and his friends use to play trucks and sports, and whatever else it is boys do."

"Okay," Kathryn burst out, "let's get our bikes and go to the lot."

The girls skipped into the kitchen to inform Grandma Hastings they were going for a bike ride.

Grandma Hastings was talking on the phone just as the two chums were coming into the kitchen. She put up her hand, halting the girls and pointed to Samantha, and spoke into the phone, "Lucy, she is right in front of me, hold on, and I'll put her on." She looked at Samantha and handed her the phone.

Samantha put the phone to her ear, "Hi Mom!" Samantha listened, took her phone our of her pocket, said, "No power, sorry," listening, "Okay, leaving now."

After a few seconds, Samantha hung up the phone and announced that she had to go home. Samantha was the youngest of her parents' four children, all daughters. Her oldest sister, Sadie, had just arrived with Samantha's newborn niece. Samantha thought it was a demanding responsibility being an aunt. In fact, she insisted that her family call her "Auntie Samantha" because it would be good for her new favorite niece to know her new favorite aunt.

"I have to go home and see my sister and niece, and YES, I have a niece, as you know, I am an AUNTIE." With a grin, Samantha overplayed her new title, "Kathryn, why don't you come over to Auntie Samantha's as soon as you can?"

Samantha smiled at Grandma Hastings, gave a light pat on top of Kathryn's head, saying, "Auntie Samantha will be waiting. You can hold the baby if you want. I'll let you."

Kathryn told Samantha that she would stop by in about an hour. "There is something I have to do, but then I'll be over to Auntie

Samantha's." They all laughed.

Samantha headed for the door, leaped off the porch, lifted her bike, pressed her foot against the kickstand, faced her front wheel in the direction of the street, turned her head toward Kathryn and yelled, "Kathryn, don't you do anything today without me!"

Kathryn smiled and waved back at Samantha, but she did not answer. She knew she was not going to do as her best friend asked.

Samantha decided to take the long way home. She made a left as she coasted out of the driveway to the empty lot alongside the Layton's house before performing her "auntie" duties.

Peddling as fast as she could, Samantha made her way down Audubon Drive quickly approaching her destination. She waved to the always smiling Mrs. Simon, who was just beginning to wash the family car with her son, Chris, and after passing the Smiths, she spotted Joey earning his allowance cutting the front lawn. A couple of quick pumps on the pedals of her bright red and chrome bike and Samantha was passing the empty lot presently under construction by two very dirty ten-year-old boys playing with orange toy earth movers. Samantha wondered why boys loved dirt.

Kathryn planned to find the Haglady's house, with or without Samantha, and she was somewhat uncomfortable with Samantha's interrogation. The odd part of the conversation had been that Samantha, who said she had passed the Haglady's house, seemed unable to see it.

Grandpa Hastings often remarked that Kathryn, her mother, and Grandma Hastings were made of the same material—they were the same person, just separated by years. So, just like her grandmother, confident in her beliefs, and unstoppable once her mind was set, Kathryn was going to do what she had planned. She had promised the lady in purple she would visit soon—Kathryn always kept her promises.

Kathryn grabbed her cell phone and slid it into her back pocket, stuffed a dollar bill and some coins in her front pocket, and rolled over her bed onto the floor, putting her in position to open the bottom drawer of the table next to her bed. She pulled the drawer open.

Kathryn looked intently at the wooden box which held the velvet pouch. She realized the drawer had not been opened, its contents, its secret, hidden since her grandmother had given her the opal the year before.

Kathryn closed the drawer and left the room.

Chapter 14

"A Year Earlier"
A Tenth Birthday, a Vacant Lot

Kathryn's grandparents thought she would want to recognize the day of the accident, so they asked what she felt was appropriate. They discussed a memorial service of family and friends to be held either in New York or at the Toms River house. However, Kathryn was uncomfortable with all the plans. She tried to think what her parents might want. Because Kathryn was unsure of what to do, she asked her grandparents if they could give her time to "think it out," and discuss it later.

Kathryn went out on the back porch and dialed Samantha. Before she knew it, Kathryn had been invited over for a "taste test." She was unsure if she was ready to discuss the situation with Samantha, but she knew spending time with her friend would help clear her thoughts, so she headed over to her Samantha's house.

About midway down Audubon Drive, Kathryn began to feel a bit lightheaded. She passed the Simon's and waved to Mrs. Smith who was putting out plastic, orange ducks and pink flamingoes on her lawn. Just past Joey Layton's house she pulled to the curb, braking to a stop. Feeling faint, she slid off her seat, felt a chill, and shivered.

She felt fine moments ago, but now, oddly out-of-sorts as if someone were watching her. Cautiously, Kathryn looked around. Nobody, except a couple of neighborhood kids.

Then she thought she could smell honeysuckle. At that instant she suddenly felt fine again. She shook off the feeling, got back on her bike and headed to Samantha's.

A few minutes later, Kathryn was walking through the front door of Samantha's house.

"Hello Miss Kathryn," Samantha's dad offered his usual greeting. He always spoke to Kathryn with a combination of formal title and first name. Samantha thought it showed respect for her best friend. As

Samantha always said, "When you show people respect, they respect you back and will always be faithful to you. You can depend on them because of shared loyalty."

Kathryn walked over to Mr. Bebout, and firmly gripped his outstretched hand for their traditional handshake, also part of their greeting.

Samantha, with orange icing on her blouse, entered the room as her dad and Kathryn were shaking. Thinking it would be fun using a perfect British accent, she asked, "Oh Miss Kathryn, would you, and the lord and lady of the castle, like a taste of carrot cake?"

Kathryn, with a botched accent, answered, "Any cow juice to go with it?"

Using her hands to mimic the squeezing of a cow's udder, Samantha began making sounds, "Mooooo! Mooooo!"

Mrs. Bebout looked at her husband, and said, "Charles, we should be proud; we are the only parents in town," enunciating each word, "with a cow for a daughter."

All the smiling eyes shifted to Samantha. She pushed out her lips, crunched her face, shoulders pulled up to her ears and looked at her mother through squinty eyes, playfully giving her a, "MOOOO!" The Bebouts and Kathryn headed into the kitchen.

"Of course, we have MOOOO juice, it is an absolute, and no dessert is complete without it." Samantha was able to milk the invisible cow, and at the same time, with a thumbs up gesture, assure Kathryn her request would be granted.

Mrs. Bebout reached into a kitchen cabinet for glasses and plates. Samantha had pulled a cake knife from a large wooden block resting next to the sink and started cutting slices, while waiting for the plates to arrive. Kathryn went to the refrigerator for the milk.

Kathryn looked at Mrs. Bebout, asking, "Milk?"

"No thank you, I'm having a latte,"

Kathryn turned to ask the same question, "Mr. Bebout, do you want milk or coffee?"

"Thank you, Miss Kathryn, a coffee for me." After a moment he said, "On second thought, maybe a small piece of cake, baked by my favorite pastry chef would be just the right snack on this cloudy day."

Samantha and Kathryn sat down on the kitchen stools. Samantha's kitchen was not your regular kitchen; her mom owned a restaurant often using their home kitchen for R&D, Research and Development, of new menu items. Samantha's goal in life was to open her own restaurant; she also wanted to build a bridge to England, dig a tunnel under the Atlantic Ocean from New Jersey to Spain, and construct the tallest all-glass building in the world.

As Kathryn's fork cut into the moist carrot cake, she recognized Samantha's special signature. Samantha always signed her food with her favorite number, which represented the month and day she was born, by using a swirling "7" on the plate or in the icing of her desserts.

The cake was delicious. Kathryn delicately pulled the fork from her mouth, rolling her eyes in delight.

Samantha accepted the silent compliment with a dignified smile. Samantha's dad said she had a much better nose and taste buds than either of her parents.

Kathryn asked Samantha and her parents if they ever saw honeysuckle on Audubon Drive.

Neither of the Bebouts could recollect any in the neighborhood except for the vines in Kathryn's yard.

Kathryn spent a couple of hours at Samantha's house eating cake, drinking milk, chatting with her parents about baseball, and listening to Samantha's ideas designing her future restaurant.

When it was time for Kathryn to leave, a heavy rain was pouring down. Mr. Bebout put Kathryn's bike in the back of his pickup and drove her home.

Kathryn thanked her chauffeur, rolled her bike into the garage, and tried to run between the raindrops to see her grandparents—it didn't work.

Her short visit to Samantha's proved successful. An hour earlier, midway through the second piece of cake, Kathryn decided that she wanted a "moment of remembrance" for her parents.

Upon entering the living room, hair drippy and shirt wet, she informed her grandparents of her decision.

"Grandpa, Grandma," she felt her voice tighten, I know what mom and dad would do if they were in my position. You know mom liked to keep family events simple, and dad was pretty much the same way."

She cleared her throat, and tried not to cry, but she just could not hold back the tears. She threw herself into her grandfather's lap and cried. Grandma Hastings glanced at Grandpa to see him looking back. There was no need to voice their shared observation; it was the first time Kathryn had cried in front of them. In fact, it was the first time she had exhibited any emotion over the death of her parents since the funeral. They all cried that night.

It took Kathryn a long time before she could begin to talk. Each time she began, the heavy sobbing continued. Finally, Kathryn sniffled, "Mom and Dad would want a quiet moment with just us in the backyard, and of course, I'll invite Samantha. Maybe she could bake special cookies, the ones dad would have liked, and we will have tea, the kind mom enjoyed."

Two weeks later, the planned day arrived. It would take place under the maple tree at eleven o'clock. All was in order, the sky was cloudless, and the sun seemed to be shining extra brightly. Samantha arrived wearing a formal afternoon tea dress, carrying a tray of fancy cookies she hoped would impress Grandpa Hastings—and they did. Grandma was inside preparing the tea. Kathryn and Samantha arranged the placemats on the picnic table, as Grandpa crossed the lawn with a boxed tea service for six. Great-Grandma Cappelli's family had brought the tea service from Italy, and it had been given to Grandma and Grandpa Hastings as a wedding gift.

Stepping from the porch, Kathryn was surprised to see Grandma wearing the dress she had worn at the birthday party the day of the accident. The plum dress was covered with bright yellow and white flowers and green leaves on pale-brown vines, and Grandpa wore his only suit, a navy blue three-piece with a red silk bow tie. Walking across the lawn from the porch to the table, on a superbly decorated silver serving tray, Grandma Hastings balanced a pitcher of ice-cold milk, a pot of honeysuckle tea, and a honey pot with a wooden honey stick. She placed it onto Grandpa Hastings' handcrafted pine table next to Samantha's assorted cookies, which were mounded on her mother's fanciest platter. The teapot shone as rays of sunlight reflected shafts of iridescent beams of greens, blues, and yellows around the table.

The tea party had officially begun. Kathryn and her parents had often had tea parties. The parties were an opportunity for her dad to enjoy valuable slow-down time. Kathryn's mom thought tea was the answer to every medical emergency or personal accomplishment: coughs, colds, sadness, an "A" on a test, scoring the first goal of the season, earning a merit badge, and any other reason she could think of. Her dad was not quite sure it was the cure-all, but he did like this special time with his "favorite gals."

Kathryn directed, "Grandma, please pour the tea." Grandma Hastings poured tea for Kathryn, and then filled her cup. Kathryn, knowing her grandfather and her friend Samantha preferred milk when eating cookies asked, "Grandpa, Samantha, milk or tea?"

In unison, they answered, "Milk please."

Kathryn said, "I live to serve my family and best friend." She lifted the milk pitcher and handed it to Grandpa Hastings, "You can take care of your buddy, Miss Samantha."

The honey pot was right in front of Kathryn. In all the years she had shared tea with her grandmother and mother, the only time she could recall seeing the honey pot was when Grandmother's tea was served. The special honey—her mother called it, "spiced honey," was a family secret. There were times when tea was served, but regular honey or sugar was on the table. She remembered asking about the spiced honey at her ninth birthday party when a guest wanted to sweeten the tea. Her grandmother said she could not find the pot, but there was regular honey in a bear-shaped container in the cupboard.

Kathryn asked Samantha to pass the cookie tray. Samantha wanted one of her tart lemon bars. Kathryn took an oatmeal-raisin cookie, and then passed the plate across the table to Grandpa Hastings who took two pignoli cookies, his personal favorite. Grandma Hasting, like Kathryn preferred oatmeal-raisin. Finally, Kathryn placed a peanut butter cookie on each of the plates in front of the two empty seats.

Both of Kathryn's parents loved peanut butter—they smeared it on everything. Sometimes the three of them experimented with different peanut butters and crazy foods: peanut butter stuffed in hot cherry peppers, peanut butter soup, and of course, best of all, chunky peanut butter on top of a grilled hot dog.

Kathryn picked up her cup, emptied it in two swallows, filled it again, and added double her usual amount of spiced honey. Her grandparents tried to fight back their tears, but they could not. They missed their daughter.

Samantha realizing this was a special time for Kathryn and her grandparents thought it was best to leave. "Thank you for such a wonderful tea party. It is time for me to go."

Grandpa winked at Samantha, and silently mouthed, "Thank you."

Kathryn snuggled in her grandmother's arms, said. "See you tomorrow. Thanks for the sweets."

After a few sips of honeysuckle tea, Grandma Hastings bent over and lifted a small, polished, golden oak stained wooden box from under the table. She placed it between Kathryn and herself. Its cover was inlaid with mother of pearl and an odd purple and brown stone Kathryn had never seen before. When the lid's brass catch was pulled to the side, the tarnished hinges creaked a bit. Grandma reached in and pulled out a small purple velvet pouch. Grandma Hastings rested the bag on the table, put the ends of the golden drawstrings between the tips of her thumb and forefinger, and gently tugged at the tightly rolled ribbons, allowing the mouth of the bag to spread open slowly for everyone to see the surprise treasure. Grandma deliberately reached into the bag, clutched the object, and gracefully, held the contents ever so softly just inside the bag.

Addressing Kathryn, her grandmother instructed, "Open your hand, my dear," and after raising it above the lip of the bag, the gift was lowered to Kathryn's waiting hand. Resting in the center of her palm was a dazzling opal pendant in a filigreed gold setting on a delicately thin gold chain.

The piece of jewelry at rest in her hand was once worn by her mother.

For a moment, a clear snapshot of her finger moving back and forth over the same gleaming opal, while sitting as a little girl on Great-Grandma Cappelli's knee flashed before Kathryn. Grandma Hastings wore the ring only those times when special visitors came to tea.

Grandma Hastings, reading Kathryn's face, said, "Yes dear, every woman in our family at some time has been entrusted with the opal.

Your mother changed the setting from a ring to a pendant, believing she could better conceal it from anyone who would want to steal it to misuse its powers. She would be happy to know it is in your possession and will keep you safe.

Kathryn had never seen her mother wear either a ring or the piece of jewelry in front of her, nor had she ever heard her talk about it. She had no recollection of even seeing it in her mother's jewelry box, and they often played "dress the princess," using her mom's fancy jewelry.

Kathryn ran her finger over the line running diagonally through the bright white stone, "What is this purple line?" Kathryn asked.

"Great-Grandmother Cappelli called it, 'Byzantine Purple,'" now, running her finger on the line, "no one has ever been to explain how the porphyry could be set inside the opal."

Grandma watched Kathryn lift the pendant, swinging on its chain twist into the sun. The porphyry streak within the opal radiated a brilliant purple high glow, then, as quickly as it emitted its energy, the light streamed back into the stone. "The stone has many powers which you must be sure to protect now that it is yours."

Kathryn confused by her grandmother's words, took hold of the golden chain, lifted it high enough so the pendant was over the mouth of the bag, and dropped it in. Then, she pulled the yellow ribbons tight, securing the jewelry in its original purple purse, placed it back into the box sitting on the table, and without displaying any sort of emotion took a bite of Samantha's peanut butter cookie.

Confused

After the table was cleared, Grandma Hastings called Kathryn down to the living room. Kathryn knew from experience that her grandmother had something serious to discuss. These conversations always ended well, though. She never argued with her grandparents— well, maybe two or three times when they all were trying to figure out how to continue their lives. But this afternoon, she just wanted to be alone.

She followed her grandmother into the living room and flopped down on the sofa.

Grandma Hastings, reading Kathryn's slow manner and slouching shoulders, began the chat in a loving voice. Grandma was curious why Kathryn had not questioned the fact her mother had never worn it. Kathryn did not have any answers other than she wanted to keep it in her room, and maybe someday, she would wear it when she was older.

Grandma Hastings needed to make a point, letting her know the ring was special. "The pendant, your pendant, is more than a family heirloom." Her grandmother hesitated, selecting her words carefully before continuing, "it is unlike any other gem in the world." Grandma Hastings told Kathryn she had a premonition, and a feeling, that Kathryn would soon need the opal. Kathryn needed to know its use and has certain elements that must be understood. "The opal is not to be given away or abused; it is to be worn only by our family's first-born ladies."

It all seemed particularly important to Grandma Hastings, but to Kathryn it seemed too much like a TV sci-fi movie. Kathryn had never heard Grandma Hastings talk about good or bad luck, other than to call it foolishness when Kathryn brought home a pink rabbit's won playing "Smack a Mole" at the Ocean County Fair.

Kathryn's head was spinning—the emotions of the tea party and this conversation she did not want to have, and her grandmother not making any sense. All she wanted to do was to go back to her room. Kathryn told her grandmother she would take good care of the gift, and she would tell no one, not even Samantha, where she hid it. The wooden box would be safe in the back of the bottom drawer of her dresser, and she would not use it except in extreme circumstances—she was sure that was what her grandmother wanted to hear.

Kathryn lifted herself out of her chair, gave her grandmother a kiss, picked up the box, and went up the stairs to the privacy of her bedroom. She put the box with its purple purse in the bottom of her dresser, crawled under the covers of her bed, and instantly fell asleep.

She wondered if she could ever have a happy birthday again.

Chapter 15

"11"

Macaroni and Cheese, the Haglady's House

Kathryn, hot and dripping, walked into the house after practicing her soccer kicks into a net her grandfather built in the back yard.

Grandpa asked, "How's that left foot coming along?"

Kathryn showing her form. "Not as good as I want it to be, but better."

"We're off to visit the Conti's for a couple of hours. There is a covered plate on the counter."

"I'm off to Samantha's after I dry off."

Grandma gave her a concerned goodbye. "Be careful. Keep your eyes open. See you later this afternoon."

Kathryn gave "sweaty hugs" to her grandparents and headed to the stairs.

She went straight to the bathroom and gave her face a quick rinse. Her mother had advised a few years earlier, "Never scrub or rub, only lightly rinse your face with a gentle soap and water." And that was what Kathryn did. Because Kathryn shared her mother's perfect complexion Samantha had suggested that Kathryn consider being a face model for Cosmo or television commercials. Her mother's brown eyes had been the same color as Great-Grandmother Cappelli's and Grandma Hastings' and passed on to Kathryn. The color sparkled when she spoke to you. Kathryn missed those eyes, and her father's voice.

Once she made her way downstairs to the kitchen, she saw a tinfoil wrapped plate and headed straight for it. A note was taped to the top: "Kathryn, we have gone to the market. Your grandfather said what every eleven-year-old needs is under the foil wrap." Kathryn already knew—mac and cheese. Her grandfather made the gooiest, chewiest, cheesiest, tastiest macaroni and cheese in the neighborhood. In fact, Nick and Nelly's father told Grandpa Hastings at the barbershop, "My kids think your macaroni and cheese is better than anything their mother cooks, and it's the only food they want for the rest of their lives." Kathryn almost agreed—his pancakes are beyond incredible.

Before she knew it, the plate was empty, and since no one was watching, she licked the plate cleaner than Chubby licked his milk bowl.

Now fully energized, she decided to leap onto her bike and visit Samantha, who had left a message on her phone to come over when she was ready. Before scooting out the door, Chubby needed to be fed. Of course, Chubby always thought he should be fed. He was weaving in and out of Kathryn's legs to get attention, declaring his hunger. She opened a can of "Chicken and Fish Deluxe" and dumped it into Chubby's bowl along with a cup of dry food. Chubby was now in the middle of one of his two favorite activities, eating, the other was sleeping—his name was quite appropriate.

Once Chubby was happily eating his barnyard and ocean combo, Kathryn went to the garage. With her bike under her, she pressed on the pedals. The bike and its passenger were at the end of the driveway when she slammed on the brakes, leaving a swerving rubber patch behind her. Kathryn dropped her bike on the sidewalk, ran back up the driveway, entered her house through the back door, glided over the snacking Chubby, and bolted up the stairs into her room, not stopping until she was on two knees in front of her dresser.

The last time she thought about the necklace was a year earlier, and now, something made her want to see it. She took a breath, then pulled the bottom drawer open, lifted the hidden box from the drawer, and turned it upside down on her bed. She grabbed the purple purse with its gold drawstrings, stuffed it in her left back pocket, and in moments, Kathryn was back on her bike. However, she was peddling in a different direction than earlier planned. She was now on a ride to that not-so-vacant lot.

As she accelerated, she became more certain of her objective. Taking a couple of turns, jumping two curbs, and executing a rear brake slide, the two-wheeled vehicle came to a sudden, but controlled stop in front of the cottage Samantha thought did not exist. The rider slid from the seat, walked her speedy Schwinn onto the sidewalk in front of a thatched-roof cottage, pushed down on the kickstand, and began to take in her surroundings. She was full of anticipation of the unknown, intently observing the building she knew she must enter.

A foggy white smoke rose from the brown stone chimney, distorting what had been a bright yellow sun that earlier in the day had warmed the summer afternoon. Now the blocked bright rays left it a dark-orange disk that appeared to be sitting atop the chimney waiting to be drawn into the stone shaft. The once warm rays no longer illuminated the lane to the Haglady's small house.

The roof's thatching was the same green as the grass on the lawn in front of her. Dark blue clapboard wrapped around the house like tape on a baseball bat. Violet half-moon framed shutters were opened so light could pass through the deep purple glass of its round windows. The winding brick pathway led from the crimson fence gate to the three bright white steps that would take Kathryn to the porch. Kathryn had never seen so many brilliant colors in one place, more than in a crayon box.

Kathryn measured the course she had to take from gate to front door, squared her shoulders, and stepped through the gate.

Kathryn felt a warm breeze move through her, guiding her, telling her what she was to do—meant to do—by some gentle, unknown power controlling all she did.

The warmth of the wind caused Kathryn to pause before moving forward. She counted to three, inhaled and exhaled, extended her left foot so her toes would first touch the red bricks just as she did to test the ocean water temperature before jumping into the surf when her family vacationed at the beach.

The softness of the bricks against her sneakers was surprising. How could bricks feel soft? She had to look at her feet to be sure she was wearing sneakers. Unlike the hard walkway entrance to her yard, the Haglady's path was almost squishy.

As Kathryn continued to put one red and yellow sneaker ahead of the other, each of her measured steps lessened the fear of the unknown, heightening the exhilaration of this quest. An unexpected confidence rose within her as she became more certain of her decision to follow her instincts wanting to meet the Haglady, knowing it was indeed the right path for her to follow. Once she arrived at the first step, her courage began to build. In three quick steps, she was standing on a porch of yellow boards staring at the Haglady's deep, dark brown, wooden front door. Her image reflected from the many layers of glassy varnish. She looked to see if there was a doorbell—none. Her eyes turned back to the door, hand ready to knock, but the door began reshaping into a storyboard. It happened so quickly; she was fascinated by what was in front of her.

Kathryn's eyes moved around the wooden door as shapes became defined in the burnt brown cedar, and then colors began to fill the woodcuttings. It was mesmerizing.

The figures appeared to be telling a story, clearly from another time, another place. She recalled seeing similar pictures in a book about ancient history. There were warriors on horseback with decorated swords hanging on their belts, foot soldiers carrying polished shields and lances in their hands, muscled oxen pulled wagons bulging with merchandise and food, a shipwreck, small boats with angry pirates, and the docks of a seaport piled high with packages to be traded. Every scene felt somehow familiar— these were from her dreams—the thought of what might be was exhilarating. What had she found at this house? How could her dreams be known by another?

Kathryn was particularly absorbed with one carving of a woman walking behind a line of dark brown covered wagons. The scene had a quality she could only describe as "Middle Ages." The lady in the wooden door wore a wide brimmed hat like the one the Haglady had been wearing at their encounter earlier. Kathryn felt her body tighten when her eyes fell upon the woodcut of a young girl with long curly brown hair standing in what looked like a marketplace wearing a yellow tunic gathered at the waist by a golden ribbon. She was the same girl fighting on the ship, and the same girl with papers in her hand standing on a foreign dock, and the same girl riding in a fancy carriage with a soldier.

Kathryn blinked, and looked again; her real world and her dreams seemed to be intertwined.

Her gaze now intent, she recognized the figure of the young girl carved into the door. Kathryn's voice gushed out, "It's me."

Looking at the entire door, all the figures, all the women, were in some way connected to Kathryn. She sensed she herself was a part of the door, and then a vision of her mother rushed into her head. She remembered seeing her mother wearing the same long dress with a belt matching like the girl in the carving. She thought she must be reacting to emotions from all that had happened since her accident.

Hot and sweaty, Kathryn wiped her face and eyes with her sleeve. When she looked once more, the door had, in a moment, changed again. Silver light shone out from the edges of the entryway, and now a message appeared on the ornate green glass imbedded in the wooden door. A golden message was etched into the glass: "Kathryn, don't bother to knock, simply give the door a good push. Be careful, I always seem to trip on the first step."

Kathryn could not believe what was happening. The note had not been there just seconds earlier. The door's woodcarvings had vanished.

Kathryn put both hands on the door and pushed. The light in the room momentarily blinded Kathryn, causing her to trip when she took that first step.

Chapter 16

Inside the Haglady's House

Kathryn found herself standing in the center of an immense room, the size of an auditorium; she could not make sense of it. The room, three or four, or even more times larger than the house she had walked up to overwhelmed her. The all-glass ceiling was as high as that in her school's gymnasium, except the ceiling of this room was constructed of a single pane. The walls of the expanse were covered in tapestries and paintings. There were platoons of lances and spears on display, luminous shelves crammed with pistols and guns, swords and knives, cabinets with bows and quivers of arrows, and helmets. Greek and Roman statues of wood and stone stood as sentries throughout the room. Many artifacts were suspended from the ceiling: there was a chariot, a trireme, and a ship in full sail. Showcases of coins, jewels, crowns and tiaras reflected twinkly lights from their glass cabinets. Ancient tools and compasses of all types along with navigational tables were set on tables for exhibit. Kathryn was so overwhelmed by the items in this hidden museum she was convinced it would take days, probably weeks, to see the vast array of treasures. Where had all the artifacts come from? How could the large sculptures and war horses with gilded saddles, the armor of ancient warriors, and covered wagons used on caravans fit through such a tiny front door? There were more wonders than anyone could imagine.

In the center of the room were two chairs and a table. They could have been made of plastic or glass. Oddly, it seemed as if the tabletop, like the ceiling, had no frame of any kind. Kathryn looked under the table and could not see its legs. It was as if they floated in place. On the translucent table, Kathryn saw a setting for two. She looked around to see who else was in the house, wondering if the table was always set for two—that didn't make much sense to Kathryn. Or had her host known about Kathryn's visit? Was she expecting Kathryn—no, couldn't be, how could she?

Kathryn moved to the table.

The place settings were prepared with off-white linen napkins embroidered with intricate yellow and green floral designs. An ornate filigreed silver teaspoon, with the picture of a palace in the center of the handle, rested next to the napkin. The tea cups and matching saucers were familiar, more than familiar; they were identical to those her grandmother used when having the family's specially brewed tea—and to her astonishment, in the center of the table was a honey pot with a wooden dipper.

There was another person in the room!

The Haglady's voice beckoned, "Hello dear. Please sit with me."

The silkiness of the voice, the soft gentle tone, made her turn her head to the source with a mixture of fear of the unknown, and an irresistible desire to talk with the Haglady.

Kathryn's eyes rested on the lady. She wore the same purple dress trimmed in soft yellow. A scarf falling loosely from around her neck was painted with blossoms, the same as those that arrived each spring on the vines climbing the fence bordering her backyard, the same blossoms and vines she remembered covering the patio trellis of her grandparents' New York City home.

"Kathryn," the soft voice beckoned as the Haglady walked into the room. Sitting down at the table, and gesturing for Kathryn to do the same, invited her to sit. "I just brewed a pot of tea. In fact, it is my favorite flavor, honeysuckle."

Looking directly at the seated Haglady, and then slowly stepping to the table, Kathryn touched the chair in front of her and cautiously sat down. To Kathryn's surprise, the seat and tabletop provided the same soft sensation to her touch as her feet had experienced when stepping on the stone walkway moments earlier outside the cottage.

Kathryn was in disbelief and disoriented from the instant she studied the front door until amazed by the incredible wonders of the room.

"My dear, you looked a bit surprised when you came to my front door?" asked the host, as she began to pour the sweet-smelling elixir from a pearl-white pot into the matching cups.

Kathryn asked, "The carvings in your door are from my dreams?"

Kathryn wanting an explanation, probed, "and how did the pictures in the door change?"

Gently revealing a difficult truth to understand, the Haglady affirmed what Kathryn already came to grips with. "Kathryn, the door, as your dreams, tells of your past," a hesitation, "we must go there."

Kathryn wanting more, questions. "Two of the carvings are unfamiliar, but I can see it's me."

"My dear, there may come a time when you will visit those carvings, but now you have a challenge, a decision before you which cannot be put aside."

Kathryn takes a sip of tea. Her focus moves to the tea service.

Drawing a sense of strength from within, Kathryn's voice burst out in a puzzling tone, "Why honeysuckle tea?"

Not waiting for an answer, Kathryn immediately barked another question in her newly acquired demanding voice: "I think you know a lot about me—why?"

In the same controlled demeanor, the lady had used when they first met, she sought to make her visitor comfortable. "My dear, I will do my best to answer your worried concerns. In fact, there are many subjects to be asked about, to learn, and I promise to answer each one of them."

For the first time, Kathryn relaxed, just a bit, and became more comfortable. This time she was making real sense of the situation. They were talking.

"Kathryn," her host began, "I take it you are familiar with 'Grandmother's Tea'?"

"How is it you know that I like honeysuckle tea? My mother and grandmother are the only two people I know who serve honeysuckle tea." A sense of apprehension enveloped Kathryn. She began to speak, hesitated for a moment, and then her voice cracked with nervousness as she asked, "How do you know we call it 'Grandmother's Tea'?"

Kathryn taking charge of her fear. "I think you know a lot about me."

"I do."

"My grandmother told me to come here. I don't know why. Well, maybe about the opal."

"To answer questions. And to talk about tomorrow."

Kathryn softens her voice, "You are the one who saved me from that creepy man, aren't you?"

"Yes."

"You know, my mother and grandmother thought I wasn't listening to them when they were talking about me and some danger. And a secret they kept from my dad." Taking a breath, hopeful in her question, asks, "Can you tell me the secret?"

"Yes."

"Mom thought I didn't know about her dreams, but I did."

"So, Kathryn, why didn't you say anything to her?"

"I was afraid she would ask me about mine."

Feeling a connection has grown between Kathryn and her, the lady asked, "What about yours?"

"I want to forget the bad ones and live the good ones."

Letting Kathryn know the unfortunate situation she is in, tells, "You can't have both. But you can try to understand them, and step into them, to be as once was. Do you wish to go to the life of your dreams?"

"My birthday wish?"

Pouring tea, allowing Kathryn time to consider the prospect of time travel. "Do you like my gallery, my collections from all the places I have traveled to over the ages?"

Kathryn took a sip of the familiar tea that had been poured from the familiar teapot, and she began to perspire. In fact, she felt herself slipping back in time as memories overlapped memories: her mother's face, remembering her mother's clothes, the visitor at her grandmother's house years ago, the accident and being held at the crash by a woman smelling of honeysuckle, and just a little while ago, the carvings on the Haglady's front door. The flood of memories and recollections impossible for her to explain almost made Kathryn faint.

"Dear Kathryn, are you okay? Do you need to rest?" The Haglady's voice brought Kathryn back to the reality of being in a house none of her friends could see, having a conversation with a woman who seemed to know quite a bit about her guest's life. Kathryn suddenly knew she MUST focus on her situation and find out all the facts. Samantha just would not be able to believe any of this. Kathryn thought with a smile, "I can't believe any of this, and I'm in the middle of it."

Kathryn took a sip, feeling the tea's familiar taste, soothing her dry throat, warming her body. She took another sip. And, then, another.

The Family Secret: Remembering the Visitor

With a knowing voice, the Haglady asked Kathryn, "Has your grandmother had occasion to discuss our special tea?" The Haglady knew the question would be quite unexpected for Kathryn, and she pointed to the white ceramic teapot. The teapot's design was the same as the pot Kathryn had poured tea from many times before.

For as long as Kathryn could remember, her mother and grandmother spent many hours enjoying conversations while sipping their tea. Her earliest recollection of the sweet tea was when she was five years old on a sunny, summer afternoon. Kathryn and her mother were visiting her grandparents' house on a sweltering day of both high temperature and humidity, a day her father referred to as a "New York oven." Her mother announced it was time for a great occasion. A special long-time family visitor would arrive for high tea, sandwiches, and sweeties at exactly 2:00 PM, and everyone was expected to dress for the occasion.

Kathryn was excited: a party, a surprise visitor, high tea, sweet desserts, a chance to dress up, and maybe, just maybe, Kathryn would be allowed to wear her white gloves.

Giddy with excitement, Kathryn knew she had the best grandmother in the world because every visit to Grandma's had a surprise.

Her grandmother loved parties, all types, whether formal or casual gatherings. She often had guests Kathryn had not met before, and many of them were special, not special important, not famous people, but special in that they were, each one of them, travelers. They had many stories to tell, and both her mother and grandmother knew all of them.

Kathryn had talked to Samantha about this subject before. She wondered how her mother and grandmother were acquainted with so many people and knowledgeable about the places these world voyagers had seen—the women in Kathryn's family were bewildering to her, especially when she grew older. The conversations were often about, as Samantha would call them, "Characters." Often the stories focused on characters who lived centuries ago, descriptions of cities that could not possibly be true, adventures her grandmother and mother were not old enough to have taken part in.

Samantha had said, "Just adults wishing they could do what their imaginations were imagining. Heck, they make fun of us when we tell them stories! I'll never understand adults." Feeling enlightened, informed Kathryn what they must do, said, "Kathryn, when we are adults, our kids will love us because we will know exactly how they feel, so remember this moment."

To young Kathryn, a tea meant a time to wear something special, wondering if she could wear her new short white gloves with fancy lace sewn on the wrists—a question that was answered before she could ask.

"Kathryn, my wonderful granddaughter, the upcoming tea is just the right opportunity for you to wear those pretty gloves your mother bought for you in the spring," Grandma Hastings announced with a big smile, "and let me help you pick out a dress. We must take a look at what you have; a light summer dress is what is needed today."

Instantly, Kathryn ran ahead of her grandmother to the closet and found the perfect dress, for the perfect occasion, which her mother had thought to bring with them this visit. Just as Grandmother Hastings stepped into the room, Kathryn was holding her choice of dress up to her neck for approval. Grandmother Hastings approved.

"My dear, you have chosen exactly what I was thinking would be perfect for an occasion like today." Kathryn's mother and grandmother **always** knew what Kathryn was thinking.

The summer cotton dress was covered with a mix of brightly printed flowers on a light-yellow background. It was sleeveless with thin yellow shoulder straps, and along with the elegant white gloves and her white patent leather shoes, and she would wear the bracelet her father had given her for receiving the *Student of the Year Award* at the End of Year School Assembly. Kathryn would certainly be the center of attention— of course everyone likes that.

She remembered Grandma Hastings going down to the bakery and choosing special desserts her family called "sweeties." The delicious delights would be two or three cookies of every type in the showcase: chocolate ones with vanilla icing, sugar cookies with sprinkles, pignoli cookies, crushed pistachios in dates, and others that dripped in honey and melted in your mouth the instant they touched your lips.

Kathryn remembered dressing very quickly wanting to be ready fifteen minutes early to sit in front of the big parlor window. She hoped this would give her a glimpse of the special guest upon arrival, so she could open the door just as the doorbell was touched.

The doorbell RANG.

How did that happen? Kathryn could not understand how the guest was able to open the sidewalk gate, come up the walkway and onto the porch steps, and ring the doorbell without being seen.

"Kathryn dear," her grandmother called, "please answer the door."

Kathryn was already moving before she heard her grandmother's request. Sliding off the windowsill box, she ran to the front door, but not without first looking in the big hallway mirror to make sure she was presentable. She straightened her dress, grabbed the glass doorknob, and pulled to welcome the tea party's guest of honor.

Just as she opened the door, her mother and grandmother arrived, placing themselves between Kathryn and the visitor.

Almost as if they had practiced their welcome, both ladies excitedly addressed the visitor, "Welcome Miss Teresa!"

The three of them hugged, and then they stepped aside for introductions—introductions at tea are very formal, and everyone is made to feel important.

Kathryn's mother took care of the formalities, "Kathryn Isabella Pangburn, this is Miss Teresa. Miss Teresa, this is my daughter, Kathryn Isabella Pangburn, the granddaughter of Isabella Hastings, and the great-granddaughter of Great-Grandmother Cappelli." Kathryn, who had practiced her greeting, looked into the beautiful tawny eyes of the guest, thrust out her hand and said, "Very nice to meet you madam."

As Kathryn tried to think about how old the lady was, Miss Teresa began, "Dear, it is my pleasure to finally meet you! Your mother and grandmother have kept me well informed. And your dear great-grandmother had so much to say about you. After you were born, she told me, "That newborn Kathryn has promise. You can see it in her eyes. She will carry on our family's…" Miss Teresa took a brief pause, looked at Kathryn's mother, and finished, "… love of tea." Kathryn was too excited about the high tea to notice the looks exchanged among the three ladies.

Miss Teresa kept Kathryn's attention. "Miss Kathryn, is it proper for me to call such a beautiful young lady, one who is dressed like a modern-day princess, Miss Kathryn?" Kathryn nodded and Miss Teresa asked, "It is grand to have you in our circle this afternoon. Are you fond of Grandmother's tea?" Miss Teresa informed, "Kathryn, I once met a delightful, very smart young girl, about the same age as you in Venice; her name was Signorina Kathryn. She had many adventures. Have you ever heard of her?"

Interested, Kathryn was ready to ask Miss Teresa about the girl who shared the same name, but her mother hastily directed the group to the back porch and onto the lawn where they would have their luncheon.

As Kathryn stepped off the back deck, she studied the visitor who moments earlier had entered the house and complimented her choice of dress. Her mom and the guest were standing next to the decorated picnic table. Even though it was so hot, Miss Teresa was fully covered in a purple outfit trimmed in yellow, wearing a matching hat with two long feathers, one yellow, the other a peacock's, which were tucked into a pale yellow lace hatband on the right side of the hat.

High tea was about to begin. Kathryn carried a tray of "sweeties" from her grandfather's bakery, and her grandmother had a three-tiered silver serving dish. On the top two tiers were finger sandwiches she had prepared earlier: cucumber and watercress, egg salad and lettuce, avocado and tomato, and salmon. Kathryn covered the bottom level with sweeties.

When the table was set, Kathryn looked at her mother—they traded smiles—and then directed their attention to Grandma Hastings.

"Ladies," Grandma Hastings gestured to the guests, "The time for our tea is at hand."

All four took their seats. On the center of the table sat a royal blue velvet covered box. Its latch was made of polished brass.

Her grandmother, in a ceremonial manner, opened the box, exposing six cups which were nestled in white velvet compartments. The beautifully decorated cups were a matching set. They were all the same shape, but each cup was individually designed.

It appeared to Kathryn, her grandmother was ready to tell her something very important. Her grandmother began, "Kathryn, the cups and teapot from this box are quite special. They have been in the family for centuries. They are important to who we are, to our family, and to be used only on special occasions. Today is a special occasion."

Miss Teresa smiled saying, "I do believe Miss Kathryn, they are over a thousand years old."

The guest of honor reached into the box and passed the cups to each of the four.

"Isabella, this is yours, and Amelia, for you, this is mine, and Kathryn, this is your cup."

"That cup!"

The gentle memory of that cup shocked Kathryn back to the present—that cup was sitting on the tea saucer right in front of her. The cup she had been drinking from since she sat down. She wondered, "How many times had the cup been filled—two, three?"

Again, the Haglady asked, Kathryn, "Has your grandmother, or did your mother, take occasion to discuss our special tea, or the tea service with you?"

Kathryn was instantly stunned by the question. The implication by her host, that her mother, her Grandmother, and the Haglady were acquainted in some way was now entirely possible. Is it possible—they must be? Why was she just now remembering a tea party from years earlier? Was this the same woman she had met at her grandmother's when she was five?

Kathryn looked carefully at her eyes!

Certainly, Grandma Hastings would have mentioned knowing her.

"I remember you. You visited my grandmother's house for tea when I was a little girl."

"I did enjoy myself that day."

"Your name is Teresa."

"It is. I do prefer that to what your friends call me."

Wanting more answers, vaguely recalls, "You told a story about my mother's opal. It belonged to a queen." Kathryn has linked her curiosity to all the events leading up to this moment, pointedly asks, "That is why I am here, isn't it?"

"You are correct. We have matters to discuss if you are ready to listen, to understand what is before you."

"I am."

"The queen's name was Cleopatra. I'm confident you have heard of her in school. Before she was queen, she heard stories of Pharaoh Hatshepsut's enchanted ring. Her vizier, Abbadon, uncovered the location of the tomb. Cleopatra secretly had the tomb unearthed and found the ring hidden in a small wooden box. It was the magic of the ring which saved Cleopatra many times after her father died and when she was Queen, a Pharaoh."

Kathryn sat motionless, immersed in the story.

Teresa continued. "Cleopatra's maid, the queen's closest friend, saw Abbadon searching the queen's chamber, opening the box which was forbidden to the touch of anyone other than the queen herself. The maid described what she saw to Cleopatra: the vizier run from the queen's room clutching a purple pouch."

Not waiting a moment for Teresa to continue, Kathryn, enthralled, asked, "What happened?"

"Cleopatra ordered her guards to capture Abbadon and bring him, bound in iron chains to her."

"Did they capture him? Did he have the box?"

"Yes. But just as they captured him, he held the ring tightly in his fist. He called on the ring's power.

"Give me many lives before I die."

The guards wrestled the ring from Abbadon and brought him to Cleopatra.

"Then what happened?"

"Cleopatra could not reverse Abbadon's wish on the opal. He escaped imprisonment days later and has been searching for centuries trying to find the opal for horrible purposes, to change history."

"What does he want?"

Teresa realized Kathryn is now ready to take the responsibility of her family line. She tells the rest of the story. "He wants to go back in time, and with the power of the prize, he can become the greatest of all pharaohs.

Realizing Abbadon's intent, Cleopatra entrusted her maid to conceal the opal where no one could ever find it."

"For the maid's loyalty, Cleopatra told her about the magic in the ring, then used the stone to cast another spell:

"My maid's youngest daughters are forever,

for good and no other,

and may they travel the ages until they die."

"Did the maid live forever?"

"She has lived many lives."

Teresa recounted the queen's trip to Rome to visit Caesar. "When Cleopatra arrived at her villa, knowing the Roman senators were disgruntled with her being there, she and the maid concealed the pouch in a place no one would consider searching—right in front of their noses, in plain sight. It was a terrible time for the queen after the death of Julius Caesar. The clouds of peril were upon her. Senators issued orders for Cleopatra to return to Egypt. Being warned guards would arrive soon, the maid and other attendants began packing for Egypt."

Kathryn interrupted, "Where, where did she, you know, the maid, hide it?"

Teresa steps away from the table and motions for Kathryn to follow and walks her to the center of the massive room stopping in front of a tall marble statue of Julius Caesar. Teresa points at the rear of the pedestal.

"Push hard against the leaf cut into the stone below Cesar's sandal. You will need both hands."

Kathryn kneels, one hand on top of the other and presses the leaf. Nothing happens. She looks up at Teresa who demonstrates a hard push movement.

Kathryn nods. She repositions herself, then thrusts her hands again at the marble cutout. Nothing. She slams her hands again, this time hitting it on the side causing a thin stone to slide sideways allowing Kathryn to press open the pedestal trap door exposing a hidden compartment.

"What's inside?"

"It's presently empty"

Kathryn riveted by the tale, asked, "Did you meet Julius Caesar?"

"Yes. He and Cleopatra were in love, but the duties of both Rome and Egypt upon them did not sit well in Rome."

Teresa resumes the story outside of Cleopatra's Rome quarters. "Servants carrying goods to wagons were being inspected by guards surrounding the villa. Cleopatra sits elegantly atop her ornate carriage ready to leave for her ship waiting at the harbor. Her maid steps up and whispers to the queen the guards would not allow the statue of Caesar to be removed. Cleopatra's eyes open wide, but not wanting to show concern returns whispered directions to the maid. The maid ran back to the home but was not allowed to enter."

"What did the queen do?"

"The only thing she could do. She ordered her caravan leave to the port city."

"You mean she left the purple pouch with the opal behind."

"She had no other choice.?

"Did she ever get it back?"

"No. Cleopatra sent requests many times to Rome for the sculpture, but never received an answer.

"Why?"

"There was bad blood between Rome and Egypt, then a war."

Back at the table, Kathryn is still engrossed in the tale, wanting more. "If you know the story. And the statue is in your room, I think I know the answer to my next question."

Teresa, delighted, responds giving Kathryn what she wants to hear. "You want to know what happened to the maid, don't you?' Teresa's lips form a smile, softly says, "I am the maid."

She waits as Kathryn mulls over all she has heard—each question becomes two.

Kathryn reaches into her back pocket for the purple bag. Both exchange glances. Teresa's face encourages Kathryn's desire to open the pouch. Reluctantly, yet, unwavering, her trembling fingers reach into the bag clutching the gold chain and displays the opal pendant on the glass table.

"Is this Cleopatra's?" She stares at Teresa.

"Yes."

"Why isn't it a ring?"

"You mother thought by changing the setting it might be less noticeable by Abbadon."

Tears well up in Kathryn's eyes as the impact of the opal on her family overwhelms her, an inner strength building, now demanding, "Did my mom and dad die because of the opal?"

"Yes. Abbadon will stop at nothing to get the stone. Kathryn, listen to my next words. Only you can change the past for your future from this point on."

"What can I do? How can a girl stop Abbadon? What if I don't want to?"

"You have the power to change the past, to destroy Abbadon, to save your daughters from feeling the same ache that is in your heart.

"Why can't you"?

"The ring and its force have been passed to you, the youngest of our line by Cleopatra's command. I can help you, but not do what must be done."

"Why didn't my mother save her life and my dad's?"

"All I can guess is she implored the opal to save you."

"Why only me?"

Teresa takes this moment to reveal the secret Kathryn has known from her dreams, but not able to identify with until now. "Kathryn, you are from the past."

Astonished at hearing the declaration from Teresa, Kathryn, questions, "The past?"

"Because of the spell, Abbadon the Assassin, like you and me, are time-travelers. You recognized your past lives in the carvings on my door."

Kathryn stands, walks for a minute contemplating her dilemma. "Teresa, if I go to my dreams, will I be lost there, forever?"

"You must first answer another question. Do you want your birthday wish of years ago to come true?"

Standing over her chair, intent on her course of action, she tells Teresa, "I do with all my heart."

"Most importantly, you must believe in yourself. You will be given help to destroy Abbadon. The people around you will not know your dreams. You cannot tell them, and they wouldn't understand.

"Will I return?

"Only when Abbadon is dead."

Teresa fills Kathryn's cup.

The time for Kathryn to decide is at hand. Teresa asks, "What will you do?"

"I'm afraid. My dreams are scarier every night, and my parents are dead. I know I can't run away, but I know very little of the past. I want you with me."

Teresa explains she will be with Kathryn but not always recognized. Kathryn picks up the pouch holding it over her heart. "I will go. When will I see you?"

"We will next meet on a rainy night in the house of a merchant and his wife. You will not know me as you do now. But, be wary, you will be in danger as you are now."

Kathryn slips the necklace and pendant over her head.

Teresa pours tea, "The tea will take you to your past. Take hold of the opal."

Teresa takes a drink, recites:

"Hold tight your necklace,

go back in time,

 revenge for a heinous crime.

With Antonio in Venice,

you can change the past.

You will face Abbadon at last."

Kathryn picks up her cup, swallows. The room begins to spin. Teresa touches Kathryn's hand, and both melt away to a shadowy past

Part Two

Antonio

Chapter 17

From Tragedy to Wealth, Port City of Varna, Bulgaria
AD 1056

Antonio's early life was one of poverty, of hunger, and of begging. It was made more fragile when disease arrived on merchant ships travelling the coastlines of the Mediterranean Sea. By age nine, Antonio was on his own, to survive if he could, to sneak around in the shadows learning how to use the darkness of the night to find food, to protect himself, to stay clear of those who stole children and sold them to ships' captains, and to steal bread from unwatched kitchens. He had to learn all of this and more.

Antonio's family—his parents and younger sister—struggled to survive on the meager wages his father and mother earned on the docks at the port city of Varna along the western Black Sea.

Because so many were without jobs, employers could hire the impoverished for near starvation wages. Antonio heard his father say to his mother, "We are paid less than slaves, at least slaves are fed."

His father and mother begged for work each day on the docks. His father loaded and unloaded ships of their precious cargos which were being sent west on caravans to Europe's growing cities or sailing east by ship to Asia's mysterious lands. Antonio's pregnant mother longed to have work in a warehouse sewing sails and making rope, so that she could bring her children to sit at her side, safe from weather and the menacing docks.

They lived as all the poor lived. They were always in search of the next meal, any meal no matter how meager. Their bellies ached, their bodies frail, and there did not seem to be any reason to believe tomorrow would bring change.

Their one room shanty was pieced together behind a warehouse along the dock. Antonio's father had stacked boulders forming two walls with one end against the outside rear wall of the warehouse. He filled the crevices with small stones, and he stuffed plant material and mud into the cracks to keep the wind and rain from coming through. The two stone walls of his three-walled shelter were held in place by a roof made from discarded bug-eaten ships' planks covered with scraps of worn sail. Protecting and providing some privacy at the front were planks sunk into the ground and tied against the roof. A thin, weather-worn blanket made of cloth remnants his mother had scavenged and sewn together hung as a door.

Death came to Antonio's family that winter. Many in Varna were beginning to show signs of an ancient disease doctors were unable to cure. The city's doctors tried all the medicines, and the clergy prayed all the prayers in all the prayer books, yet they could not stop the sickness.

Stories of the disease came first, told by seamen and travelers, but now the virus had found its way to Antonio's shelter. Smallpox did not care about a victim's wealth or status. The pus-filled blisters covered infants and grandparents; the scabs could be seen on nobles and beggars. Its fever did not kill all those who had the sickness. Many recovered, but those who were weak of body, especially the hungry, were not strong enough to fight the enemy inside their bodies—they died.

When Antonio's mother first began to show signs of scabs on her skin, she pleaded with her husband to take the children and leave the city as others had even though there would be no one to care for her. His father could not miss work, for if he did, others would take his place. He had been without work for so long and could not let them go hungry again.

Antonio had no other family. They were poor—no help at hand, no doctor, no relatives, not even anyone to pray over them—they only had each other. Once the sickness came to their hovel, they unknowingly spread it to each other within the drafty, cold, damp makeshift shelter.

One by one, his family succumbed to disease. His infant sister surrendered to the sickness only two days after her skin reddened. And then, Antonio could only watch as his father, hot with fever, was brought to their shelter after collapsing on the dock. He died the next morning. All Antonio could do was sit in the corner of the shack as his mother lost her strength and will to live after the losses of her daughter and husband.

"Antonio, Antonio, my son," her cry woke the exhausted boy. He was so weak from lack of food he could barely raise his head to look at his mother. A faint sliver of morning light found its way through a hole in the cloth and rested on his mother's face. For a second, Antonio felt relieved that all had been a bad dream, but his hope was quickly dashed. "Antonio, please listen," came a plea. "You must listen to me."

On hands and knees, he crawled to his mother. Wanting to be held in her arms, to be kissed on the cheek, to be told all was going to be as before, was dashed when Antonio stared at his sickly mother. In a sharp tone, his mother insisted, "Antonio, don't touch me, you must save yourself." When he started to cry, her heart melted, but she knew what must be done, so she continued in the soft gentle voice he loved, "Antonio, please listen. You are to leave—never to return. You are to promise me you will follow my directions."

Antonio, with tears in his eyes, nodded. He looked behind him. His father and sister were only inches away against the wall. The dead looked grey, old, like the ghosts in stories told to frighten children, to make their dreams terrible. A stench hung in the air. Antonio could smell death.

Terrified, he knew what her eyes were saying. She was giving her last goodbye. Those eyes that once made him laugh and offered comfort were distant with fever.

Her loving eyes met his, and she smiled the softest of smiles. "Antonio, my love, we will meet again." She leaned back on her blanket, her eyes closed, and she fell into a sleep.

She was not able to answer her son's whispered cry for help, or his wish for her to stay alive, or his questions about what he should do.

Antonio did not follow his mother's directions. He stayed with her that day. Later that night she stopped sleeping. She had stopped breathing.

Antonio, his arms crossed against his chest, rocked back and forth, with no one to look after him, and no one to touch him…no one.

Antonio remained in the room with no one to talk to, no one to care for him, no one alive. Hunger replaced his disbelief, so Antonio stepped outside and walked to the dock for help.

Antonio watched as a cart approached his home. He pointed to his house of stones and sticks, the home with a cloth door, the room in which he had been born. He talked briefly to the men outside his home, describing what had happened. Antonio stepped to the hut and pulled back the shabby curtain. He watched as two men dragged the bodies out into the air—they had tied a rope around the ankles of the dead, not wanting to touch them. The men stuck long thick branches under the corpses to roll each body onto a plank, then, they lifted the boards above the cart and with a tilt, the lifeless bodies, one by one, were dropped onto the bed of the wagon.

Antonio did not recognize the bodies. He knew who they were, but they did not look like his parents or his sister.

His eyes burned with tears, and his heart burned with loss watching the ox cart pull away. He had no one to talk to, to console him, protect him.

Antonio stood alone.

Many weeks later, Antonio was filthy from living as a street urchin so skinny from lack of food the same clothes he had been wearing for weeks were now hanging on him as if they were intended for a much larger boy. Standing alongside Antonio was Gregorio, another boy of the streets who was a year older, and who was as grimy and hungry as his new friend.

The boys did not ask for their lot in life. No child would want to be without food, without a home, or without parents, but they were. The boys were cold in the winter, wet when it rained, afraid for their lives, and they saw what happened to those who could not escape the men who captured and sold children.

Gregorio's parents, who fished along the Sicilian coast city of Agrigento, were not able to feed their children, so they offered him as a cabin boy to a sea captain hoping he could become more than his poor family could offer a young son. But, months later, the captain left Gregorio on the dock at Varna when he no longer had use for him.

Antonio's mother, Helena, came as a newborn to Varna with her parents from Trieste. Her father and mother tended to animals on a merchant caravan that traveled to fairs throughout Europe. When the caravan left for Kiev, Helena and her mother were left behind. Helena never met her father, and her mother died of fever a few years later.

It was on the docks of Varna that she met Antonio's father, another youngster without a home.

The boys were two of the many beggars in the city who began each day holding out their hands on the streets of Varna. They stood outside the city's churches hoping some gentleman of substance on his way to work, or a woman of wealth on her way home from early morning church services, would open their purses to a parentless hungry child. The penniless hoped someone, anyone, would feel compassion for the malnourished, and find in their heart some kindness and drop a slim coin onto the beggar's palm, as they had dropped offerings into the church's brass box when they entered to say prayers.

Antonio and Gregorio also prayed, not in the pews of the church they could not enter, but on the steps waiting for a handout which could provide enough bread to ease the groaning in their hungry stomachs for three days, maybe a week.

But their morning was without bread. They had not eaten anything more than the scraps they found at the back door of a local tavern two afternoons ago.

By mid-day, Antonio and Gregorio wandered along the busy docks, and stood at the doors of warehouses, shops, and factories, asking for a chance to work, no matter how small a task for food. The temperature and a misty rain began to fall. Gregorio, who was shivering, went to rest at the fallen down shack Antonio's family had once called home. The two of them were now family—two orphans barely surviving.

That late, very cold winter afternoon, when the season's sun was low on the horizon, almost ready to fall below the edge of the sea, Antonio was looking for protection from nature's chilling wind, a wind that is never kind to a boy like him. He crouched close to a warehouse wall behind tall clay pots filled with olive oil ready for the next day's tide.

Antonio, carefully making sure he was not seen, inched forward so that he could see down both directions of the dock. Walking past Antonio was the laziest watchman on the dock. Antonio was hopeful this watchman would fall asleep in a warehouse sometime after darkness covered the city, as he had done many times in the past, allowing Antonio and Gregorio, to take advantage of the sleeping guard. They would wait for him to begin to snore. The snore was their guide. It let them know when to slip into the warehouse to fill their bellies with the next day's shipments of grain or salted meats. On a rare occasion, when luck or the fates were with them, special tasty riches were to be stolen. They would take off their shirts, tie them into a ball around their hands, and smash containers of honey or olive oil, then sneak out and run to safety, licking the golden and green liquids until their bellies were full.

Antonio knew this dock guard, like most guards, did not do his duty when the weather was foul as it was on the dock this late afternoon. This guard walked his post until the wind made him shiver, and then he went to the warmth of the tavern. He only came out once every couple of hours, just long enough to look at the dock and return to his tavern seat or hide in a warehouse.

This would allow Antonio to take advantage of the night. He knew once darkness settled on the port, with the guard in the tavern and the docks clear of merchants, the timing would be right to quickly smash open one of the clay pots, drop the wad of hemp in the oil, and return to Gregorio, so his friend could lick the olive oil to warm his sick bones. With the plan settled in his mind, and remaining out of view, Antonio waited for the hours to pass before taking the liquid treasure from the pots that surrounded him.

The booming voice of a ship's captain, ordering his sailors to adjust the ropes which held the ship to its moorings, traveled with the wind across the dock. Now paying attention to the ship's activity, Antonio crawled forward to get a better look, but stayed hidden in his position, concerned that he would be found.

The captain suddenly fell silent in the middle of his directions, distracted by the sound of carriage wheels and horses moving in Antonio's direction. Antonio curled into an unseen ball. Then he heard the captain's heavy boots stepping on the gangway.

The captain walked halfway up the planks, facing into the wind while sleet, like knife points, cut into his face. A gentleman's carriage pulled by two matching dark bay horses raced up to the ship. The horses' hooves clattered on the dock, but the deep-voiced merchant's calls found the captain's ears. Hearing his name invoked so loudly, the captain's instincts took over. His hands crossed his body, putting a hand on each of the two daggers tucked into his belt, ready for action. When the captain recognized the passenger in the unfamiliar carriage, he relaxed his hands, dropping them to his side. He walked across the gangway and onto the dock.

A cloud of steam created from the cold sleet coming to rest on the hot backs of the horses blew with the wind along the path from the carriage to the gangway.

From his initial position, all Antonio could see were polished boots standing on the gangway. Silently, in the shadows, he flattened himself against the wet dock like a cat ready to catch a mouse. Antonio crawled to see what was so important on such a miserable day.

He watched curiously, making sure he was out of sight as two, well-celebrated, important men in Varna—a ship's captain and a merchant—held a business discussion on the dock, just a step from the gangway. Antonio was too far away in his cramped position to hear the exchange between Master Delyan and Captain Zoran. No matter how hard he strained his ears, the westerly wind and increasing mixture of rain and sleet beating on the jars and dock carried their voices seaward.

The captain, known by sailors, merchants, longshoreman, slaves, and beggars was Captain Zoran Ducik. No one on the docks knew about his past—he never talked to anyone except for business, and about the sea. Sailors said his voice was like that of the Pechenegs, who lived north of where the Danube River spills into the Black Sea. He was a captain of few words, communicating many orders through his first mate. His seamanship was well-known on both land and sea. Captain Zoran had commanded ships for two decades. Stories are told that he seized the opportunity to command at nineteen when the captain fell overboard after drinking too much wine. Without discussion, he took control of the wheel, and none of the crew challenged him. Many of the crew whispered the original captain might have been "helped" overboard during the night.

As a captain he always took the helm during foul weather until his ship was safely through a storm. On the docks, Zoran personally negotiated the cost of his cargo, sure to get his percentage first, and never compromised a contract or backed down from a fight.

At times, when the ship came under attack by pirates, Zoran led with his cutlass, and his blade was the bloodiest when the fight was over. The captain's orders to his crew were sharp and crisp; all aboard moved instantly.

Those who sailed with him feared him. He was quick with the lash for any disobedience and would put any laggard ashore if his orders were not followed. Nonetheless, the dock was filled with sailors wanting to sail with Captain Zoran; he always brought them safely back to port, money in their hands, and ready to sail as soon as the cargo was loaded and the next tide on its way out.

He always stood hatless. His long black hair pulled back behind his head was tied with intertwining threads falling below his shoulders to the middle of his back. His leathery skin, like an old neglected saddle, was deep-brown, darkened by the sun. Creases and cracks cut deep along his brow and out from the edges of his deep-set, dark black eyes. His face, weathered by days and nights on the stormy decks, spoke the story of a lifetime at sea. His nose was long and thin. A grey-black beard, as greasy as the hands that stroked it, fell onto his chest. The captain's faded, heavy, oiled goat-skin coat extended down below his knees, and his tall leather boots, were white with salt from waves crashing across his decks.

Many who sailed on the open sea gave up their youth to sign on as cabin boys, but not all went to sea by choice. Some disappeared from the docks, some sold as slaves to work the oars, others ran from lives of crime, and most were attempting to escape a hopeless life.

Zoran chose the sea to flee the crush of tribal war. Captain Zoran had no house to call home. His home was his ship. His country was the sea. Zoran had given up all notions of family long ago, erasing the past from his memory.

The merchant, Pavel Delyan, was familiar to Antonio. He was the wealthiest merchant on the docks. He owned at least eight warehouses, many businesses in town, and he came from one of the noble families outside of Varna. His family had been extremely important a half century earlier. His Grandfather, Peter Delyan, the grandson of the great Tsar Samuel, once ruled Bulgaria, if only for a short time.

Delyan was half a head taller than the captain. He wore a stiff, wide-brimmed leather hat that protected his face from the heavy rain.

The rain fell from his hat to his shoulders which were covered by a matching leather coat with leather strings that wrapped around five whale bone stick buttons starting from his neck to the middle of his thighs.

The captain stopped when both feet were firmly on the dock. The merchant walked quickly to the captain. He had in his hand a single rolled document held together with a thin cloth ribbon which he handed to the captain.

The captain did not take it.

The merchant yelled to his carriage. A servant holding a large cloth umbrella ran to the side of his master protecting both men and the parchment from the downpour.

They obviously knew each other. The men exchanged words, but no sign of friendship, although no evidence indicated a problem between them. The merchant did most of the talking; the captain nodded his head occasionally and pointed to the opened document now protected from the rain. It appeared to Antonio some sort of agreement had been struck.

The servant took a candle from his pocket, lit it, and turned it over the paper. The merchant opened his cloak and untied a bag the size of a man's hand from his belt. From it, he took out a tool and pressed it into the red bubble of hot dripped wax.

In what appeared to be a final business agreement, the captain and the merchant nodded to each other. The captain, now holding a leather encased tube, turned toward his ship, and walked up the gangway. The servant stepped quickly to the door of the carriage and opened it for his master.

While walking to the carriage, the merchant lifted his coat to replace the bag to its original position on his belt. He stepped into the carriage and gave directions to the driver. The horses responded instantly when the servant snapped the thick reins over their backs. Gracefully raising their thick, powerful necks, and with heads held high as gentlemanly as their owner, the pair of horses were ready to return to the protection of a stable to be wiped dry by a servant boy. The carriage pulled away.

The meeting on the dock completed, Antonio decided he would check one last time before breaking the wax cover of the clay pot for the night's olive oil.

Carefully, slowly, his eyes wide with caution, Antonio crept out from behind the wide amphora jars, making sure no one could see him. It felt good to stand, to stretch his legs. He looked and saw no one. He took another step forward and saw a figure off to his right. Antonio stiffened. Lazlo, the dock guard, trying to stay out of the wind, had been standing against the same warehouse wall as Antonio. He had observed the same exchange at the ship's gangway.

Lazlo began to step in the direction of the ship, the spot where the captain and merchant had met moments ago when he noticed Antonio. However, he quickly shifted his eyes back to the ship then back at Antonio. Scared, Antonio thought to run, but the guard was not concerned with the street beggar. Lazlo kept looking back at Antonio, and again to the ship, telegraphing a secret Antonio could not decipher.

Antonio's eyes moved in the direction of the guard's focus.

In an instant, Antonio was running like he had never run before. Not from the guard, but in the same direction as the guard, headed for a treasure on the ground. Antonio did not know why the pouch was important, but he, like Lazlo, wanted the trophy.

A certain collision of different forces—a poor waif with a miserable fool, a hungry boy without a future, and an oaf having wasted his past—both living for the moment, knowing only one can survive.

Antonio glanced at Lazlo to measure the distance to the prize, and he heard Lazlo's vile curses and threats, and saw a knife in the hand of the overweight guard. The guard's last sprint forward surprised Antonio.

At full speed, Antonio reached down and grasped the rain-soaked pouch of Pavel Delyan. As he dipped, he heard the blade of Lazlo's blade split the air above his head.

The next few steps were strides for life or of death. The pushing wind aided Lazlo's pursuit of Antonio. He was only a step from the boy, a mere arm's length from his prey. Antonio could hear Lazlo's frenzied breathing close behind; Lazlo was so close Antonio could smell the derelict's onion breath.

Lazlo slashed again, stumbling in Antonio. They both slide on the wet dock. Lazlo grabs for Antonio. The thin shirt melts away in Lazlo's hand. Antonio jumping up runs.

Antonio's fear was greater than Lazlo's want—Antonio was fleeing for his life. Antonio never stopped running until he was safely far away from the dock and its guard.

Chapter 18

The House of Master Pavel Delyan

Afraid of capture and terrified of the beating he would receive from the angry guard, Antonio pushed through his pain, his heart pounding, certain his body was not able to continue, but he kept running. His throat was dry, and it ached as he gasped to breathe the harsh winter air, but he kept fleeing. Antonio's knees were raw and dust-red, and an ankle twisted after stepping in a ditch and falling when he turned to see if the guard was close behind. His legs felt heavy like the animal no longer able to outrun the predator; he had to escape the blade which his pursuer meant to use on him.

In the first few moments of the chase, Antonio, could at times, hear Lazlo's flat feet closing the distance between them, and hear the frightening voice. Antonio's young legs ran faster. Antonio did everything he could to evade his hunter. When he came to the end of the dock, he turned quickly and dashed straight for the city. On the city streets, he could take the alleys that only the street children followed, moving over fences, changing direction, and stopping to take a momentary glance. Lazlo still followed. Antonio ran through the empty market square to the road taking him out of Varna.

Certain his enemy must be lost, Antonio stopped to catch his breath, but the pursuer was still stalking his prey. The guard continued the hunt but falling farther back succumbing to exhaustion. Fear pushed Antonio to run again. Remembering a place, where he often went with his father, Antonio changed direction, running into the forest on the outskirts of the city. The forest was full of places to hide. Once he was far into the woods, and just over the top of a hill, he turned and crouched behind a stone wall to watch for Lazlo. The hunter was no longer in sight. But Antonio was still in danger. Lazlo would undoubtedly tell the police about a boy who stole from a nobleman, and they would surely come after him.

Everyone knew of other beggars who had been caught stealing from the rich. They were whipped in public to teach other thieves a lesson, and then sold to slave merchants never to be seen again.

Antonio knew there was only one chance if he was to survive, and time was running out, so he needed to act quickly. Antonio jumped up and ran again.

Antonio knocked on the door of Master Pavel Delyan. There was no answer. The heavy wooden door, surrounded by brown and grey stones, must have been thicker than a ship's decking. He knocked longer and with greater force, scraping the cold skin covering his knuckles, causing them to redden. He continued to knock. On his right he saw a bell rope hanging next to the door. He yanked it and waited. He tugged harder and waited, repeatedly—the same result. Just as he was ready to pull again using two hands to strengthen his effort, he thought he heard voices on the other side of the door. Antonio put his ear against the door, and as he did, he heard someone was coming up behind him.

The door opened. Antonio recognized the servant who answered the door as the carriage driver for Master Delyan at the dock earlier in the day. At the same moment, two large hands came from behind and crashed onto his shoulders, forcing Antonio's knees to buckle under him. The pain was excruciating when his raw, bare knees were crushed on the hard brick entranceway, fresh blood oozed.

Looking up, Antonio saw the man behind him was not Lazlo, but a monster of a man, a slave.

Turning his head back to the door Antonio saw the squinting eyes of the servant looking down at him. The house servant's face, twisted in anger, was not concerned about the boy who was kneeling in front of him.

Antonio's shoulders hurt as the slave holding him to the ground applied more pressure. For a second, Antonio thought his decision to come to the master's house had been a bad one, but he had come too far to let this possibility pass.

The powerful hands of the monster holding him down caused his voice to crack with pain as he demanded to be let go.

Antonio, trying to sound as Captain Zoran had on the dock, was straining to speak, but ordered in a loud cry, "You dumb ox of a man, let me go! I come with news for Master Delyan." In a louder voice, he demanded, "Let me go or your master will punish you for your stupidity!"

Antonio was trying to stand, but the weight of the monster was too great on his back. He could no longer feel his knees. He yelled again, trying, hoping for relief. Antonio's attacker finally released the pressure on one shoulder. The free hand sent a stinging slap across the boy's face knocking him to the ground.

Antonio groaned from the sting.

The house servant leaned over, yelling, "Silence!"

Antonio looked up to see the servant no longer standing at the door, but bent over, hands on his knees, staring at him. The slave reached down, grabbed Antonio by the shoulders, and lifted him so violently, Antonio could hear his neck and back crack.

The servant, surprised by the visitor's late-night knocking, and disregard for a nobleman's privacy, was even more shocked that such a filthy, wet street beggar had the audacity to come to Master Delyan's house.

"Boy, never come here again, or I will have you whipped, then sold to sea." Then to the slave, the servant ordered, "Remove this vagabond to the street. Throw him or drag him, whatever pleases you. Be sure to give him a beating he will always remember before coming to this house."

When the brute readied to hit again, Antonio felt the grip on his shoulder lighten. He instinctively jumped forward, freeing himself from the slave. The force of his jump caused him to fall forward toward the doorway of the house knocking into the house servant and both landed inside the doorway on the marble floor. Just as he found his footing the slave grabbed Antonio by the hair and pulled him back out of the house.

Antonio's screams were not of pain—he could not feel anymore—they turned to screams of survival.

He felt the slave's hand grip his throat trying to stop Antonio's ear-shattering call for the master.

Antonio could see through the doorway; the master had entered the hallway to see what all the noise was about.

Antonio yelled again, "Master, I have your--" but never finished his announcement. He was hit by the giant, this time with a fist against his mouth. Bleeding, tasting his blood, Antonio continued to yell, and now he started kicking and swinging his fists.

"Master, I have the master's wax stamp!"

The fist came again, landing just above his right eye—Antonio's eyebrow was crushed by the blow. His vision in both eyes dulled, his body went to the ground.

When Antonio awoke his eye was tender and throbbing; he reached up and felt a soggy cloth covering it. He slowly ran his finger under the rag to find the spot that throbbed with pain. When he looked at his fingers, they were wet with his blood. He moved his fingers to his swollen, bruised lips.

It took a moment for Antonio to realize he was on a rug—his mother and father had never lived in a house with a rug. For as long as he could remember, every night of his life had been spent on the ground, except for those times, when he and Gregorio had hidden in a barn covering themselves with straw as shelter from the cold.

Antonio's body was warmed by the red-hot logs of a fireplace. In winter, his parents would start a small fire outside to cook, and after, the rocks from the fire were pulled into the shelter at night to temporarily keep back the cold of winter from their sleeping bodies.

Antonio was sore from the beating, from the escape. Once the smell of blackened bread and cooking meat found its way to Antonio's dulled senses, he sat up quickly. The hearth warmed the air around him. To the side of the fire pit, resting next to the hot embers was a large black cooking pot. Steam rose above the lip of the pot; a stew had been prepared and was ready.

He surveyed the room. Antonio was sure he was inside the master's house. He had only been in a rich man's house once before, when he had helped his father with a delivery, a story his sister always wanted repeated. They had delivered special packages to the mayor's house which came aboard one of the ships that carried goods from the other side of the Black Sea. A caravan, with merchandise from the Spice Islands, had crossed from India to the Black Sea.

Antonio, trying not to think about his family, looked around the room. Directly across from him was a giant of a man, arms like tree trunks, a huge head, and a face covered in hair—he did not seem like a man, more like a monster. Antonio looked at the hands of the slave—the hands that had pressed his knees into stone, the hands that had slapped him. Those hairy fingers left long red and blue marks on his throat. Those powerful fists had hit his face, opened his lip, put a deep gash above his eye, and left a raised red welt on his opposite cheek.

Antonio thought, "I will never forget that face."

Also, in the room was the house servant. Both the repulsive servant and the ugly giant were staring at Antonio, no longer concerned with tossing him to the street. What had happened?

The servant, without expression, pointed to a tray on a table near the fire, gave directions to the slave, and left the room. The slave moved to the table, picked up the bowl from the tray, went to the fireplace, and ladled the contents of the cooking pot into the bowl. He grunted and placed the stew on the table. The servant returned to the room, saying the master would be coming soon, but first he wanted "the boy" to eat.

The servant said, "Boy, do you have a name?"

Certain this change of attitude from the servant and slave was due to the orders of the master. Antonio decided to take advantage, speaking in the manner of a nobleman, "You may call me…Antonio."

Not wanting to show his pain, not giving the brute and servant any satisfaction, Antonio stood slowly, and then walked to the table, lifted the bowl of stew to his nose, and inhaled the scent of cooked, warm food that he had not had in many months. He opened his mouth and let his lips touch the edge of the hot bowl. He lifted it, letting the lamb stew fill his mouth. Life returned as the healing liquid washed over his tongue, swirling in his mouth, flowing down his throat, and filling his empty belly.

"Slow down. There is plenty for you to eat. Take some bread—you can take the night to gain your strength."

Master Delyan was but three or four steps from Antonio, his voice caring; his slave and servant were on the other side of the room.

Antonio twisted to see Master Delyan, nodded a thank you, reached for the broken piece of bread on the tray, pushed it into the bowl, watching the broth soak in the bread, and put the saturated morsel in his mouth, sucking the juice, and closed his mouth over the delicious crusted bread.

Master Delyan watched in amazement at how much the skinny Antonio ate. He ordered the servant to bring more bread.

"Antonio, I understand that is your name?"

Antonio in full voice and staring directly at Master Delyan, said, "Yes, Master Delyan, it is."

"Antonio, how is it you had my purse in your possession?"

It was just at that moment Antonio realized the stamp purse was not in his hands; it was being held by Master Delyan.

Antonio, now with a warm belly and knowing his position since arriving was now in his favor, answered in a polite fashion but with a strong voice, "Master, you dropped it this past afternoon on the dock when you were talking to Captain Zoran of the *Sea Serpent*."

Continuing, Antonio told the story. "I watched you and the captain talking. I had hoped for a day's bread after your business, but you raced away in your carriage"—Antonio paused, staring in the direction of the servant—"before I could ask, as I did not want to interrupt you." Antonio was stretching the truth, unsure if it mattered

"The guard on the dock saw the purse, and I was sure he would rather sell it than return it to you. That guard, Lazlo, is a lazy man who steals from the warehouse he guards. He hides at night and never patrols as he is paid to do."

Master Delyan listened with interest as Antonio re-counted the incident. "I raced to pick up your package before the guard. He chased me but could not find me. I came here, certain the guard would report me as a thief, hoping to claim a reward."

"What is your full name?" asked Master Delyan.

Standing straight, staring at the merchant, Antonio humbly said, "Sir, our family is so poor, we never had a need to use it, but my father told me his father was called Dimitar."

"And where is your father now?"

"Master, my family is dead from the smallpox."

"Antonio, I am sorry. Where do you live? What family do you live with?"

Antonio, sensing the master's real concern, dropped his defenses and answered, "I have no family. I live with another boy. We beg for food. We are happy with scraps, and sometimes ladies will give us coins when they leave church."

"I see. Antonio, you said you did not want the guard, the lazy one who steals from the dock, who would sell my name stamp rather than return it to me, to get a reward by turning you into the city authorities."

"Yes, master, he would see me in jail if he could get a reward."

"Boy, I mean to say, Antonio, what is it you want from me for returning this valuable stamp?"

"Sir, all I want is a day's bread for me and my friend. And, if I may, can I have a cup of the stew for my friend Gregorio, who is sick and without bread, and with fever?"

"Antonio, do you feel ready to go outside?" asked the master.

"Sir, if it is not too much to ask," looking at the table with bread and fruit, "can I have a loaf of bread to keep us for two days?"

The servant broke into the conversation: "Don't ask the master for food! Just leave this house without being sent to the city's jail."

Master Delyan, looking curiously at Antonio, raised his voice, without turning his head, addressed the servant by name, "Radomir, you will take Antonio Dimitar to the place of his friend, bring them both back to this house, and make a place for them in the barn. Give them food and drink for the night, and if they are still here in the morning, bring them to me."

When Antonio returned with Gregorio, the ailing boy was shaking from the cold, hungry, and sweating with fever. Hot stew, bread, and blankets were brought to the barn. Antonio told Gregorio what had happened. They ate. They slept. They stayed.

Before the boys were brought to Master Delyan the next morning, they were made to wash, and were given new clothes.

Master Delyan and the boys talked for many hours. Of interest to the master was how much detail they had about the workers on the dock, the merchants, and the ships' captains. An unwritten contract was offered to the boys. They would work for him while he looked to find them a master. The boys would do as they were told and to live by the "Golden Rule." Antonio and Gregorio agreed—they ate every day and slept on a rug in the barn—and began working on the docks.

Lazlo was caught stealing by Master Delyan's agents and sold to a ship needing oarsmen along with the hairy slave that beat Antonio. Gregorio was nursed back to health, and two months later, he was offered the opportunity to sail as a cabin boy with a Greek captain trading cargo through the Bosphorus Straight to Constantinople and west to the Mediterranean Sea. The boys promised to be each other's brother; they were a family. Over the next few years, they crossed paths many times whenever Gregorio's ship came to Varna's port.

Antonio began working as a clerk's assistant in one of Master Delyan's many warehouses. As the years passed, Antonio's natural gift in mathematics, his strength of character, and his outgoing, easy manner were useful tools for Master Delyan, earning Antonio the respect of captains and merchants passing through Varna. Each year, he was given greater levels of responsibility.

The young boy, who Master Delyan was so interested in learning about that evening in his house many years ago, became more than a valued employee of Varna's most successful merchant. Antonio's skills crossed over to all aspects of business: his business calculations were never wrong; he always made sure his scales were exact; and his reputation as an honest employee—both with merchant clients and sea captains—was never in question. Most who met the teenager on the docks tried to hire him away from Master Delyan.

Chapter 19

From Varna to Venice

AD 1064

When Antonio was seventeen, his master decided that the young clerk should accompany an important cargo headed to the port of Venice, Italy. Antonio was respected by all men on the docks, merchants and sailors, government officials and cutthroats, bankers, andthieves.

Over the years, Antonio, while at the master's side, had learned to read a man's face, determining who was a friend and who would use a dagger in anger. With tutors, he practiced math, learned how to read a map, and studied the lands beyond the docks of Bulgaria.

Antonio lived the life of a wealthy man, a man who worked harder than his workers, planned each day's events the day before, never guessed about business, made sure each contract was understood, never cheated a customer, treated all people—the rich and the poor—with respect, while also being the first to strike if danger was at his feet.

Antonio learned never to underestimate a man in business or in a fight. He feared no one, and he was held in high regard by all who met him.

For Antonio, this trip to Venice was to be more than as a guard and seller of goods. Months earlier, Master Delyan had travelled to Venice thinking the time may have come to expand his holdings. Upon his return, he sat down with Antonio to share his thoughts.

"My Antonio, our world is changing. As you are quite aware, our volume of trade has not grown in recent months. Captains that once stopped in Varna now pass our port heading to the Bosphorus for Constantinople and continue through the Sea of Marmara to the Mediterranean Sea. The populations of North Africa and Europe swells, and their ports become busier each month, while we have fewer cargos to buy and sell."

Antonio did not move a muscle listening to his master describe the workings of Antonio's love: the business of trade and ships.

"We must make a change or be lost." Master Delyan explained, "Antonio, those who stand still, fall behind those who can see the future."

With a list of questions growing longer with each word by Master Delyan, Antonio spoke, "Sir, I can see in your face that you have made a decision which will not be reversed, and I understand tomorrow will not be as yesterday. What is it you want of me in your plan? What is our next move, and do you have a timetable to follow?"

Master Delyan smiled with pride as the boy who boldly knocked on his door, the street beggar with bloody knees was now a man of Master Delyan's equal. He thought to himself, "This boy has brought happiness to my life. He brings a smile to my face. This boy makes me feel comfortable in my own home."

Sitting back in the same chair where he had asked the young Antonio questions the first night they met, Delyan said, "Antonio, I have purchased a warehouse in Venice. While there I met with your friend, our Gregorio, who has made quite a fine fortune for himself. He now owns three ships and is ready to purchase another. It did not take much on his part to convince me of our future in Venice. While his ships sail from Genoa, they sail in and out of Venice to buy for his customers along the southern European coast and North Africa."

Further describing the business potential, "The future of that city and your opportunity will be shaped on its location at the top of the Adriatic Sea. The city is built on islands safe from land attacks, and too far north for raiders by sea to consider, and across the lagoon are avenues to the cities of Europe."

The master could see thoughts of adventure beginning to bubble on Antonio's face. Watching the young man—who was like a son to him—anticipate the possibility of going to a new port, Master Delyan took his time to pique Antonio's eagerness for travel.

"The Doge of Venice and the Emperor of Constantinople have ambassadors traveling in secret to and from their cities. Antonio, you know there are no secrets in this world. My friends report those two rulers have conspired as trading partners to regulate all the goods from Constantinople to Europe and back, pulling trade from North African and Black Sea port cities." Running his finger over a map, he drew an imaginary line from Ceylon to the Black Sea, and another from Britain south along the coast and east touching every port in North Africa and onto Venice, and finally from Venice to Constantinople and back. "This will take many years, but these two men are acting as one to command all trade."

"And Antonio, the Venetians will put into place a shipbuilding capability no other city can equal; it is estimated the Venetians will be able to put a new ship to sea every week. The Doge of Venice has directed his city's planners to expand the dock works and clear the city's canals in preparation for triple the number of ships at its wharves."

With a quiet and serious voice of secrecy, the master hesitated, and said, "The Venetians will be the bankers for all future trade in the Mediterranean Sea. Antonio, this you must learn: Those who control the banks, control trade."

The master stood up, called for the servant to bring the meal, and addressing the young merchant in front of him, said in a hearty voice, "Antonio, our business must go to Venice, and you will lead the way."

On the wharf a week later, Master Delyan's carriage arrived while Antonio was examining the cargo being off-loaded from the Corsican ship, *Scorpion*. A message came from Master Delyan requesting Antonio to join him at the house after the ship's manifest was fully marked.

Antonio especially liked working the docks while a ship was unloading. Usually, this was a busy time as negotiations for goods being bought and sold happened quickly, money passed hands, and debts were covered.

He arrived within the hour anxiously awaiting the unplanned meeting that likely concerned the trip to Venice. It was rare for Antonio to be given short notice of any change in business plans. The master preferred to keep business figures at the warehouse office, and talk at home focused on shipping, trade, competitors or new partners, or science and geography.

He walked in the house and sat next to Master Delyan at the table closest to the fireplace—the same table Antonio had leaned against when eating bread and stew that first night in the house. A plate of cheese and dried fruit, along with a porcelain cup were at his place. The cup had been a gift to Antonio by a ship's captain returning from the eastern port of Kerch, on the Sea of Azov a year ago. A shipment had been miscounted at the dock by both the ship's first lieutenant and Antonio's assistant. When Antonio reconciled the list days after the transaction, he found the captain had been underpaid. The correction was made and the difference in payment was held until the captain returned five months later. Antonio met the ship at the dock and gave Captain Zoran the miscounted profit.

The captain sent a note calling on Master Delyan to visit his ship and to bring Antonio along. The next day, the captain, the master, and Antonio were on deck. Captain Zoran, addressing Master Delyan, proclaimed, "Sir, there is, at the dock in Varna, the most honest man in the world. His name is Antonio Dimitar." He gave Antonio a box decorated with colored ribbons woven between its reeds. The captain, still overwhelmed by Antonio's honesty, inquired, "Antonio, I must ask, why didn't you put the mistake in your pocket? No one knew about it, least of all me."

Antonio said, "Because it was the right thing to do. I only want what I work for. If I take what you have earned, you have been cheated, and I am the cheater." After answering, Antonio lifted the lid by pulling the reed lock from its catch to see a white and blue porcelain cup from the Indus Valley. Antonio had been rewarded for "doing the right thing."

Master Delyan and Antonio ripped sections of bread from the large dark loaf sitting on the table to dip in the shallow bowl of olive oil resting between them. They both sighed when the silkiness of the olive oil touched their tongues. They swallowed.

"Antonio, you are to travel to Venice within the week. Your ship will be the *Scorpion*," directed the master.

Some ships' captains would declare a portion of the cargo water damaged and not able to be sold at the original price, keeping the profit, knowing the merchant who shipped the goods could not validate the sale. When the profits were high, most merchants allowed this to happen, but Master Delyan, always dispersed profits according to the signed contracts, expecting merchants and captains to be honest, and most were if they wanted to continue business with Varna's most successful merchant. But, this captain, a Corsican known to sell cargo at any price for a quick profit, was not one to keep his word—he would sell his brother if he thought he would fetch a good price.

"Captain Asim is not to be trusted, but the profit, even as he steals our fingers from our hands, will still be quite fat.

"Master, if he is taking care of the sale, why am I going? I thought I was to lead our new operations."

Assuring the protégé of his position and responsibility, Master Delyan answered, "Antonio, you will be our future. But there is more to business than a sale. To begin, you must establish yourself in a new marketplace. You must sell yourself, and then you can sell your wares."

Continuing, but embarking on the chief purpose of the conversation, "Antonio, you will be carrying our most important property to Venice. It will have more value than a year's worth of profit."

Antonio was flabbergasted. How could that be? He knew every trade of his master's business. He knew every contract; in fact, Antonio usually wrote the contracts for the most detailed of accounts, having knowledge of every piece of cargo in and out of Varna.

"Master, I am bewildered. What could be worth that amount of profit?"

Master Delyan began, "You will stay in Venice to perform two duties. You will oversee the building of new warehouses and learn the businesses of the new port and correspond with Gregorio in Genoa who will assist our trade alliances with the western coast cities of Europe."

Shifting in his seat, Master Delyan motioned with a raised finger, "Most significant of your duties will be to establish relationships with all who communicate with the palace and whoever it is designated to lead the new trade policy with Constantinople. You are to learn about the people of Venice."

"Antonio, you know I have no friends, no interests other than my work. I have given you all I know. You know my wealth, and you know the men of my businesses, all but one. Outside this room there is only one other I trust."

Master Delyan's voice became somber, he instructed, "Should the time come," took a moment to consider his words, "should anything happen to me, a messenger will be sent to you. My friend since boyhood will be a ship's captain. You know this man as a captain, but he is my friend. He is Captain Zoran. It is too complicated to explain now; you must accept my word. You will follow his directions as if they were my words." The master paused for a moment measuring young Antonio. "Do you understand this is your duty to me? You are my family, no less loved than any man's son. I have not called you son, but I think of you as such."

Now with the heartfelt voice of a father, "Antonio, may I call you, Son?"

Antonio was stunned with pride at this title he had longed, fancied, to hear from the man he adored as a father. His soul filled with love and devotion for the man standing in front of him, Antonio answered with words that drove deep into the heart of Master Delyan —two words changed the master's world, fulfilling the life of a man who had everything—Antonio whispered, **"Yes, Father."**

With a wide smile, Master Delyan stepped forward and put his arms around Antonio and kissed him on both cheeks. Antonio's body warmed. Not since he was caressed as a little boy by his mother had anyone held him. Quickly, he regained his composure and responded with an equally hearty embrace.

An invisible wall had been broken; they now spoke with each other as father and son.

Master Delyan joyously said, "You know we are alike, the two of us, both without family, both with only a single friend. You have your friend, Gregorio, who visits us but once or twice a year, and my friend Zoran. We live only to work because we work at what we love; of that, many are envious. We value a person's character; not what they say they are going to do, but what they have accomplished. And we can see tomorrow."

"Father, I like the sound of that. Many on the dock think we look alike, and all those new to Varna believe I am your son, and I have never corrected them."

They smiled and broke in laughter.

At the Dock Ready to Sail

Antonio packed his personal items into a carpet bag, thinking back to his early life and what he had become. He wondered if others his age, readying for a long voyage, had a family treasure, a trinket to carry, a ring, a bracelet, a piece of cloth, some item to be touched, or gazed upon, that would bring to its owner, sweet memories of family, of loved ones, of a home. He possessed nothing. Antonio closed his bag, carried it to the carriage, not knowing it would be the final time he would close the door he first entered as a boy, the last time his eyes would gaze upon the house he called "home."

Waiting for him when he arrived at the dock was Master Delyan. Antonio was surprised to see many of the master's workers and servants, men and women of the docks, and captains who were in port. It was unusual for the warehousemen, the dock laborers, the servants, and merchants, to demonstrate this expression of friendship, of respect, knowing he was to sail that morning.

Antonio was unlike any other on the dock. Since Antonio was a member of Master Delyan's house, and all knew how the master thought of Antonio, he was considered like the master's son, a man of wealth, a man of the upper class. But Antonio never felt noble, aristocratic, or superior to any other person. Antonio remembered that he could have been one of those who were lost in the world, one of the unremembered, the dirty, the poor, or one of those stepped on by men who think they are important because of their family name, the value of their business, or because they own a stable of fine horses. Antonio only had to touch the scar above his eye to remember, whether by chance or destiny, on a wet, cold, windy day, his life had been changed.

One by one, men he had given bread to when they were hungry humbly bowed their heads and thanked him, and ladies who had been given medicine for their sick children gave him flowers, and merchants whose cargoes had been lost, but were given funds to start again, shook his hand. Two fishermen came forward, shook Antonio's hand, and presented him with a gift. Years earlier, the men had come to Antonio asking for a loan to buy a fishing boat. They had been the hardest, steadiest workers on the docks, and Antonio arranged for the loan. The two men of no means were given an opportunity and because of their will to succeed, did so. The gift was a beautiful knife with a carved leather sheath. Its bleached white ivory handle was inlaid with lapis and the blade was forged of Damascus steel.

With the ship ready to sail, father and son, now stood alone, apart from the others on the dock, two steps from the stained planks connecting sea to land. They exchanged last words, not sure when they would meet again.

Handing Antonio the first of two packets, Master Delyan said, "My Antonio, in this you will have all the letters and information about the Venetian trade plans with Constantinople. Study them well. Build relationships with all those named. Learn about them before you meet them, understand why they do business, obtain information about their families, discover what they like and hate, and use it to your advantage."

Handing him the second envelope, "My son, in this envelope is a new name if you choose. All preparations are completed for you to be called 'Antonio Delyan.' From this point on, in this city you will also be called Master Delyan. I know you will not take the title, but it is yours if you wish."

"Father, you honor me with more than I can repay. From this day forward, I shall be Antonio Delyan."

"Antonio, Antonio!" Captain Asim yelled, and then with a loud laugh, he pointed to the gangway, "We are pushing away from the dock, so either climb on board or swim to Venice. The tide waits for no man!"

The father and son grasped hands, held tight, and smiled.

Antonio jumped aboard the *Scorpion*.

The planks were pulled from the dock at the same time the lines once holding the ship to the Port of Varna were cast from the ship by its sailors.

The tide had changed. The Scorpion with wind in its canvas sailed to Venice.

After quickly stowing his bags, Antonio walked to the stern of the ship, facing the city of his youth, and the docks where he had become a man—the home he loved.

Standing on the distant dock, watching him sail away, was Antonio's father whose proud shoulders slumped, arms hanging straight. Antonio could not see the pain in his father's heart, or the tears rolling down his face.

Chapter 20

Brains and Bravado
Venice, AD 1066

It was early morning. Antonio Delyan was negotiating the price of goods which had arrived the night before on trade vessels from Carthage and Athens. Documents showed two ships, one from the North African port was filled with large clay jars filled with spices from Alexandria. The other, a Greek ship, had sailed from a port in Anatolia, its cargo packed in dark brown wicker baskets tied tightly to protect the bundles of beautiful silks from Mosul. As Antonio bartered, a very well-dressed third party broke into the conversation.

In a deep, graveled voice, Signor Moretti addressed Antonio, "Scusi, Signore, I would like to discuss the price you are negotiating with my clerk." The other man in the sale looked at the new participant, nodded in deference, and took a step back.

Antonio looked up to see the most powerful man on the piers of Venice, Signor Matteo Moretti. He was well known on every dock in the Mediterranean Sea. This powerful man owned many businesses throughout the Italian peninsula and Greece. His shipbuilding docks in Venice produced the finest merchant ships on the sea. However, his influence as a counselor to Doge Domenico Contarini, gave him unspoken authority. The merchants and bankers, captains and seamen, every laborer on the dock, each restaurant owner and all the fishermen, ambassadors and beggars, all knew the weight of his name. He oversaw all business activities in the city and controlled the flow of goods in and out of Venice. Signor Moretti's decisions impacted prices in Greece, Anatolia, all northern Africa, Europe and beyond.

Antonio remembered his father's lesson to know all who were powerful in Venice. The lesson would be tested as Antonio was aware of this man's influence and knew the intricacies of his business. Deciding to stand his ground, and leading Signor Moretti to think he was not recognized, Antonio struck first in the negotiations.

Antonio gave the nobleman a broad smile and told him, "Signore, I will be happy to do business with you after this sale is complete. And I doubt the man you interrupted needs your help, as I deal fairly with all customers."

Signor Moretti broke out in a hearty laugh. Realizing that the young salesman had taken control of the conversation, he decided to test the skills of the precocious youth. He turned to the original buyer for a brief conversation, and then he turned back to Antonio.

Antonio watched as the man bowed to Signor Moretti, sending a telling glance to Antonio that Signor Moretti was now in charge of the purchase.

Signor Moretti asked, "What is your name, young man?"

Shifting to place himself directly in front of his adversary, he addressed the question, "Antonio Delyan, Chief Clerk of Trade for my father, Master Pavel Delyan of Varna."

"Well, Antonio Delyan, Chief Clerk of Trade, the price you have discussed with my clerk is 10% too high."

After the initial uneasiness of meeting such a high-ranking person subsided, Antonio felt the excitement of the contest, a match to challenge the second most important man in Venice. But he had to remain shrewd. This was to be a match of guile, most importantly a contest of traders, a test of knowledge of cost and value. Antonio knew he must manipulate the negotiations, careful not to offend, remembering the guidance he often heard at the warehouse: "Antonio, business is business. It is not personality, like or dislike; it is only the buying and selling of things."

Antonio spoke with respect, professionalism, and without emotion, "Signore, I will not move on my price. And, furthermore, how can you discuss the price of olive oil if you have not tasted the product?"

Signor Moretti was shocked initially. It had been many years since anyone questioned his business decisions.

In a strictly business voice, Signor Moretti continued the conversation with Antonio. "Signor Delyan, most people are more concerned about the price than the taste. And you will still make a handsome profit with the price my agent offered."

Antonio cleared his throat, "Signore, if I may take a moment to establish my price and your offer." Again, clearing his throat, Antonio continued, "First of all, I doubt you know the price I paid for the contents of the ship in question. Secondly, you do not know my customers. I have several discerning patrons with an appreciation of quality. I take it you are a merchant. So, you may, in fact, have some knowledge of my costs and customers, but you do not know my ability to conduct business."

Many in the crowd laughed quietly. Signor Moretti humiliated.

"Delyan," Signor Moretti's voice, now commanding, dropped the obligatory signor from the exchange, was speaking as if he was talking to an underling, rather than negotiating, drew the attention from all who were on the dock. "I know your costs. I know your customers, and I know much more about what happens in Venice than anyone on this dock. Now give me what I want for the price that was offered!"

Antonio, remaining calm, leaned forward, and so as not to embarrass his adversary any further, quietly offered, "Three days ago you bought olive oil from a Greek ship for three-quarters of what I am offering today. But the oil was of poor grade. A portion of the oil was putrid, and you sold it for less than half of what you paid. In all, you sold that oil at a loss." Antonio stood straight up, never taking his eyes off Signore Moretti, never changing his expression.

Stepping away and turning his back on Signore Moretti, Antonio reached to his side and pulled his ivory handled short knife from its leather sheath. The knife was the envy of all who had seen it. Antonio cut the twine wrapped around a basket of silks, reached into the basket, and gently removed one of the folded silk fabrics. He took an end in each hand, allowing the wind coming off the canal to lift the luxurious silk in the air, showing all who were watching this contest; its color and beauty, its bright white background fluttered in the wind, its brilliant threads given life from the bright noon sun, before allowing it to rest for display on the box it had traveled in from its origin in the Middle East.

Then Antonio walked to a small amphora, and with the back of his knife handle broke the wax seal inside the narrow mouth of the jar as he had as a starving boy hungry in Varna. Antonio took a handful of cardamom seed, walked back to Signor Moretti, grabbed his wrist exposing his hand, and poured the seeds onto his palm.

The crowd listened as Antonio, now in control, with respect, but with command in his voice, said, "Signor Moretti, touch the fabric of Persia, taste the spices of Africa!"

The crowd applauded.

Antonio stood and waited.

Signor Moretti reached for the silk, held it for a moment. He raised the limp product to his face. He hesitated, put it back atop its basket, and looked at Antonio. Then he pinched the spice between his fingers and tasted.

Antonio heard a throaty sound of pleasure from his trade opponent—he knew he had won.

Now, it was Signor Moretti's turn to whisper, "Are you free to come to my home later today? At sunset is best."

Antonio was on time at Signor Moretti's house that evening. A servant apologized for the master's lateness and indicated he would arrive soon. Antonio was escorted through the house up to the rooftop garden.

Antonio had been to the houses of other merchants of Venice, but this house was at least three times larger than any other he had visited. It had many more servants and was furnished with the finest of carpets, furniture, pottery, paintings, and tapestries, one of which he recognized as having passed through his hands.

When Antonio arrived on the rooftop, he was directed by a different servant to a table set with food and drinks. Of interest to Antonio was the location of his host's home. He leaned on the ornate iron railing surrounding the roof of Signor Moretti's luxurious home. He was overwhelmed by the view of the fondomente, where Venice's busiest trading stalls lined both sides of the Grand Canal. Just hours ago, across the canal on San Marco, Antonio had received his invitation to dinner, and with it, an opportunity to learn more about his host.

Waiting, Antonio reflected on his father's advice, about the future of Venice. The city of six islands was quickly becoming Europe's foremost port. Antonio was expanding into new businesses, added stores for buying and selling of precious metals and jewels, and he opened a factory for manufacturing decorative ornate iron gates, fences, and railing, like those around the edges of Signor Moretti's roof garden.

Signor Moretti arrived, breaking Antonio's concentration on present and future role of Venetian trade.

He asked many questions of Antonio, and Antonio did the same of this powerful man; both men were taking measure of the other. The dinner of fish, fried in an herbal olive oil, and fresh vegetables was splendid.

Antonio could only wonder at the wealth of the man sitting across from him.

Venice was a new city, built on a swamp to protect frightened farmers from marauding tribes. Over time it grew to become a city of trade, a center of vision, of art, of wealth. Many of its merchants came to its islands sensing possibility and seeing what could be if a person worked harder and smarter than the next.

With the dinner ended, and having established a familiarity with each other, Signor Moretti chose to speak less businesslike with his new acquaintance, "May call you Antonio?"

Antonio returned a gentlemanly nod of approval.

"Good, and please call me Matteo. We have much to discuss. I have been watching your success, rather your many successes in my city. I am sure you will accomplish much, continuing to open new businesses as you have already, and eventually buying the businesses of some of your competitors."

Antonio, not sure what was coming next, thought his host might be ready to make an offer to buy his holdings.

Signor Moretti swallowed a piece of white cake covered with a lemon icing both sweet and tart. He was curious about their business on the dock earlier in the day. "Antonio, I was impressed that you knew of my loss at the market. How did you know and why did you not make an offer on the oil?"

Antonio was quick and to the point, saying, "First, the captain of that ship is as corrupt as any who visit our great city. Second, my father told me never to buy without seeing the goods, and, pardon my boldness, that is what happened. If the deal is too sweet, you know something is sour. Also, I always offer a fair price and I never budge. I never take advantage of another."

Signor Moretti was extremely impressed with his guest's response, thinking this is a man with a future in Venice—this is a man who I want working for me.

Signor Moretti, settling down to the reason for the dinner, said, "Antonio, I asked you here tonight—"

He was interrupted mid-sentence by two ladies who had just arrived on the terrace.

An excited, "Papa, Papa!" changed the atmosphere of the conversation, fully claiming all of Signor Moretti's attention. The younger of the two ladies ran across the terrace to the open arms of her father. Her mother, Signora Moretti, elegantly dressed, was a step behind. After a moment, Signor Moretti began introductions.

"Antonio Delyan, this is my wife Signora Moretti, and my daughter, Serena."

From the moment Serena stepped onto the rooftop, Antonio could not take his eyes off her, and Serena, once introduced wanted only to look at Antonio.

Signora Moretti nodded to Antonio and said to her husband, "Is this the Antonio who embarrassed you on the dock this morning?" Turning to Antonio, she continued, "Antonio, it is rare when my husband is made to look the fool. But rarer is for him to admit it and to praise the man who got the best of him. I commend you." Now, looking at her husband, with an eye back to Antonio, "Beware, Antonio, he may be looking to take the clothes off your back."

After a laugh from her husband, she continued, "Please Antonio, let me have a few minutes of my husband's time, and we will let you return to your discussion. Remember what I told you. Serena, stay and talk to Antonio."

With a bow, Antonio said, "As you wish, Signora, and thank you for the advice. One never knows if an adversary will become a friend or family."

A few minutes later, Signora Moretti addressed her daughter, "Serena, we are ready to go. Serena?" There was no reply to her mother's call.

"Antonio, Antonio, my wife and daughter are leaving."

Antonio and Serena had shut out the world the moment their eyes met.

It wasn't until Signora Moretti stepped between the two, and gently taking hold of Antonio's arm, did he realize more than two people were on the terrace. "Will we be seeing more of you, Antonio?"

Mother and daughter were leaving the terrace, but just before stepping through the doorway, Serena turned with a smile to see Antonio watching her every step. And her mother looked at both, and under her breath said, "Brava!"

Signor Moretti and Antonio sat down, and the conversation began where it had left off. "Antonio, I asked you here tonight to offer you a position. But, now that I know you, I am sure you will not take it."

With a smile, Antonio replied, "Signore, I am honored and humbled at the offer, but as you have guessed, I want to be independent of any other, except for my father, who I expect will join me soon, hopefully within the month."

Signor Moretti spoke in a more casual manner, "Again, your answer is as I expected, yet, I want us to be friends. But we will be competitors, honest in our dealings. I have influence in every part of Venetian life. Please call on me when needed. I think we should meet often, discuss business, and the future of our families," hesitating and with expectation in his grin, "I would like that."

A servant dressed more formally than the other house servants, Signor Moretti's most trusted personal employee, walked up to the table, looking at Antonio, said, "Scusi Signore," then addressing his master, handing him a document. "Master, there is a ship's captain at our door. The one you requested to come as soon as he docked. Do I bring him here or will you be meeting in the downstairs parlor?"

"The parlor, we will be there momentarily."

"Antonio, we must go. There is an urgent matter I must attend to. I have had news from a distant port that must be verified, please follow me downstairs." Signor Moretti's face had changed after reading the note.

Uneasiness came upon Antonio. He felt as if something had gone terribly wrong. Certainly, the messenger from another land carried a note of great sorrow.

Once downstairs, Signor Moretti asked Antonio to wait while he attended to the business at hand.

Opening the parlor door, Signor Moretti looked at Antonio, "There was news earlier in the week of a tragedy off Greece. Pirates attacked one of my ships and all but two men died. The details of the attack and of those onboard came with this note."

Standing at the parlor door, Signor Moretti, said, "Antonio, there is a man here to see you." The door was pushed open. In the room was Captain Zoran.

Antonio's father, Master Delyan of Varna, had been killed during an attack near Pylos, off the coast of Greece two weeks earlier.

He had been on his way to surprise his son.

Upon returning home, Antonio sat alone in his room. In his hand was a familiar leather satchel. It had belonged to Master Delyan. Antonio told Captain Zoran he would meet with him in the morning.

After sitting for some time, Antonio lit two candles, unbuckled the case's leather strap, and pulled out three documents.

On top was a letter of instruction from Master Pavel Delyan's lawyer. A month ago, Master Delyan had sold all his holdings except for a single warehouse; there was a keeper in Varna waiting for final instructions.

The second document was Master Delyan's will. In case of his death, a fixed amount would go to Captain Zoran, but the rest of his estate was to go to his son.

The last document certified by the Mayor of Varna was the official adoption record of Antonio Dimitar. And with it was his name change: Master Antonio Dimitar Delyan. He held his father's leather satchel gently against his aching heart. It would be cherished his entire life.

He felt his life was darker than a moonless night.

He at last had a family treasure, the name of Delyan.

Part Three

Kathryn and Uncle Antonio

Chapter 21

Venice, Italy AD 1072

Over the years, experience was second only to the guidance of his father, Master Delyan. Antonio found his way into the mainstream of merchants growing wealthy on the docks of Venice. He opened offices in Ostia, Roma, Genoa, Napoli, and his agents bought and sold goods at almost every port in the Mediterranean Sea, in Baghdad, Damascus, and east of Constantinople, and across the Black Sea where ships sailed to the Sea of Azov meeting caravans delivering caches from India and Cathay.

As he grew in wealth, so did his influence among the city's elite, and with government officials. Many men offered partnerships to Antonio, but he politely chose to stay on his own. Antonio wanted to be the only one responsible for his success or failure, thereby never allowing himself to blame others.

The one businessman Antonio looked up to was Signor Moretti who was always reminding Antonio he could be a part of the family business. Signor Moretti would say, "Antonio, when you are ready, all you have to do is tell me, and the deal is firm". Antonio always answered, "I doubt that day will come, but should that day arrive, I will call on you."

Late one day, after especially difficult negotiations with buyers of expensive mosaic tiles, Antonio sent a messenger to Signor Moretti's office asking to meet at the earliest convenience. The messenger returned asking if the next day at two o'clock was suitable.

It was.

Antonio's barge crossed the canal from his home and office complex on San Polo to the Rialto section on San Marco, the home of Signor Moretti. Stepping off the transport and onto the brick entrance to the house he was met by Signora and Signorina Moretti.

Signora Moretti was the first to greet their guest. "Antonio, it is wonderful to see you. And it is nice to see you dressed as one would be if asked to a formal dinner."

Looking in Serena's direction, he was pulled back into conversation by Signora Moretti, she asked, "What is this important business you wish to discuss with my husband? Is it of interest to me?"

"Yes, Signora, it is. I must sit with your husband today to discuss family negotiations, and I am sure you will be informed immediately of the result." He tilted his head, and raised his eyebrows, "But may I ask you a question?"

With a smile, she answered, "You may."

"Signora, may I expect today's discussion to be agreeable to all, both your family and me?"

Signora Moretti could not mask her excitement of what was to happen, and with a twist of her head in the direction of the steps in front of them, replied, "Antonio, your answer is waiting on the terrace."

Antonio smiled at Serena; she returned his smile and blushed, as he took the first step to meet Signor Moretti.

Unlike Antonio's first visit to the house, Signor Moretti was waiting for Antonio.

Antonio received his answer.

Renovations at the Church of San Giacometto in Venice were completed just in time for the wedding. Pillars, scrubbed and polished, reflected the glow of hundreds of candles lighted for the special day. The sun touched stained glass windows, showering the many guests with every color of a Venetian rainbow. Beautiful mosaics, woolen tapestries, and artwork of skilled painters covered the walls, and the marble floors were covered with flower petals of red, and pink, white, and yellow.

Antonio's old friend, Gregorio, his wife, Amelia, and their infant daughter had arrived a week prior to the wedding on one of Gregorio's ships. They were married a year earlier in Tangier, Morocco, where the waters of the Mediterranean Sea and Atlantic Ocean touch. The four of them had shared many meals together, especially during a port visit during the early months of Antonio and Serena's engagement. On this visit they stayed with Amelia's sister, Paola, in Castello.

Also, in attendance was the Doge of Venice, Domenico Selvo, a special guest of Signor Moretti.

Outside the church doors were hundreds of well-wishers. In the crowd were dock workers, sailors, captains, tavern owners, factory workers, men, women, and children of Venice.

Master Delyan had instructed the young Antonio to treat every person the way he wanted to be treated when he had nothing. "Antonio, now that you are never hungry, and have a place to sleep, you must always remember being hungry and cold, and alone."

Just as he had in Varna, Antonio cared for his workers. He always treated his customers with respect, and whether a beggar or nobleman, they were alike to him.

As Antonio and Serena exited the church to the awaiting carriage, the crowd cheered, threw flowers, and each and every one wished the young couple long lives and many children.

Chapter 22

Kathryn's Tragic Arrival in Venice

Antonio's holdings were growing faster than he had imagined. He was working extremely hard, and Kathryn was working just as hard. Serena was concerned that Kathryn, who Antonio now depended upon, was not living the life of a young woman. Many girls of wealth were sheltered in the house, promised to wed, and none worked. Antonio told Serena that Kathryn was smarter than any man he employed, and she had a better business mind than most in Venice—she worked harder than any two.

Nonetheless, Serena made sure Kathryn devoted two hours a day to studies. She reminded her husband of the education he had received as a young boy. The tutor was always surprised how quickly Kathryn learned her mathematics—everyone knew she had learned to complete a ledger and calculate on an abacus at the side of Antonio. And she had a better understanding of geography than people twice her age—she learned by listening to the stories of sailors and always asked questions of the captains who came to port in Venice.

Kathryn lived with Uncle Antonio and Aunt Serena.

Five Years Earlier

Five years earlier at the Delyan's Venice home, Teresa, who had been hired by Serena, answered a knock at the front door on a late rainy, cold night. Paola, the sister-in-law of Antonio's closest friend, Gregorio, stood in the doorway soaking wet with a rolled-up leather packet in her hand.

Teresa, concerned, bids her to come in, "Signorina, come in out of the rain," turning her head, calls out, "Signor, Signora, come quick!"

Antonio and Serena arrive quickly to see the unexpected Paola shivering in their foyer.

Serena alarmed, asks, "Paola, has something happened?"

The teary-eyed Paola nods. Serena takes Paola's hand, guiding her to a seat, "Please come sit."

Antonio sits alongside Paola, inquires, "Paola, what is the matter?"

Shaking, unable to control her tears, looks at Serena and Teresa, faces Antonio, tells him, "Emelia and Gregorio and their daughter were aboard a transport, near Messina. Many were lost. Survivors said it was the pirate Red Hood who attacked. There was a fierce battle, many jumped off the ship rather than be captured. Gregorio sent Emelia and their daughter overboard.

Serena in disbelief, "What news of Emelia and Gregorio?"

"Gregorio died in the fighting. Emelia never made it to shore." Paola breaks down, sobbing.

Serena continues, "And their daughter?"

Paola hands Antonio the official-looking envelope from within the leather carrier.

"Please, come, sit next to me. We will share the bad news."

Antonio unfolded the document titled: *The Official Will and Testament of Gregorio and Amelia Cappelli.*

Antonio first turned to the last page of the document—where he found the familiar signature of his long-time friend. Antonio flipped back to the first page and he began reading. As Paola had directed, Antonio found his name: *"That upon my death, and that of my wife, my brother and friend, the only man I trust is Antonio Delyan who is to be the protector of, and responsible for the life of my most precious jewel, my daughter, Kathryn Cappelli."*

Addressing her, he said, "Paola, it shall be done as Gregorio and your sister wished."

Paola stood and walked to the front door. The door left open, Antonio and Serena watched as Paola went to meet a small figure waiting under an umbrella outside his gate. She returned, leading nine-year-old Kathryn by the hand to the front door of a stranger's house.

The girl walked into the house, head held high, clutching the gold chain hanging around her neck.

Serena put her arm around the child and guided her to the sitting room. "Kathryn, it has been a long time since we last saw you. You might have been three years old. I remember the first time we met, your mother carried you in a bassinette," looking at Antonio, "on the day of our wedding."

"Antonio and your father were closer than friends, more as brothers, so we will do whatever we can for you. Is there anything you want to ask of us?"

Kathryn lifted her head, eyes weepy, and spoke softly through quivering lips, "How do I address you?"

Antonio answered, "You are part of our family. I am sure your father and mother would want you to call us uncle and aunt."

Over the following days and weeks, months and years, Antonio and Serena discovered that Kathryn was as her father had said, "a most precious jewel." And more than once, Antonio looked to the heavens thanking his friend Gregorio for the gift.

Attending Class

Antonio and Serena invited Corrado Russo, considered the most learned teacher in Venice, to their house for dinner. Corrado was surprised that he should receive an invitation from the House of Delyan. The men had met two or three times at the Doge's Palace but had shared no more than a friendly greeting.

Knowing it would be an insult to decline an invitation to the home of Signor Antonio, he readily accepted—his curious nature was baited by the request. What was the real reason to join him for dinner, he was certain it was not to discuss business or politics?

The evening air had been clear and warm, and they instantly felt comfortable in each other's company. The three discussed geography, the future of trade on the Mediterranean with Venice as the primary port city, bigger merchant ships, and if in partnership with Constantinople, Venice was ready to be the banking center of Europe.

When he felt the time had come to inquire about the evening's invitation, Corrado asked, "Signore, Signora, your table is exceptional. As a host you are gracious and I enjoyed our conversation, but you asked me here for a reason. What is that reason?"

Antonio looked at Corrado, and said, "I am told you are the finest teacher in Venice." The dinner guest grinned accepting the compliment. "As you are perceptive enough to know there is more than what one sees on the face of a host, I have indeed asked you here as my guest to answer a single question."

Serena, serious in tone, wanted an important question answered by this man of cultured tastes, asked, "Who would you have as your child's teacher if money were no object?"

Corrado looked first at Serena, then Antonio, and answered without hesitation, "Me!"

That night Corrado became Kathryn's tutor.

Kathryn and her tutor spent afternoons together, arranging their study time around the arrival and departure of ships. As she grew, so did her responsibilities, and like her uncle, she loved the docks. The waterfront was alive with men of adventure who told tales of their world travels. Talk of travel with Corrado was the most important part of her studies. He tied math and language to geography knowing Kathryn was a quick learner and always wanted to know more about each subject.

The two-hour class with her tutor was a wonderful time. Corrado taught her Greek and she improved on her Latin; she had a gift for languages. They discussed history, plotted points during geography, as well as mathematics, geometry, and astronomy. He told tales of the many places he had visited as a young man sailing the Mediterranean and while at war as a soldier in the Byzantine army. He recounted the stories of incredible people of other lands with different traditions and customs. Best of all, he taught history through the eyes of a traveler, making the world come alive. They laid out maps on warehouse desks and consulted captains when they arrived from foreign ports. His teaching of Homer's Iliad and Odyssey, Caesar's life, Greek and Roman gods, and every imaginable subject filled Kathryn with a love for life, a love of adventure, and the desire to travel the world.

Kathryn's unquenchable thirst for knowledge also demanded explanations of her dreams. Often, she spoke in detail to Corrado about her nightly imaginings. He listened, often confused, and repeatedly, could not answer her questions about worlds he did not know.

She described a machine that appeared in her dreams. She drew a contraption with two large wheels that a person could sit on. Each wheel had spikes from the center to an outer rim like a wagon wheel covered in black, but he could not recall ever seeing or hearing about such an apparatus and they could not figure out how one sat on it without falling over. In her dreams, she sometimes dreamed in a different language, the language of sailors who came from Britain.

It did not take long for Uncle Antonio to become more than just an uncle to Kathryn. He became an adoring uncle, and she in turn adored her Uncle Antonio. They became inseparable—and she was almost always with him on his trips to the dock.

On a mild but blustery February day, after his noon meal, Antonio was sitting in the courtyard, as he often did if the weather allowed, informing Kathryn of a change to his afternoon plan. She handled his appointment calendar and needed to be aware he was going to visit a merchant at Saint Mark's Square. After that, he would go to the warehouse at Palazzo Navagero to prepare orders for the next day knowing Kathryn would be there. Then, putting his arm around Serena, he said, "Kathryn and I will be home just before sunset for dinner," and with a playful scowl on his face, "that is, if she approves of my work." He gave goodbye kisses to Serena and Kathryn.

Antonio met with the investor as planned. They agreed it was good business to see the buildings together at the Arsenale, located in Castello, to study the future of shipbuilding at that location as an expansion to the factory's primary function of repairing weapons. When his meeting was concluded, he walked to his warehouse office.

Just as he arrived, one of his shipping clerks, Massimo, obviously unnerved and panicked, ran up to him, "Signore, Signorina Kathryn has disappeared!"

Antonio's heart stopped, and his belly turned bitter. In a loud, frustrated tone, he demanded, "What do you mean she has disappeared?" Antonio's face became red with worry, and with urgency in his voice, he asked, "When did this happen?"

"No one has seen her since she left your house. Signora Serena came to see her; we did not know the Signorina was coming."

Massimo did not give the answer Antonio wanted to hear. Antonio's face became stern, and he demanded information. "She has been missing for four hours, and *NOW* you come to tell me?" Antonio, knowing Kathryn rarely traveled alone, demanded information, "Who was with her?" He waited a second. Again, pressing the inquiry, but this time in a whisper, each word slowly being formed, "Who was with her?"

"Your wife has asked the question already. No one knows."

"Where is Signora Delyan?"

"She is out looking for the Signorina."

With fear in his eyes, Massimo said, "We looked for you as soon as we knew. We could not find you at the square."

Antonio realized that he could not have been found because his appointment had moved from the square to the Arsenale. It didn't lessen his frustration.

An immediate concern for Antonio, his stomach still tumbling with nerves, were the stories of many young men and women, often children, kidnapped from the docks. What was he to do next? His mind raced; he would sweep every dock, every warehouse, and every house if needed to find Kathryn.

He never realized, until this moment, just how important she was to him.

Kathryn wanted to know why Teresa seemed fearful of her safety when she found her. "Teresa, you looked frightened when you found me. Why? I often travel the docks by myself."

"What did you feel just before I found you?"

"What did I feel?"

"Yes."

"Come to think of it, I thought it odd I was chilly. In fact, I had those arm chills some people call goosebumps." Kathryn was perplexed by her word. "Teresa, I don't think I ever used that word before. I know, it was from my dreams."

"Kathryn, did you feel like you were in danger? Or see anyone you thought threatening?"

"Just before you walked up, I did happen to look around thinking someone was watching me."

"We talked about danger on the docks."

"I remembered when I got those bumps. I covered my necklace with my hand as you told me. And I felt better."

Just as Antonio was ready to bark orders, Kathryn and Teresa walked around the corner of the warehouse. She approached Uncle Antonio with an inquisitive expression. Her voice broke the fright in all their hearts.

Antonio felt a tide of relief run through his body. He asked for an explanation of Kathryn's whereabouts.

"Teresa found me at the market, informing me that Aunt Serena was concerned about my safety." Kathryn's eyes were trying to read the faces of the men in front of her. She asked, "Uncle Antonio, Massimo, what is the matter? Why do you have tears in your eyes?"

Uncle Antonio took a step toward Teresa and gave her a kiss, "Thank you, you are always at the right place at the right time."

Kathryn learned how important and how loved she was by all the people around her. Uncle Antonio spoke personally to every member of his house and business staff. He informed them that the safety of young Kathryn was their most important responsibility. Kathryn also knew she must be responsible in all her travels and actions on the docks.

Chapter 23

Kathryn's Surprise **Venice, AD 1095**

The bell hanging inside and above the front door in the Delyan's home sent its ring throughout the house. Kathryn loved answering the door—never knowing what interesting person might be on the other side. She did her best to reach the door before any of the servants—the servants always gave her time to get to the door first.

It rang again just as her hand touched the handle.

Greeting Kathryn when she opened the door was a messenger holding an envelope for delivery. "Buon giorno, Signorina. I have a letter for Signorina Kathryn Cappelli."

"I am the person you seek." She then held up her hand asking the messenger to wait, Kathryn said, "Un minuto per favore." She disappeared, ran to a dish on the foyer table, and returned with a coin, thanking him for the delivery.

Bounding into the kitchen, Kathryn dropped the note on the flour covered marble slab and grabbed a fresh-baked cookie resting on a plate which had just been pulled from the kitchen's wood burning brick oven. It was so hot she tossed it from one hand to the other, dropped it on the table, sat down and told the Teresa what had happened. "A few minutes ago, a messenger delivered this envelope, it was for me. I have no idea what it may be. What do you think?"

"Signorina, your birthday is tomorrow. Now let me ask, what do you think?"

"I think you should quit cooking and become a fortune teller."

With hands moving as if ripping a make-believe envelope, Teresa asked, "Signorina, why are you staring at it? Open it!"

That was the push she needed. When Kathryn flipped it over, she saw the orange wax stamp with the Moretti family crest in the middle of the envelope. She quickly broke the seal and read the note.

She spouted, "Teresa, you are right."

The letter was an invitation. It read:

To Celebrate the Twelfth Birthday of Kathryn Cappelli

"Signorina, what can I bake to make your birthday special, cookies, pastry?" Teresa, taking a moment to think what might be special to Kathryn, said, "Or, how about an extraordinary, fancy cake that looks just like our Doge's Palace?"

The idea of an unusual cake caused Kathryn to pause for a moment, thinking she knew of such a cake baked for another occasion, but quickly answered, "Teresa, there is nothing in this world I need. Knowing you are here when I need you is all I ask. You are always near when I need a friend. Remember last year, you just happened to be walking by the market when I fell between the two boats in the canal?" Kathryn leaned so their shoulders would bump, lifted her body off the seat, and gave Teresa a squeeze. "I should have told you sooner that I am happy you came to this household the day I arrived. I believe we are connected. Someday, we should tell each other all about our pasts."

"Somehow, Kathryn, I think you may be correct. I'm sure our families have met many times."

"Teresa, have you ever seen a wooden door that has stories cut into it?" The sound of the front door closing halted the conversation and brought Kathryn to her feet. She ran to see who arrived. It was Serena.

Trying to act surprised, Aunt Serena asked, "Kathryn, it is late afternoon, and you are in the house. I hope you are not sick?"

Not fooled, Kathryn tried to go along, "Aunt Serena, today is a very odd day. This morning Uncle Antonio said everything was in order, and he didn't need me. I know he needs me. You know he needs me. He knows he needs me. If a ship arrives at our docks late today, we will be overwhelmed, and tomorrow's orders will be behind. Anyway, then Corrado became sick and left early. He seemed fine to me."

With the last of Teresa's cookies in her hand, Kathryn offered it to Aunt Serena who put up her hands and said, "No grazie, Signorina." With that, Kathryn bit into the last almond paste and pine nuts cookie.

Keeping an eye on her aunt, she continued, "And then, about an hour ago, a messenger came with a letter for me, for Kathryn Cappelli. Guess? Go ahead and guess who sent me a letter?" Not waiting for an answer, she continued, "Your mother invited me to her house for a birthday party."

No longer able to keep a straight face, Aunt Serena told Kathryn that she and Uncle Antonio, along with her parents, had planned a party.

Giving her aunt a big hug, "Aunt Serena, I love you and Uncle Antonio, and I love your parents." Taking a second, she stated, "You know you don't have to give me anything special. I could not want for any more than you have already given me," and with a laugh, "well, maybe you could ask Uncle Antonio if I could train an assistant. Someday, I will be traveling around the world, and who will take care of Uncle Antonio?" Thinking aloud, "Maybe to a land not yet discovered. No one has sailed far to the west. No one knows if there is a land beyond the sun. Corrado thinks that is the short way to the land of the Khans."

The next day, Kathryn was at the office early checking to make sure no ships were in the channel. She set up the schedule for the day and went over to the Rialto market for some vegetables she had promised to buy for Teresa. She helped everyone in the household whenever she could. Uncle Antonio was serious about everyone in their house taking care of one another. No house, especially wealthy houses, would allow girls to work as Kathryn did or assist the hired help.

As a young girl, Serena never had to lift a finger in her home, nor had her mother. Servants were there to do everything. At first, when visiting Antonio's house, Serena was astounded he did so many things for himself. She was also surprised he had only a couple of servants and that was because he was out of the house most of the day. Even now, he seemed quite happy living the same as he had lived many years ago. Serena liked the way they lived. In fact, Serena was learning to do chores she had not learned as a young girl. She found a love of cooking, and on occasion gave Teresa time off so she could prepare the family's meals which often included the staff—sometimes good and other times not—and the staff never made a face when her recipes flopped.

Kathryn was back at the house early. She wondered what was planned. Could it be a scavenger hunt? Or possibly, did they plan a race in the square? She wondered if they would hide a prize inside the cake.

Kathryn was wearing her usual red slippers with yellow fringe.

Aunt Serena, always impeccably dressed but fully aware of Kathryn's taste in fashion, recommended a yellow tunic with a golden ribbon to be tied around the waist.

The launch was ready at the slip for the party goers. The rowers quickly made it to the other side, coming to rest at the dock.

When Kathryn stepped off, she thanked each of the four rowers, and the coxswain. Each of the crew wished her a joyous birthday.

Signor and Signora Moretti were there to greet them. "Kathryn, Serena, Antonio—today will be a joyous day for our family," began Signor Moretti.

All the house servants were lined up to receive the guests. Trista, the youngest and most spirited of all the servants, who was always delighted to see the Signorina, addressed Kathryn with her usual animated greeting, "Signorina Kathryn, you look wonderful," and with a bit of surprise in her voice, "Your hair is so long and curly, it is nice to see you dressed for a party."

Another servant, Elena, commented on Kathryn's eyes, "Signorina, I think your eyes have changed color over the years, the green has disappeared. They are clear, like the brown sapphires in the earrings you are wearing."

Kathryn was overcome by all the attention. She thought it peculiar within the past two weeks, three people commented on the color of her eyes; even Uncle Antonio had remarked on them.

Serena's mother directed everyone past the sitting room, through to the garden. The house was built in a square and all living spaces on the second and third floors had interior balconies looking down on the beautifully manicured gardens and fountains. The garden was always in full bloom.

A handsome iron and tile table and chairs sat on the garden patio. It had been a New Year's gift from Antonio and Serena made in their San Polo factory.

Kathryn, seeing Signor Moretti with his lawyer, Signor Rizzo, figured they were completing a last-minute business deal. But she became puzzled. There were no papers on the table. Both men had glasses of wine, and they did not seem to be conducting trade. Kathryn met with Signor Rizzo when she brought or retrieved contracts for his review. She walked up to him and extended her hand. He stood, bowed, and in keeping with his usual practice of shaking her hand, said, "Signorina Kathryn, it is a great pleasure to see you today."

Kathryn's anticipation grew as she sensed everyone, Corrado, the employees, even the servants, knew about her birthday surprise—and no matter how Kathryn tried to pry information from Teresa and the others in her home about the birthday party, they would not give her even a hint of what was to happen.

Antonio and Serena stood ready to address those in attendance. With a tap of a spoon on his glass, Antonio began, "Kathryn, today is a special day—your 12th birthday. Over the past year, Serena and I have been discussing your future. We have asked Signor Rizzo to help us, and that is why he is here. We love you like a daughter. We think of you as our daughter, just as the Moretti family thinks of you as their granddaughter."

Serena stood and before addressing the guest of honor, gave her husband an adoring look, and with a smile from her mother, began. "Kathryn, we have no children, and will likely not have any. But, if we had a dozen, you would be as dear to us as any child. We have a question of you, a question that does not need an answer today. We want you to be our daughter, according to the laws of Venice. While that sounds so formal, simply put, will you allow Antonio and me to call you," Serena needed a moment, "to call you, daughter?"

Kathryn was not ready for this surprise. Her eyes met with everyone in the room, and last with Uncle Antonio; studying his face, his eyes, she felt as if she could see inside him.

Looking back and forth at Uncle Antonio and Aunt Serena, she stood.

"Uncle Antonio, Aunt Serena, you honor me more than I deserve. Signor and Signora Moretti, you are so incredibly special to me." Looking back at Uncle Antonio, her eyes glassy, she continued in a softer voice than when she began, "We are alike in many ways. We both lost our parents and found a house to call a home. We found our future in the business of the home. I love the docks as you love them. I'm happiest when we are the busiest. But what is different for me is that I still dream of my parents. You became Antonio Delyan as a man.

I am still a girl. Sometimes, in my dreams, I see their faces in worlds I do not know. Yet, in each of those worlds, their faces are the same."

Because of the tears in her eyes, she could not see the tears on the faces of her uncle and aunt, and Signor and Signora Moretti. She felt tears running down her cheeks; one fell on her hand. She lifted her other hand, and with a finger, softly touched it.

"You took a scared little girl, with no parents, into your home. You let me call you 'uncle' and 'aunt.' You allowed me to grow, always listening to my thoughts. On the docks, many think I am your daughter, and I never correct them. Our lives, our worlds, always change and we must recognize, what once was, cannot be again."

Taking a breath, Kathryn continued, "Uncle Antonio, Aunt Serena, Signor and Signora Moretti, you know the memory of my parents is still with me, and I want to keep their love for me, always," the secret in her heart, now exposed, did not stop her longing to express the deep worship she had for all in the room, "so, if you are willing to accept that, and if you are able to understand that I want to keep my parents name, and if you are willing to call me Kathryn Cappelli Delyan, I will happily, joyously, be your daughter, and your granddaughter, because that is how I feel about you already."

Everyone in the room was overwhelmed with emotion; every hand touched the tears which welcomed Kathryn as daughter and granddaughter.

Teresa had honeysuckle tea ready for Kathryn Cappelli Delyan when she arrived back from her birthday party.

Business over the past week was completed by noon. The mid-August afternoon sun drove all but a few from the docks, ships sitting silent, crews finding a cool shade, which meant Antonio and Kathryn could leave early once the morning's accounting was tallied.

The warehouse doors were swung wide releasing the heat within. Kathryn, Antonio and two warehousemen stepped outside the warehouse. Except for a couple of stragglers sitting on barrels a few yards away, the waterfront was empty.

"Signor, we will close-up shortly, after the baskets for Naples are counted."

"It's too hot," Antonio wipes his brow, "go home. Come in early when the morning air is gentle on our face."

"Thank you. Be safe, this hot air makes men's minds do stupid things."

"We will." Antonio and Kathryn begin walking.

Kathryn pauses. She rubs her hands on her forearms. Antonio two paces past Kathryn stops, turns to her, "Why are we stopping?"

Alarmed, her face stern, Antonio worried.

"Kathryn, what is it?"

Kathryn, anticipating, searches the docks, answers, "Can't you feel it?"

"Our docks are empty. What am I to feel?"

"Father, I need to talk to you. I am not who you think I am."

With a slight smile, asks, "Are you the princess of some far-off land? Or a maybe a fortune teller who has news of our business?"

Serious, Kathryn brings her face back to him, "Father, I'm like a fortune teller".

Antonio puts his arm around her, asks her, "We have to get home, so, please enlighten me as we walk."

"Father, have you ever thought I'm different than others my age?"

"Of course, yes, smarter and excellent balancing our accounts. How you can learn to speak so many tongues so quickly has me stumped, especially the language of the sailors of the northern seas?"

"Please be patient with what I am going to tell you."

Antonio stops, ready to listen, "So, tell me."

Kathryn stiffens, sees Abbadon a distance away on the dock, his hand in the air. She spins to see the two men who were near their warehouse rushing towards her and Antonio.

Kathryn screams, "FATHER!"

She screams louder, "HELP US! HELP!"

One of the Abbadon's henchman swings a club, knocking Antonio to the ground with the blow to the head. The other grabs for Kathryn who initially fights him off, but his weight overwhelms her; he grabs her by the throat sliding his hands down for necklace she holds tightly in her hand. Her continued screams bring workers out from Antonio's warehouse who come to their rescue. The attackers flee when they see workers running toward them to rescue Antonio and Kathryn.

Antonio and Kathryn are helped by the workers back to the warehouse providing a bench and a wet towel for the gash on Antonio's head.

"Thank you, Luca. I'm fine."

Kathryn, caring, guilty, knows she is the reason for assault. "Father, how do you feel?"

"Thank goodness they hit my hard head."

"Are you sure you're okay?"

"Yes. Only a torn shirt, and lump on my head. I'll be fine." Concerned about Kathryn, he inspects Kathryn whose hand is still covering her pendant. "Oh, my, your neck has red finger marks and scratches."

She releases the pendant and runs her fingers up to her neck, flinches. "Stings."

Luca hands her a wet cloth, instructs, "Signorina, the cool of the towel will ease the pain."

"Thank you, Luca," she stands and gives him a kiss on the cheek, "you and our men saved us today."

Antonio ponders the scuffle. "That has never happened to me. I've always felt safe on our docks," he gives Luca hug, "thank you for saving my Kathryn."

Luca, trying to hold back his emotions, "Signor, Signorina Kathryn is Our Kathryn."

Kathryn and Antonio are sitting alone on the bench. Antonio is curious and wants to know the meaning of her words before the attack. "Kathryn, you knew we were in danger, didn't you? You said so, and I didn't listen."

"Yes, father I did."

Recalling the moments before being hit, Antonio asks, "Who was that man you were staring at on the dock?"

Kathryn takes a few moments to answer, sure her father will find what she is about to say unlikely, but she must tell him, "His name is Abbadon. You have heard him called Red Hood."

The initial expression on Antonio's face is what Kathryn expected, but quickly changes. He has known for some time Kathryn has hidden abilities and knowledge about things no one else has seen. "How do you know this?"

"That is what I want to talk about."

"You asked me earlier if I thought you were, let us say, different. Well, yes, and you did say something about fortune telling. I thought you were joking."

"Father, please be a good listener. Let me finish what I have to say, then you can believe or not believe me, or ask any question. I will do my best to explain, but I must tell you, there is much I do not understand."

"You are a special girl. And it is my duty as your father to protect you. But I need your trust to help me do what I must do."

"Father, I have come to you and mother because of an undertaking only I can complete, and now you are a part of it."

"What do we tell your mother?"

"We cannot tell her. I did not want to tell you, but you need to understand me and protect our family. Are there any questions before I continue?"

"Okay, we will keep this to ourselves. There is one question that has always been in the back of my head."

"About Teresa?"

"Ah, there is that intuitive skill which makes you the most respected and loved on the docks," Antonio tries to read Kathryn's face, but she seems to have an answer ready, "Do you, or should I ask, did you know Teresa before she came to our house?"

"And that my dear father, is our other secret," Kathryn smiles at her father, puts her arm around his waist as they walk off, "now I'll tell you more of what you must know."

Chapter 24

The Sharkfin Pre-Boarding Day
AD 1095

Finally, the most important and busiest day before the trip had arrived—pre-boarding day. The days over the past fortnight had kept her busier than she could ever remember. The ship they contracted had arrived two days late because of a problem with its rudder. The captain said he needed a day to complete the repair, and loading could not begin until it was fixed. Nonetheless, he had assured Antonio it would be ready to sail on time.

Still, Antonio was concerned about the time it would take to unload the goods and then load his products bound for Constantinople. The goods that could not be sold immediately once the ship arrived would be the responsibility of Massimo to either find buyers or have them stored in his buildings, and at the same time, Antonio was reluctant to bring goods from the warehouse and let them sit on the dock until ready for loading; he preferred to safeguard products from weather and thieves.

Weeks earlier, once they had agreed on a merchant ship, Antonio and Kathryn had worked every day to prepare the shipment for their new market in Constantinople. They calculated every square meter of cargo space on the *Sharkfin*. They knew what products were to be stored in the holds below deck; items that could withstand weather would be lashed down topside.

Kathryn had arrived at the gangway of the *Sharkfin* twenty-four hours earlier, checking lists against the offloaded boxes and bundles, determining how much of what was said to be in the boxes and crates actually had made it to port. She was quite aware many hands touched the goods from the time they left a distant city until stacked on her dock.

Of course, the most vigilant captain had much to gain if the cargo arrived intact at its final destination by getting an extra percentage of the dock price. Nevertheless, other captains made stops before their final destination if they thought they could barter a better deal.

The long hours the day before paid dividends. Kathryn was able to have the ship unloaded rapidly and had reached a proper accountability of goods; then they went to the market for sale. It was always good to have extra coins to entice the ship's lazy crew to unload the products immediately and carefully from ship to the dock. A few more coins could quickly get the stevedores to move goods from dock to market.

The business at the port always excited Kathryn. She loved being a part of the buying and selling, and she was always ready for the morning's activity.

Kathryn learned, "The way to success is to be prepared, identify what you have, and know what it is worth—not to you, but to the customer. And always be the first one at the dock. The late and the lazy will never have what those that work hard have."

She was always organized for each day's sales, and when an incoming tide brought new products on arriving ships, her pricelist and customer list were side by side.

Kathryn was very aware of all that was happening around her. Over the preceding years, she was able to learn the languages of trade, and could hold conversations in Greek and Latin, and understood the North African dialects. She was becoming particularly proficient speaking English, which came to her tongue more easily than other languages. She often surprised herself when she used words with the English traders that she was convinced she had not heard before. To her amazement, the Englishmen remarked at her command of their language.

Kathryn understood the tempo, the language of trade, and the faces of those who work the docks. Business was often cutthroat. Each buyer was trying to negotiate a lower price than what the seller asked. Some sellers sailed on the tide to sell products for a quick gain, cheating the unsuspecting buyers, and before the truth became apparent, the swindler disappeared. Buyers and sellers needed to know whether they could gain more profit on the docks of Venice or wait for a caravan's buyer who might pay more to take goods to market squares on their routes to foreign lands with unfamiliar names: Clermont, Lyon, or Paris in France; or London, New Castle, or Edinburgh across the English Channel. There were also the trade centers of Calais and Bremen, or Metz, Vienna, and Cracow, or others as far away as Danzig and Riga.

Kathryn seemed to know everyone in Venice. At times, the office was filled with people stopping to talk to her, or ask her opinion: women introduced their sons, merchants tried to hire her, and city officials wanted her to speak to her father and grandfather on their behalf. No one cared that the girl was only twelve years old.

Kathryn's usual merchant customers were on hand after runners had been sent to inform them of goods they would want to purchase. Antonio was known for the fairest prices on imports. He did all he could to maintain quality customers. He never sold damaged or inferior products, and everyone on the docks knew "his promise was set in stone."

A Year Later

Late one morning, after her business was complete, and all the goods that had not sold and those received in trade were moved to the warehouse, only one shipment remained on the dock to be completed, and it turned into an angry dispute over goods intended for the palace. The dispute resulted in Antonio being summoned to the palace to answer questions directly by the Doge of Venice.

What had happened was a ship carrying goods had arrived and been unloaded at the dock in front of Antonio's warehouses. The manifest for those goods had been checked and contracts were to be signed for purchase by the ship's captain and Antonio as soon as he returned from San Polo, which was expected to be later in the day.

However, another merchant went to the ship's captain to buy the already promised goods. The captain wrote a new contract, sold the goods at a quick profit, and the goods were removed from the dock.

When this happened, Kathryn immediately sent a runner to alert Antonio.

When Antonio returned, he was furious, but there was nothing he could do because the ship had sailed immediately upon selling the goods and a court could not be established.

A large portion of the shipment was to be delivered to Doge Vitale

Faliero's purchasing agent, and the price had been fixed.

The next day, Antonio delivered the goods as promised. To keep his promise with the contract he had with the palace's buyer, Antonio bought the goods at market price, double the dock price in the original contract.

A day later armed soldiers knocked on the door of Antonio's house. His servant alerted Antonio of the guard's arrival, and he was the one to open the door. The captain of the Doge's Guard said, "Sir, are you Antonio Delyan?"

"I am," answered Antonio.

"You are ordered to stand before His Most Serene Prince, the Doge of Venice. You will dress accordingly."

Uncle Antonio was walked to the palace flanked by the guards.

Serena was at her parents' house when the soldiers arrived for Antonio. As soon as Antonio left, Teresa sent servants to the Moretti household and to fetch Kathryn at the office.

Vitale Faliero, the 32nd Doge of Venice, a nobleman who had been elected to the most powerful position in Venice almost 11 years earlier, wanted to know the details when he was informed of the swindle over his goods on the dock. He was especially interested in Antonio's keeping to his part of the contract, even though he would lose a lot of money. When all the information was presented and Antonio was established as a man of firm personal integrity, the Doge was certain he had found the right man for an important mission.

Vitale Faliero knew Antonio on two fronts, as the son-in-law of Signore Moretti, Chief of Trade for Venice, and they had talked briefly on occasions at palace receptions. But, more importantly, Antonio's reputation was untarnished.

Past doges had been in negotiations with Constantinople for many years and the time was now ripe for a trade partnership.

The Doge had prepared a secret diplomatic message for Alexius I, Emperor of the Byzantine Empire in Constantinople. Only three people would read the words on the document: the Doge of Venice, Emperor Alexius I, and an unnamed agent to complete the undertaking. The agent needed to be someone outside the Doge's inner circle, who would not draw attention to the task, who was able to be silent about the trip—a person of integrity, and someone who had permission to speak for the Doge. This person's words, his decisions, and his signature would carry the weight of Doge Vitale Faliero, himself.

Hours later, Antonio left the palace with a new responsibility. Antonio Dimitar Delyan was a diplomat to the court of Alexius I—and he would be carrying a secret pouch.

Antonio returned home late that afternoon and went straight to the veranda. At home, he was always cheery, happy to be with his wife and Kathryn, and he rarely spoke about his work. Often, he unsuccessfully encouraged Kathryn do the same. He had instituted a family rule: talk of business ended once they walked through the home's threshold at the end of the day. That rule however, had failed. He could not stop Kathryn from telling him what was next, how to do a task more efficiently, and what she thought was the future of Venice.

Serena was standing anxiously at her third-floor window waiting for news from the palace. As soon as Antonio stepped off the transport, she made her way to be with her husband. Serena was unexpectedly handed a plate with Antonio's favorite sweetie and hot tea by Teresa.

When Serena walked onto the veranda, she sensed he was going to keep something from her. Serena was often frustrated because Antonio usually did not tell her what he planned or what he was thinking. She knew he needed to "think it out" because that was his way. He believed there was no reason to discuss, "What has not, and may not happen." He preferred to "show results rather than express hollow words." He realized this annoyed her, and the last thing in the world he wanted to do was disappoint her or hurt her feelings. He did not do it on purpose. There was nothing he could do; it was who he was.

Antonio smiled as soon as he saw Serena walk onto the veranda with Teresa's lemon torte. He was tapping a jagged piece of jade on the table. It had broken off a handcrafted candleholder made in Mumbai. The broken piece, the size of a pigeon's egg had fallen to the floor as the warehouseman pulled back the protective reed covering. The jade was like many of the new products introduced by Antonio to Europe—it was what his customers wanted, but not needed.

Serena placed the tray on the table and sat down next to her husband. "From as early as I can recall, I have loved looking at the canal. Of course, my view, until you stole me from my parents, was from the Rialto to this side. The boat traffic has more than doubled in just the past few years."

Antonio could see Serena's concern for his safety had been heavy. He decided to be straight-forward with her as she would certainly want to know all that had happened at the palace and what he was thinking. But exactly how to say it was going to be tricky. His scheme had two points: he had to gain her support for taking Kathryn on a long trip, and the other to conceal the reason for the trip.

"Darling, I think it is time to expand to Constantinople." He held up the broken jade. "New products are coming from the East, products many customers will want. Our ships arrive with riches seen for the first time. We must be the family to show Europe what they could have. There is a new world opening to those who want to touch it, taste it, smell it, and feel its treasures. I must travel to Constantinople, find an agent to represent us there, and open a trading office."

Seeing Serena's interest, he kept explaining, "I should be gone no more than a month, maybe two. All I will need is a clerk who—"

Stopping Antonio with a sharp tone in her voice—the voice of a mother who is protecting her child—Serena said, "You can't mean what I think you mean? You aren't talking about a 'clerk' are you?"

Trying to use his smile as a shield, he said, "Yes, a clerk. And it has to be the best clerk I have. And, of course, it has to be a clerk who can speak Greek." Trying to make the uncomfortable situation easier, he asked, "Do you know such a person?"

"Antonio, you can't take Kathryn! She is only 12. Yes, she is the most mature 12-year-old anyone has met, but still, you can—"

"Serena, darling, Kathryn is the perfect choice. And she will be 13 years old while we are away." Thinking he could make the sale, "Could anything make her happier? She could walk the streets of a city only foreign sailors and caravans visit. She could see the city she reads about. And she told us the city has been in her dreams. Serena, what are we going to say when she asks to go?"

Kathryn ran from her launch the moment it landed. As soon as she spotted them on the veranda, she yelled, "Don't tell the story. Wait for me! I want to know every word of what happened."

Kathryn was out of breath after jumping out of the boat and running as quick as she could to them. After giving each of her parents a kiss on both cheeks, she sat down, reached for the finger cake on the tray, put the whole thing in her mouth, and began to chew while looking directly at Antonio.

Antonio, making the face of one who was offended, said to Serena, "I am not sure if the Emperor of Constantinople would take her head off or simply have her drowned in the Golden Horn for exhibiting such bad manners." Still ignoring Kathryn, "I suppose as her father, I would be tortured for being responsible for the embarrassment to his court."

Kathryn glanced back and forth at her parents, not understanding the full flavor of the conversation.

Serena followed with, "I am sure foreigners are not beheaded or sent to jail for such behavior, but they are probably cast from the city as one would toss an old bone after a meal." Then Serena asked Kathryn, "You are the one with all the knowledge of Constantinople. What do you think would happen to you?"

The glimmer of anticipation, then understanding the largeness of what was being presented to her, brightened Kathryn's eyes. Trying her best to control her anticipation of what was to be, unsuccessfully giddily, said, "Should I be so lucky as to have the opportunity to visit the city of Constantine, to walk inside the Hagia Sophia of Justinian and Theodora, I would be the perfect lady, dress accordingly, and display the finest courtesies expected of a Venetian visitor!"

"Kathryn, your father has plans to visit Constantinople in the upcoming months, and I cannot accompany him..." Serena, head bent down, putting her two hands on the small bulge of her belly, and looked at Kathryn, "... in anticipation of our family's newest member. Your father was curious to know if you might want to accompany him as chief clerk on this trip."

The table almost toppled. The dessert plate and its contents catapulted up as Kathryn's body jumped with excitement. Kissing her mother, then bending over and putting a kiss on her belly, she slid over and jumped on Antonio's lap, hugging and kissing him. "Yes! Yes! And...Yes again!"

She was so excited she scurried back to Serena, "Thank you, Mother.

I love you. Each time I say 'Mother,' I want to say it again, and again."

As if telling all of Venice, Kathryn shouted toward the canal, "Kathryn…Cappelli…Delyan is traveling to Constantinople!"

Then, she asked, "Does anyone know?"

"No, your mother and I decided—let me take that back—your mother cast the deciding vote a few minutes ago."

"Can I be the first to tell my grandparents?"

"You can. We will be seeing them tonight?"

"I must tell Teresa."

"Go tell your friend Teresa. But she probably knows. She seems to know what will happen before it happens. Anyway, she will surely be happy for you. We need to start our planning in the morning.

After additional kisses, Kathryn skipped her way to the kitchen.

Greeted by Teresa, who had tea already in cups, she said, "I understand you are to join your father on a trip to see the Golden Horn."

"How did you know? I just learned of the adventure myself."

"My dear, the sounds of all that has and will happen, travel through the walls of time quickly." Changing the direction of the conversation, Teresa laughed, "Poor Corrado, you will make his life difficult trying to teach you what he does not know."

"Teresa, I wish you could be with us."

"My dear, I will be with you in all you do. Constantinople is the most beautiful city of cities."

Kathryn brings her teacup to her nose. Your tea has a familiar flavor I've had before coming here, but I don't remember when."

"You will. Grandmother's tea has been a part of our family since the time of Cleopatra."

Kathryn is absorbed in another thought. "I saw the man who wears red in my dreams last night. He is the one who attacked father and me at the docks, isn't he? I know you know him. Will he follow us to Constantinople?

Kathryn stares at Teresa waiting for an answer.

Teresa pours some tea, warns, "Abbadon knows you have the ring. You must safeguard yourself and Antonio.

Kathryn takes the ring out from under her blouse. "I know he is near. What should I do?"

"My dear, he will find you. Be careful. The ring will be your protector. You will need its power and most importantly, do not let his yellow eyes frighten you. He is not ugly because of his eyes, but because of his yellow heart.

"I had to tell Antonio."

"Time and circumstances have connected the two of you. Our secrets are safe with him. He will fight to the death for you, and you must do the same for him."

Kathryn wraps her arms around Teresa.

Teresa is warmed by the arms around her. She smiles yet takes in a deep breath of worry for the young girl who through no want of her own, will shoulder the wonders and dangers of duty.

Kathryn picked up two more of Teresa's cookies and went to her room. The exhilaration of the last hour and the long day made her eyes heavy. She dreamed she saw the four horses of the Hippodrome, in a building in Venice, which did not exist.

She looked forward to the ship's sailing, a chance for an adventure and to read. Corrado gave her Homer's Iliad and Odyssey as a gift two weeks earlier for her to take on the trip; she began reading immediately, and she planned to complete them on the way, rereading them again, and again. Antonio knew she would ask hundreds of questions before arriving at port in Constantinople. She wasn't sure how long the trip would take. One of the deck hands on the ship said it would be no longer than two weeks, with at least one stop because of weather or for provisions.

Kathryn could hardly sleep the night before they were to leave because she knew she needed to complete her responsibilities at the office and on the dock before they could sail.

When Kathryn skillfully presented a convincing argument to Antonio for an assistant after two new warehouses were purchased, he agreed and asked if she had anyone in mind.

She did—Massimo.

For the past two weeks, she had instructed Massimo on all he would need to learn while she was away for, "four, maybe five weeks."

She was not sure if she or Massimo was more nervous about

the trip. He had been a part of Antonio's house for many years. His father, Ciro, was the first person hired by Antonio when he began his business in Venice. When Ciro died a few years ago, Antonio immediately brought Massimo into his household so that he could afford to care for his widowed mother and sister; Ciro's faithful dedication to Antonio needed to be repaid.

Chapter 25

Venetian Docks

The Venetian docks were alive with activity this day, as they were most days. Here was the place where foreign traders and local fishing boats tossed their ropes to shore, so the wooden transports could be tied tight, just close enough to kiss the dock, allowing the ships' wooden planking to span from the quarterdeck to the wharf.

Floating vessels and crews from the entire Mediterranean Sea and beyond came to Venice. The warships carried sailors and soldiers to the friendly Venetian canals: merchant ships brought traders ready to barter goods for gold and silver; and diplomats exchanged secret packets from sultans and kings to gain, resolve, and build alliances. From every corner of the world, adventurers were traveling to exotic ports and would find their way to the islands of Venice.

Each of them disembarked to shake off their sea legs in the city atop the Adriatic to eat the islands' fresh foods and drink the clear wines, to sell the goods pulled out of their holds, and to fill the ships with possibilities for other lands. They longed to share tales of far-off lands, the stories of kings and queens, of emperors and empresses, of pirates and warriors.

The Canal of San Marco, the entranceway to Venice, called sailors from every sea and ocean to its docks. Here they would resupply the warehouses, and prepare for their next voyage, always hoping to return to the "City of the Lion."

Ripples excitedly pushed away from the wooden ship, rolling to port, back to starboard, and back again, as the ship's crew lifted and heaved cargo to be stacked on the deck across the connecting planks, and then carefully lowered for storage in the transport's belly, while other crates were being tied down on the open deck.

The captain barked orders at the cargo handlers, "Move along, move quickly! You are costing me money and time, neither of which I have enough of to waste, and you will pay for any damage to the crates your miserable lives cannot afford."

The captain's face was intent on his task—of utmost importance was to have his ship at sea, to have wind in her sails. He pressed his crew to have the *Sharkfin* ready before tomorrow's outgoing tide. The contract demanded that he arrive in Constantinople in a fortnight.

Kathryn had completed the ship's manifest of goods. She accounted for every roll of English wool, regarded for its durability and weaving quality by rug-makers, and watched to be sure the boxes of dry goods, clay jars filled with spices, and the bundles of wheat were secured for the voyage.

Antonio was a merchant—considered by many on the docks, the most knowledgeable merchant in Venice—who understood the buying and selling of goods. He often schooled Kathryn on how to be successful at the docks.

"Kathryn, you need to understand how sellers of goods—like you, me, and the other merchants we work with—buy and sell, why our customers want to spend their gold, and what they want to spend it on. More to the point, we give them products they did not know they wanted. We convince them to buy what arrives at the docks. Once you know the world is organized and built on finding the supply of what people want, then, we will meet their demands. Remember this, the prince who controls trade, controls an empire.

"Kings have been fighting their neighbors over trade since the world began, and I am saddened that it will never change. For you and me, we work in the shadow of kings like Emperor Alexius I Comnenus in Constantinople, and here in Venice, our Doge Vitale Faliero, or Philip in France, or William Rufus in England. Our fortunes prosper and fail on the whims of those in power.

"Venice is positioned to be the center of all Mediterranean trade—a crossroads of trade and banking. Our trading partners in Constantinople are influential managers of money and shipping, at the most important port in the world, able to connect the East and the Orient to our Western markets.

"We will be there soon. In Constantinople, you will touch East and West."

Chapter 26

Sailing from Venice
AD 1095

Antonio's carriages arrive at the dock just before the appointed sailing time. Antonio, Serena, Kathryn, and Teresa step down onto the dock. Teresa walks behind the carriage, her face searching the warehouses and docks. Porters transfer luggage to the ship.

Serena, tears welling up, takes Kathryn hands. "Kathryn, please take care of yourself and that amazing father of yours. The trip, while important, is not more important than your safety. I have never been comfortable until Antonio returns from his trips, and now you will be away from my arms."

"Mother, I love you. I will be safe." Kathryn slowly raises her hand to the pendant.

"My darling wife, I'll make sure we return on the first ship returning to Venice with new goods to sell what our buyers do not need but believe they must have."

"Go you two."

Kathryn looks for Teresa. She quivers, rubs her arms. Sees Teresa facing away from her. Looks past her. There in the distance alongside a warehouse is Abbadon watching them. He turns away slowly going out of sight.

Captain Okeanos calls to Antonio, "Antonio, get aboard. The wind is our today."

Antonio and Serenas hug. "Kathryn, we must board."

Teresa comes to Kathryn. "The time has come for you to fulfill your destiny."

The weight of what Teresa said is heavy on Kathryn's shoulders. "When will I see you again?"

"Soon my dear, soon."

The *Sharkfin's* sails began to swell with a northerly breeze as it cleared the channel through the Lido, a barrier island of sand and scrub pine. With Venice behind them and shrinking from sight, the voyage was underway. That first day, Kathryn walked to the bow of the ship, its sail billowed with air blowing from the north, cut through the blue water of the Adriatic Sea. The chosen route was to sail south along the Italian coast, then east from Otranto at the heel of Italy's boot. Should strong easterlies blow, they would drop anchor at the port of Gagliano del Capo until favorable winds were at their back.

On the third day, off the coast of Brindisi, the captain stood next to the tiller steering his course. He looked intently at the growing clouds, calculating the increasing winds, weighing if he should try to outrun the advancing storm, or put into a port early.

The ship's two voyagers were standing at the rail, adjusting to the cadence of the slow rolling waves just as the sun was rising from the sea. Captain Okeanos greeted his two passengers, "Buon giorno, Signore e Signorina."

"Captain, your name is Greek, isn't it, meaning 'ocean'?" asked Kathryn.

"Si, my mother told me she could see me under sail in her visions while I was still nothing more than a low tide in her belly. So, my name was decided before I was born. And, as you can tell, my mother could tell my future."

"And, Signorina Kathryn, you are from Venice, but your name is not Mediterranean."

"Si, my ancestors were Gaelic, but my home is in Venice."

Addressing Antonio, warning of bad weather ahead, the Captain said, "We should enjoy the next few hours, for our gentle sea will change its face. It looks like a storm behind us wants to find out if our sails or its winds are stronger. The westerly winds are sending dark clouds lower in the sky. We will feel Poseidon's wrath just before tomorrow's dawn. His powers of rain, wind, and current will test my seamanship and that of my crew."

Antonio agreed about the conditions as he too studied the advancing sky. He was curious about the plan to stay far from the coast, wondering why the ship was not looking for a safe harbor until the storm passed.

"Captain, your experience at sea far exceeds mine, yet I hold the contract for this ship, so I must know why you don't sail closer to shore or find a harbor and safety against a western shore. It seems that there the blow could be broken rather than taking the full impact of waves and wind. Another day added to this voyage is but another day, why chance to lose our lives and cargo?"

Captain Okeanos was quick to answer. "These waters are crawling with pirates, mostly brigands looking for a quick mark." With a snap of his finger, he continued, "They come on a ship quickly with small scows, but with more men than we have, and they are skilled with their swords and crossbows. All they care about is today. They know their lives are counted in months; not one of them thinks of old age. They live by the loot they take and bring to port, wasting it in a few days, and then must look to the sea to find their next meal. I do not plan for this ship to be anyone's next fortune."

The captain continued to educate Antonio and Kathryn. "These bandits act as any animal would. Like the shark, they prefer to eat the weak or slow fish. Signor Delyan, we are a slow fish compared to those outfitted for robbery, for killing, and for capturing survivors of the attack to sell as slaves." The captain looked at Antonio, shifted his eyes to Kathryn, then back to Antonio—all three understood his hidden message.

Kathryn wanted to hear more about the pirates. She realized both men seemed to think she was in the greatest of danger should there be an attack. She asked, "What is the likelihood of pirates attacking in these waters?"

"They choose their target, swiftly advance with small oared boats on slower ships of sail, like us, and decide if they have an advantage. Next, their small craft will pull alongside, grappling hooks will be thrown, and quickly secure both ship and scow as one. In their hands will be a sword or mallet. Should a show of force be demonstrated before they come alongside, they may back off and wait for the next score. But if it has been a long time since their last cache or if they think they can take a small merchant ship like ours—knowing its holds are full of goods which can be easily sold on any Adriatic dock—they will quickly recalculate their chances against their gains."

Captain Okeanos decided he was going to outrun the storm.

Just off the coast of Brindisi, the wind gained strength and the waves grew. The captain informed Antonio that they were changing direction to the southeast. He began bellowing orders to the crew. The ship came alive with activity, the ropes holding deck boxes were checked, and checked again. This was done not to save the boxes, but to prevent them from interfering with the crew's duties, and to avoid any possible injuries from moving boxes should they be hit by heavy winds and high seas.

The storm hit with a fury. Neither Kathryn nor Antonio could sleep. During the long black night, the ship was battered. The captain had the sails taken down and secured. The craft now belonged to Poseidon. Waves were coming over the rails, its bow rising quickly to the black sky, and just as quickly slamming down as each wave caused the ship to rise and fall, rise and fall. With each wave, the ship climbed a higher mountain of water and descended in a violent plunge to a collision of wooden ship against the sea's unbreakable surface. Containers broke loose, toppling, opening, and their contents sliding on the deck and flying in the air, catching on the rigging and tangling. Much of it went overboard.

Antonio, Kathryn, and the crew were on the deck, in danger of the debris tossed across the ship, in danger of being tossed overboard, no one wanted to be below should the ship break apart.

Captain Okeanos, standing tall on the deck, pitched back and forth, blasted with water from an angry sea, his legs straining to hold position while he cursed the spirits that swim the sea. He continued to hold fast with both hands to control the tiller guiding them through the storm, and to save their lives.

The captain called out to one of his crew to help. Kathryn watched as the sailor untied the leather strap that held him to the ship started to crawl across the deck. Before he was halfway to the captain, the ship drove up a wave, rolling over its crest, and pointed to the bottom of the swell, it landed against the side of the cresting water. Another wave crashed over the starboard side; its driving power lifted the sailor off the deck. The sailor cried out for someone to rescue him, but his cry was not heard, he was swallowed by a wave and disappeared over the port side.

Kathryn held tightly to her father. Antonio's grip on Kathryn was so tight that she screamed in pain. Then another wave larger than the last covered both Antonio and Kathryn.

Wave after wave hit the ship. Captain Okeanos standing against the storm, fighting, not willing to give, held his place.

The tempest tried but failed to sink the *Sharkfin*. As it moved past them to the east, the waves were now slowly rolling. The sun, only half visible in the clouds, had climbed above the horizon showing the damage from nature's anger, and the crew trying to return the ship to seaworthiness again. Boxes had been lost overboard; others were waterlogged. The mast had held but was cracked. Many of the canvas sails, ripped and shredded from the storm, hung from their crossbeams. They needed to be mended.

The westerly winds from the torrent had carried the ship farther to the eastern coastline than was safe. Now at the mercy of the current, and without sail, the *Sharkfin* could only navigate with its rudder for the next two days.

What Kathryn, Antonio, Captain Okeanos had no inkling what lay ahead was…

More Dangerous than the Storm.

Kathryn and Antonio were on sitting on deck eating crackers. She felt a cool breeze pass over her. She stood. Antonio, not sure why she was shivering under the warm sun, studied her face. "Kathryn, you look cold fearful."

A frightened shout called the crew to attention, "CAPTAIN, LOOK TO PORT!"

A second later, another sailor yelled, his panicked voice cried,

"PIRATES!"

Kathryn was quick to the rail followed by Antonio. Three boats, each with men pulling their long wooden oars, cut down through the blue swells closing the distance to the *Sharkfin*. In one boat stood Abbadon.

Stavos, yelled, "Captain, it's **Red Hood**."

Captain Okeanos quickly reacted to the alert. His voice clear and in charge organized for the certain fight. "Stavos, Telemon, prepare your men. Three men forward and three amidships on both port and starboard."

The captain ordered Antonio to battle, "Hide the girl and grab a pole," he shouts, "Cutlasses and poles to the ready!"

Kathryn crouched between two boxes was covered by a piece of torn canvas in the stern directly behind the long heavy tiller controlling the rudder.

The two boats drew nearer, near enough to see the faces of those on the hunt—those who came to plunder, to kill.

The captain gave control of the rudder to Francisco and he went off to the rail preparing for the fight. Captain Okeanos shouted, "Keep your weapons out of sight. They see our mast and know we can't outrun them. They think that we will give up our stores, not willing to fight. We will let them move close."

"Bowmen make your marks when ordered. Poles hold them off, cutlasses in your hands if they board."

The two attacking boats coming straight at the bow, oarsmen straining to build speed, separated to board on each side of the *Sharkfin*. Okeanos was deciding his next move.

The pirates were almost alongside on the right side of the ship.

"Bowmen, go to starboard!"

Stavos and Telemon ran to the starboard side and began their flight of arrows. Antonio and crew waiting, ready to fight.

"Francisco, take the helm. Men, you know your duties. Wait for my orders.

As the first boat closes with the Sharkfin, the captain commanded, "Bowman, ARROWS!

The arrows cover the attacking boat. Two of the arrows were on target, but it did not stop the attackers.

The first craft is quickly alongside, its grappling hooks first, catching hold of the *Sharkfin*.

Antonio grabbed a long pole to push it off, but it was useless against the steel of a sword, allowing the villains to climb up the merchant ship. He now slashed at the grappling ropes, but men were jumping, climbing up the sides. One of the pirates stayed on his boat and jumped on as it reached amidships and climbed aft.

When the first wave of pirates climbed aboard Stavos pulled his weapon but was slashed and left bleeding on the deck. Antonio was now fighting with his knife. The captain, with the point of his lance, saved Telemon who was on the deck with a pirate standing over him.

On the portside, the pirates still in their boat were close to boarding.

As pirates come over the rails, one says, "Look for the girl. Abbadon wants her necklace."

Kathryn under the canvas recognizes the man who had his hands around her neck at the dock.

Captain Okeanos went to the portside rail, and not looking back yelled, "Francisco, push hard, push hard to port, ram their boat!"

The captain did not know Francisco was wounded, when he stopped the pirate who was the last to leave his boat and came over the rail next to him.

Everyone was engaged with the attackers on board. Kathryn, realizing the situation, tossed the canvas back over her head, ran out from behind her boxes, and charged to push the bar once held by Francisco. As soon as she was in the open, a pirate noticed and ran in her direction. "The girl. I'll get her."

Captain Okeanos yelled to Antonio. Antonio broke from his fight to help Kathryn.

As Kathryn put two hands on the tiller, a slash from a cutlass passed her face but its tip cut a thin line opening her flesh from the bottom of her shoulder to her elbow. Two men crashed into her, one Antonio, the other the pirate. Seeing the men fighting, rolling on the deck, Kathryn knew what she must do. Her body hurting, she rose quickly from the wooden deck and rushed to shove the thick tiller to turn the rudder. Captain Okeanos came to Antonio's aid, slashed with his sword opening a large wound in the pirate's leg, and slashed again at the neck causing the pirate to release his weapon. No longer able to fight, the captain lifted the pirate and tossed him into the sea.

Kathryn took the wooden shaft to it farthest position. Pain ran up and down her arm, but she continued to hold it in place. Her clothing, arm and hands were now scarlet from the blood spilling from her left arm.

The ship responded to Kathryn's action; it quickly began to turn to port against the smaller boat just as the pirates were ready to board—their oars snapped first, then the sound of the smaller boat being crushed against the boards of the larger, its pirates sent to a watery end along with their boat crushed under the *Sharkfin*.

The pirates onboard were now outnumbered. The score to be quickly settled by the crew of the *Sharkfin*. Some of Abbadon's pirates jumped overboard, others wounded or dead, tossed into the waves.

Kathryn looks in the distance to the third boat which never entered the fight. Abbadon's red hood shadowed his face, but Kathryn cannot see, but can feel his dastardly smile. He orders his men to row, leaving those in the water to drown.

Nonetheless, Antonio, Kathryn, Captain Okeanos, and two others had felt the steel of the pirates' cutlasses. Three crewmembers did not survive the fight.

Kathryn's ribs were sore, and her arm throbbed from the tourniquets Captain Okeanos had tied tightly to the top of her arm and just above her elbow to stop the bleeding. "You, young lady, are very brave. Without your quick thinking, we may all have been tossed overboard."

Antonio commends the captain, "Your crew fought well."

"As did you Antonio."

Kathryn looks at the tiller. "Captain, no one is at the tiller."

"Our ship is at the mercy of the sea. Our rudder was broken when we crushed the second boat. But the current takes us towards friendly shores. All we can do now is watch and wait."

The *Sharkfin* and crew had survived the attack. Now adrift, its ability to maneuver, unable to steer a course and without full sail. They drifted, carried by the current the rest of day and into the night.

Then!

The *Sharkfin* hit a reef. The sound of cracking wood broke through the waves and wind. **The boat began to break apart**. The darkness of the moonless night added to the confusion, the mayhem, and certain death from the unknown. The captain's orders went unheard. Everyone onboard now followed another master, their will to survive, as the sea was carrying out the final destruction of the *Sharkfin*.

Sailors who knew the dangers of the sea, the stories of tragic shipwrecks, but never thought it could happen to them, realized they were now in a struggle more violent than any pirate attack. They were in a contest against Poseidon, and they knew, except for those who might hold a lucky charm, no one can survive the force of an angry Mediterranean. The *Sharkfin* had won against the storm, and able to defeat an attack, but the sea decided to raise its mountains to touch its prey.

The ship's hull was torn, its distorted boards holding it tight to the rock, but the Sharkfin twisted and turned with the waves, pitching the crew and contents like stones skipped across a lake. In the chaos, Antonio and Kathryn were knocked into each other in the black night. They had to shout to each other to hear. Antonio grabbed Kathryn, holding her tight while holding onto the ship's rib.

"Kathryn, can you reach the rope behind you?"

She looked over her shoulder, nodded. She held onto Antonio's extended hand, and with the other she attempted to reach the rope. As her fingers touched the rope, a wave slammed into Kathryn, hands no longer touching.

Kathryn, now sliding away from Antonio, looked at him with terror in her eyes. Just as Antonio let loose of his position to follow her, the *Sharkfin* rolled onto its side.

A huge wave rose above the rail and crashed down on the open deck, sending Kathryn, sliding, colliding backwards into Antonio, both engulfed, and out of control on the rocking ship.

Extending his arm, Antonio caught Kathryn's shirt as she washed up against him. Kathryn was still holding the rope.

Antonio tied a loop on each end of the rope for them to put an arm through as a lifeline should they lose their hold of each other, the other hand free to hold the ship's aft rail.

Watching the bow's oaken boards splinter and swallow men into its cavity, Antonio, yelled above the noise, "Kathryn, we must jump or be sucked down. Hold tightly to the rope, but if I sink, let it go. Do you understand?"

Kathryn looked at her father in disbelief. She instinctively moved her hand to the necklace to grasp the pendant dangling from its chain.

Before she could answer, Antonio reached around his daughter and pulled her to him. Unable to hold on, the wooden deck almost perpendicular to the sea, they rolled over into the roiling water. Kathryn and Antonio landed hard against the water. All those who could, swam away from the ship, swimming for their lives in the dark, cruel sea.

The *Sharkfin* disappeared under them.

Kathryn fought to breathe, but each time she tried to gasp for air, she swallowed a mouthful of the furious Mediterranean. Antonio smashed his head on the fallen mast when they hit the water.

A hand pulled them to the surface, dragging the two Venetians to the beach.

Antonio's face bruised. His shirt open, his leather satchel tied to his waist, and his knife on his belt. Kathryn next to him is unconscious.

Once on land each struggled for life, finding the other alive, initially thinking each had been the other's rescuer. A vine was wrapped around their arms. Kathryn had seen this vine before; it was in Teresa's kitchen.

"Kathryn, Kathryn!" Antonio coughing from the sea water.

Kathryn stirs, throat sore, groans in pain. Antonio crawls through the sand next to her.

She looks up. "Father, I didn't see you after we jumped. I started sinking."

Not all the crew found land after the ship's belly was ripped open and water filled its hull. In the darkness, in the wind and rain, Antonio, Kathryn, and four of the crew were on the beach. Captain Okeanos was not one of them.

A fisherman rushes up to them, kneels. "Thank the gods you are alive. You and a few others are the only survivors on the beach. Your ship hit a reef. A lady pulled the two of you ashore with those." The man points to the vines.

Antonio asks, "Who? Where is she?"

"I don't see her. She left right after saving you."

Kathryn fondles her vine, smiles, touches her pendant. In a whisper neither Antonio or the fisherman can hear, says, "Thank you."

The message from the Doge to Alexius had been saved. Inside his father's leather bag, which Antonio had strapped to his chest, were the secret papers wrapped in oiled cloth. He had also kept a money belt tied tightly around his waist.

Part Four

Constantinople: The Court of Alexius I

Chapter 27

A Caravan, an Emperor, a Princess, a Captain

The caravan had been on the road since before the first rays of sun began heating the scorched, rocky, uneven track, on its destination to Constantinople. The difficult roads and the sun were conspiring to slow the march of wagons, and the caravan's guards were on watch for bandits who might attack the dusty merchants at the bottom of a narrow pass, or around the next mountain of rock.

It had taken three days before Antonio and Kathryn could continue the journey to Constantinople. And they had to do so by caravan. The *Sharkfin's* hull had been torn away against the shallow bottom on a small island not far from Igoumenista, a Greek shipping center. They were lucky to find space on a wagon headed from this small trading city to Constantinople. It was their only choice; there would not be another ship in port for weeks.

They were only able to purchase a single set of clothing and necessities as the caravan leader directed. Their first chance to outfit themselves was a week into their trip at Thessaloniki, where the caravan rested their draft animals for two days and to purchase food for the final march to Constantinople.

Mother Nature, no longer able to accept more heat, chose to return the sun's favor by sending shimmering veils of warmth skyward. The unrelenting heat was almost unbearable for the animals. The caravan needed to begin the day very early and to find shade or raise canvas by mid-day to protect the animals and themselves from the heat, and then they would try to press forward for a few hours at the end of the day when the scorching, yellow sun turned red on the horizon.

After the last full day of travel ended before the next day's arrival in Constantinople, Istvan, the caravan's leader, gave his final orders to the travelers. Istvan's first order was for the sentries to take their positions, making sure the wagons and animals were safely inside their defenses, and to prepare the camp for the evening. Antonio was to act as a sentry from dusk to midnight. Along with all the men and women of the caravan, Kathryn obeyed the second order which was to make sure the horses and oxen were tended to, and each wagon's axles and wheels checked ready for the last day of travel.

Kathryn looked forward to the march. Before Antonio went on duty, he sent her to the wagon to rest for the next day's trip, but sleep did not come to her quickly, for tomorrow would be an adventure to a land from her dreams. Excitement overwhelmed her, and she stayed awake well into the night talking around the campfire with the merchants who spent their lives on caravans. Two of the men had sailed into the great city, and each of them told Kathryn of the beauty, the wealth, and the magic of Constantinople.

When the call to rise rang about the camp, Kathryn had been in a deep sleep. She experienced a dream so vivid that she wondered for a moment if the unknown kingdom really existed, where candles without flames lighted rooms at night, and homes had boxes in the wall for cooking, and wagons without animals to pull them moved on black streets.

She needed but a moment to realize that she was not in the bed of her dreams. In most of her nighttime imaginings, she could not understand this night's fantasy. She remembered seeing a light shining through a window spraying its glow over a bed and touching a wall of glass crystals. She had dreamt this before, described it to Corrado, but he could not interpret the dream. The unusual parts of her dreams were the surroundings of her dream world. The voices were not of a language she spoke—they were the foreign words she was learning on the docks. In the dream, however, she was able to understand and speak with others.

She felt as if she knew the people of her dreams; they were familiar, as familiar as friends, even family, but she could not recall anyone's name or the circumstances. She couldn't reason why she could remember an outside table set with dishes, sweet foods, and three people, including her, and all wearing oddly styled clothes.

Kathryn had always been a person of habit, of routine. She remembered a dream of a girl, one her own age, telling her, "Always be ready for a new day. Know what you are going to do and write a list. If you do it all the time, success will be your habit." Kathryn did as her dream instructed. In Venice she always planned for the orders in and out of the warehouse, checked on ships, and had plans ready.

On the caravan, she learned how to take care of horses and oxen, how to hoist a wagon with a broken wheel, was taught to cook on an open fire, milk animals, and had assisted in childbirth—and to keep a safe distance from the men hired to protect the caravan.

Before she left Venice, knowing she would be sailing across the Mediterranean to Constantinople, through the famous waterways traveled by ancient mariners and conquerors, she knew she was to be on a trip through the history lessons she had studied with Corrado. She would pass through the Hellespont, where Darius and his Persian troops crossed to attack Greek city-states at Marathon, and then to the Bosphorus Strait, and disembarking at voyage's end. It was the place Corrado told her had formed when the Marmara Sea and Black Sea had overflowed, spilling into the hole made when the land parted. But now she would enter in a more dramatic way, by caravan.

The last morning of the trip had arrived. She had been in the same clothes for over a week, and had decided the night before to change clothes for the final day of travel, not that the new clothes were much cleaner, but she had tied them on the outside of the wagon the day before to let them freshen in the hot air. After dressing on the floor of the wagon, she brushed and tied her hair in a knot, and jumped out. The smell of burnt pita bread cooking on the open fire made her move as fast as a hungry puppy.

Having dressed quickly, she jumped outside the wagon and, as usual, sipped the sweet tea Guido had prepared. No matter what time of day or night, Guido was always awake. Guido was assigned as Antonio's wagon handler. She followed her nose to the bread Guido had spread with mashed fig and honey.

"Is Signorina Kathryn hungry? Would you like some?"

"Oh, yes. Please." Guido slides the bread off a flat pan and hands it to her."

"Guido, this may be the best bread I have ever eaten."

"My young traveler, hunger makes the most basic a banquet."

Kathryn continues to stuff her face, but requests, "Is there enough for my father?"

"He was here an hour ago. He is on guard duty," Guido continues after a bite of bread, "Signorina, we are lucky to have each other. You and your father needed to travel to Constantinople, and I was without passengers."

"Thank you," Kathryn's mouth is full, she swallows, "for teaching me about this part of the world."

"Do you prefer to ride or walk today? Me, I like to have the reins in my hand, so I can see far ahead from my seat."

Kathryn vibrates, giggles, "The uneven road shakes my body sitting next to you, but my feet feel every rock and hole."

The rough and rocky trade routes traveled by the caravan rattled the bones of those in the wagons. Most of the travelers, like Kathryn, chose to walk alongside the wagons rather than absorb the shock of ruts and uneven grooves cut into the sand road by thousands of previous adventurers

Guido stood about five feet tall, and it seemed he was just as wide. Guido's bald head was always shiny clean. Everything about Guido was neat, clean, and orderly. Guido was a library of knowledge. He was never without a book, and always interested in discussing new ideas and experiences, especially with new members of the caravan—Guido and Corrado would have been good friends.

He was a wheelwright. Almost daily, when a wagon broke down, Guido was called to mend a wheel or repair an axle, and always with only a short delay, he had the caravan back on the road to its destination—Constantinople.

The nervousness and excitement of the road's end could be seen on everyone's face and heard in their conversations, even the animals were moving at a quicker pace somehow anticipating their arrival to the journey's end.

After a couple of hours on the road, Istavan the caravan leader, road up to her wagon on the largest, most beautiful chestnut horse Kathryn had ever seen.

"Is my friend Guido talking your head off?"

"Sir, I love every minute of it. I sometimes think I am in the famed library of Alexandria."

"We are almost to a city of libraries." Back to business, "Guido, after this rest, we will stop early to prepare for our last day. In the morning, pull your wagon into first position so our Signorina is first to see the city."

"Sir, thank you."

"My great pleasure is the have you see the sun rise over the capital of Byzantium."

When the caravan leader rides away, Kathryn asks, "Guido, do you believe in dreams?"

"Of course. Everyone does. Don't you?"

"Sometimes my dreams are pictures of places and people I don't know.

Guido, reins in hand, steered the sun-bleached canvas-covered wagon which carried the few personal belongings of Kathryn and Antonio that were found ashore after the shipwreck. Easing the boredom of the road, Kathryn often sat alongside Guido. They talked to pass the time on the road. Guido educated Kathryn about each city they visited on their trip from the Greek coast to Constantinople. Guido's account of the Greek and Persian wars and his knowledge of the road systems built by Roman soldiers made Kathryn want to learn more with each tale. He described the aqueducts she would see. The utter mass of their stones, cut perfectly and put in place was outshone by the straightness of the elevated tunnels carrying water and the engineering of their arched construction supports. These supports often rose 80 feet high from the ground supporting the water trough tied into the city's wall.

Guido's story of engineers building a city's lifeline of water began with the naming of the Valens Aqueduct. In the year 368, Byzantium, now Constantinople, celebrated the completion of the waterway which brought water flowing into its city from the far springs of distant Thrace. The source of the water from 200 miles away filled deep underground cisterns built to hold the city's growing need.

Kathryn barely slept. Her dreams and the excitement of the next day's travel caused her to twist and turn entire night. The morning did come. Antonio accompanied Kathryn and Guido in the wagon was in the wagon. The conversation was about languages. Guido stood on his seat; his face bright with animation. "Kathryn," Guido announced mid-conversation and pointed at the walls of Constantinople rising on the horizon, "look, up ahead. The city." Kathryn's heart jumped.

Antonio looked proudly at the young woman with him. She had changed since arriving at his house a frightened, little orphan girl. Now, she was the self-confident young woman he called daughter.

He thought how their young lives paralleled each other and the path each took to a door in Venice—maybe it was meant to be, planned by some destiny not to be questioned.

Antonio recalled the strong-willed girl trying to overcome tragedy. He could not remember her sulking or crying after arriving at his home. She had spent hours in his gardens. She needed hours to herself. As time passed, she spent less time seeking solace among the flowers and trees, and more time in Antonio's library and trading offices.

Kathryn could see into a customer's thoughts. Kathryn had business instincts. She could determine if a merchant was negotiating a fair price or trying to take advantage of Antonio's traders. In the past year, Kathryn had been able to establish a fair market price for most commodities, which became the standard among Venetian trading houses. Because she was but a young girl, merchants would try to take advantage of her, thinking she was inexperienced, and that Antonio was foolish to let her book trades. But once the trading was completed, a ship's captain or vendor walked away from the dock satisfied they had made a fair trade with a knowledgeable businessperson.

When Antonio had decided to give Kathryn trading responsibility, he knew this was going to be a big step for someone so young, but more importantly was the fact that only men bartered on the wharves outside a merchant's storefront. Each day, Kathryn gave bidders the list of items and prices, dependent on orders of customers throughout the Mediterranean rim. Antonio took note that Kathryn often sensed a bargain and directed the salesmen to bid on products others did not buy. Her bargaining instincts often turned a substantial profit for the House of Delyan. She correctly predicted the daily outcomes even before his agents traveled to the docks. Kathryn understood the inner workings of the docks, the shipping schedules of products coming to the docks, and the products necessary to fill ships leaving for ports of call. Antonio's customers regularly bypassed the usual ordering procedures by going directly to Kathryn, knowing she would be sure to give their orders her special attention.

The incident that caused Antonio to give her freedom to make decisions occurred at one of the trading wharfs on the island of San Marco, which is just across from Dorsoduro. Dorsoduro is home to the primary docks for ships entering the Grand Canal, the trading waterway of Venice, and to the Doge of Venice.

An envoy, representing Robert Curthose, Duke of Normandy, placed an order with Antonio for a special azure-colored stone, which was to be a surprise for the duke's wife, Sybilla of Conversano. The Egyptian merchant who carried the highest quality lapis lazuli was expected from Alexandria within the month.

Since ancient times, lapis lazuli, the stone of azure, had been considered the most beautiful of all rocks. The mines far to the east, in the lands of the Afghan, were perhaps 3,000 years old. The multiple blues, deep in color were mixed with white and creamy greens crisscrossing the stone with metallic brass veins, flecks, and splashes.

Upon arrival at the Port of Venice, the Egyptian jeweler, Badawi, who had sold many gems to Antonio in the past, was invited to visit Antonio's office. After a friendly opening conversation, the salesman opened his case to display three lapis stones. One was more beautiful than the others, worthy of the finger of the Duchess of Normandy. It was a flawlessly polished, perfectly shaped oval. Rising from a thin gold pedestal, the stone's smooth, rounded edges rose to become a half moon boasting its many shades of deep azure blue.

The discussion of the stone's price was almost concluded when the young Kathryn, who had been intently listening during the negotiations, interrupted the trading conversation. Antonio always told his agents, "Never, never go above the price I determine for a product, and never drop the price of the product we offer."

Antonio's trading opponent was pressing him for a final price, and without so much as a "Scusi," Kathryn came between them reached up and took hold of Antonio's lapels and pulled him down to her. She knew something about the numbers appeared incorrect.

To say the least, he was quite taken by surprise and met her eyes with the frown of a man embarrassed. But before he could utter a word to her, Kathryn in a subdued, but determined voice said, "Your prices for the lapis are wrong. You must not make this sale. Compare the costs of columns two and three." She wrote on the paper.

Kathryn shoved the price sheet in front of him, pointing to a number next to the word "Normandy." Antonio looked at the price sheet he had prepared that morning. Kathryn always checked the cost sheets for the next day's trading but having left early the day before to do another errand, Antonio checked the purchasing sheets.

To the surprise of both, she turned around, faced the Cairo trader, and told him, "Signor Badawi, the trading is suspended, but only for the moment. We know you to be a fair man. There has been a mistake. Please, while the correct prices are determined, share a plate of our finest Spanish olive oil and freshly baked bread."

The Egyptian trader smiled and asked with a sense of good humor, "Signorina, will you be joining us during this break Antonio has asked for?"

Kathryn returned the smile and answered, "No, signor, trading is not my business."

With a twisted smile, a look at Antonio, and speaking to Kathryn, "My apologies, but I think you are mistaken, you are the trader in the family."

Antonio had quickly realized the error of his mathematics and responded, "Badawi my friend, if you do not mind, I would like my Kathryn, my newest business agent, to join us. I know this is not work for young girls—the wharves are often dangerous, and trading can challenge gentlemen as well as thieves. I assure you, no one on this dock can match her business skills. I offered you a price for your lapis that was well over market price. Thanks to Kathryn, I did not insult your honor as a businessman with an unfair quote."

"Signorina," Badawi, with an optimistic tone questioned Kathryn, "If you worked for me, what price would I ask?" Antonio passed the price sheet to her outstretched hands. Kathryn used her stylus to write figures, turned the paper over, and recomputed. Seeing that both numbers matched, she wrote a figure for both men.

The men put their mark to the paper and the business was complete. She spent only a few moments with them tasting the crusty bread drenched in the rich, dark green olive oil. She excused herself and went directly to the office to review her uncle's work.

Chapter 28

Entering Constantinople and the Captain

Everyone in the caravan was happy to see the end of the journey, especially Antonio. Excited to share this moment, an adventure, and the exhilaration of the unknown, he put his arm around his daughter. "Kathryn, prepare for the sights and sounds of the world. Constantinople is the city the world longs to visit. When people first come to this city, seeing the strong, high walls of massive stones and concrete, they believe it was built to defend itself from invaders. But the truth is the strength of the thick walls surrounding the city was engineered to hold within it the energy of its visitors trading in the many languages echoing throughout the marketplaces."

Alexius I monitored the population of his great city. He regulated the balance of trade to assure his city retained its importance as the gateway between the Orient and Europe. He was especially vigilant of his borders and watchful for enemies throughout his vast empire. His custodians of public safety inspected each person, the animals, and foods entering under the welcoming arches. Braying donkeys pulled wooden carts which rattled on the stone streets as they made their way to market. The aromas of smoky cooked meats and seasoned vegetables wafted from the many food peddlers enticing the community of buyers and sellers to their stands. Golden cooking oils fried just-slaughtered lamb and boiling water in large pots steamed freshly caught fish at the busy docks for the hungry sailors to fill their stomachs after weeks at sea. The merchants and dockworkers lined up to get spicy specialties from charcoal grills. Antonio told Kathryn she would soon see the famous Hippodrome. Kathryn knew all about the legendary stadium, famous for its gladiatorial contests and chariot races.

News of their arrival preceded them. Before entering the city, a palace guard of four horsemen rode up to the caravan, stopping its progress. The captain asked Istavan for Signor Delyan and his daughter.

The cavalry and an ornate carriage of the Emperor's Palace Guard galloped up to their wagon.

Guido said, "Signore. Ahead," all three were watching the soldiers advancing, "It is either trouble or a welcoming."

Captain Stefano of the Guard halted his troop.

"Signore, by order of Emperor Alexius I, you and your daughter will travel in the Emperor's carriage. I am to take you to your living quarters." The captain exchanges a glance with Kathryn.

Kathryn kisses Guido, "Will I see you again, Guido?"

"That can only be answered by the Fates."

Antonio lifts Kathryn from Guido's wagon and she is assisted into the carriage.

The Palace Quarters

Antonio and his daughter, guests of the emperor, were guided to their palace living quarters.

On the way to their rooms, Antonio was greeted by a soldier holding a small ornate silver plate. On it rested a single piece of white parchment folded in thirds and tied with a purple string.

"Signore, this letter arrived moments ago. It is from the secretary of our glorious Emperor. A messenger stands outside your door. He has been directed to wait for your answer."

The soldier dismissed himself as soon as Antonio took the note from the tray. He handed it immediately to Kathryn. She gently grasped the letter between her thumb and forefinger as if it would break should she drop it. Antonio smiled, saying, "Finally a chance for you to practice your Greek. Let's see if your teacher of languages has earned his salary. What does Alexius want of us?"

Kathryn read the letter to herself before offering her translation to her father. With confidence in her voice, she began.

"Signor Antonio Delyan and Signorina: Welcome to the city of Constantine. I am sure your living spaces are comfortable. Anything you want will be made available. Should your needs not be met, send a request to my clerks and all will be resolved." Kathryn paused, trying to be a sophisticated nobleman's daughter, but unable to hold back a smile, looked at her father, enunciating each syllable of the signature: "Alexius I, Emperor of the Byzantine Empire."

She passed the letter to Antonio. "Father, please read this handsome letter as I am not sure my reading was entirely correct. I guessed at a few of the unfamiliar words."

With letter in hand, Antonio quickly read. "Very well-done Kathryn, remind me, once we return to Venice, to give Corrado a gift and another year of employment."

Antonio called the waiting messenger: "Please tell the secretary my daughter and I thank him for the gracious welcome. We are here to serve the emperor's will." The messenger hastily left.

When they arrived at Antonio's room, he said, "Before you go to your room, come inside to see my accommodations."

Both the Delyans were stunned by the lavishness of their surroundings when they walked into the room. Waiting for Antonio were two male attendants to serve him.

One of the attendants advanced, "Signorina, I will escort you to your room where maids are prepared for your arrival."

Antonio and Kathryn recognized the familiar face entering the doorway as one of the soldiers, the captain, who had intercepted their caravan and brought them to the palace.

The soldier, no older than 17 or 18 years of age, wore the uniform of the Emperor's Guard. He marched into the room, positioned himself directly in front of Antonio, and saluted. He then reached into an ornate cloth pouch hanging at his side and pulled out a folded card with a representation of the Hagia Sophia in gold on its cover. The soldier quickly peeked at Kathryn, and then presented the letter to Antonio, announcing in a practiced voice. "Signore, my Emperor directed me to carry your answer to him as soon as possible." Antonio opened the letter and began to read.

After reading, Antonio stood and addressed the soldier. "Tell your Emperor, that my daughter and I," he directed his gaze in Kathryn's direction, "are humbly thankful to be invited to his palace. We will attend at the time and place of his direction."

The soldier saluted Antonio, "Signore, by your leave." Then he turned to Kathryn, and in a quite formal manner, obvious to Antonio, the soldier wanted to impress Kathryn, addressed her. "Signorina, I apologize for not introducing myself earlier. I am Captain Stefano, and

I welcome you to the Court of Emperor Alexius I."

Kathryn could not take her eyes from the soldier in front of her. She felt her face warm, and answered, "Kathryn." Taking a second to compose herself, she answered, "My name is Kathryn Cappelli Delyan. I am comfortable with Signorina Kathryn."

The soldier's eyes seemed to search Kathryn's face in those few seconds while wanting to hear her name. Once heard, he spoke it in a long slow voice, "Kathryn." Taking a moment to choose his words carefully before continuing, the anxious soldier began, "Signorina Kathryn, I look forward to escorting you to the palace tomorrow." And then, as if he had just awoken from a trance, he wheeled and nervously looked to Antonio. "Of course, Signore, I am to escort you and Signorina Kathryn to court tomorrow. You are to travel in the emperor's carriage. Please be ready to leave 30 minutes before your appointed time."

"Captain, did you have any other responsibility attached to our meeting?"

"Yes. I am to deliver any papers you carry to the emperor."

Antonio took his father's satchel from his shoulder, lifted the flap, reached inside, and pulled out papers. "I trust you know the importance of these documents?"

Taking the papers in his hand, he answered, "I do. Signore, Signorina Kathryn, I take my leave." He bowed and left the room.

During this conversation, Antonio noted the unspoken exchange passing between the soldier and Kathryn. He decided to tease his daughter to see if his instincts were correct. "Kathryn, don't you think the soldier was well spoken?"

"Yes, he was very nice." Kathryn's short answer carried a quiver.

Her father continued, "He did look handsome in his military robes, don't you think?"

With that question, Kathryn sensed that her father was baiting her. "Yes, father, his uniform is neat, colorful, and soldierly, but I can't say that I noticed if he was handsome or not." She had to turn away from her father; she could feel her face blush. Kathryn had never had anyone stare at her with the intensity like that of the soldier from this new land.

Captain Stefano took a deep breath as he stepped onto the gray and black granite porch outside the visitor's guesthouse and leaned against one of the many white marble columns holding the massive terra cotta roof. The soldier had never had anyone look at him in the same way this young lady from a faraway land had stared at him.

Chapter 29

Meeting Alexius I

Kathryn rose early in the morning. This day promised to be one of discovery. She stepped out of her bed and to her surprise she was greeted by one of the two maids assigned to her. Multiple outfits for her to wear were draped over chairs and hanging from a rack, and in addition there were belts, sashes, and other accessories that lay on the dressing table awaiting her approval. Her few clothes and personal items that had been wrinkled and stained from the trip to Constantinople had somehow overnight, been cleaned, pressed, and ready for wear. Her excitement however centered on the new clothes of silk and soft fabrics from lands unknown to her. There was little doubt the fashions of Constantinople would fit her.

She bathed and for the first time in many years, allowed someone else to comb and shape her hair. She asked for it to be styled in the fashion worn by the ladies of this court. Kathryn chose clothes from the new wardrobe to wear for the audience with Emperor Alexius I.

Kathryn took a light breakfast with her father. An enameled pot of steeping tea accompanied a tray holding various sweets, candies, cakes, nuts, and edible flowers. Of immediate concern to her was the protocol for the visit.

"Father, do you know why Alexius called us to his court? And how does one act when in the presence of an emperor?" Without allowing for an answer, Kathryn continued, "Also, what do you expect of me during the visit? What should I wear? Oh, never mind, I'm sure the maids will tell me." With a bit of concern, she continued, "You did not tell me we were to visit the emperor."

Then directing the chat on a different path, she looked for an answer, noting, "My dear father, you changed the conversation quickly after Stefano left yesterday afternoon."

Antonio's laughing response came quickly, "Oh, so it is 'Stefano,' not 'Captain Stefano'?"

"Father, you think you are being funny—my mistake, Captain Stefano. And to answer your question from yesterday, **yes**, I think he is handsome. But you have just tried to change the discussion again about the documents you handed Captain Stefano. What is it you don't want me to know?"

Antonio waited for his business companion to take a breath before answering. When Kathryn stopped, he took the opportunity to put her at ease. He smiled and began, "I do know the reason for the personal invitation. I am here by order of the Doge of Venice. Venice and Constantinople have much to gain if our Doge and Emperor Alexius can strike a trade agreement. I am the voice of Venice in this matter. And, while I do not believe any secret is a secret, I am fairly sure there are only four people who know why we are here—you are now the fourth.

"In the past, my business was completed before going to any court activity. In fact, I met briefly with the emperor's staff during my previous trip, only to answer questions about trade and travel."

Antonio took a bite of a date dripping with golden honey and followed it with a sip of a mint tea before continuing the conversation. "Just be yourself. That does sound easy to say considering it will be your first time at a royal court. The emperor is a shrewd judge of people. Therefore, and most importantly, one should only be who one is. Do not try to impress or attempt to fool those who can see through the thickest mask."

"And to your final question regarding my expectation of you: stand by my side, keep your eyes and ears open to opportunity, and please add to the conversation."

Concluding the conversation, Antonio stood, took his daughter's hand, and led her to the door. With love and a genuineness in his voice, said, "Kathryn, you know I depend on you. You are my most important assistant. Today will be a wonderful part of the adventure I promised you before we left home." With a gentle push on her shoulders, he said, "Kathryn, go get ready for our visit at court," and making sure his words were heard, he deepened his voice and spoke very clearly, "and by the way, the young soldier will be coming for you," waiting but a second, now speaking as a father, he continued, "I mean to say, he will be coming for *us*, within the hour."

With that direction, Kathryn ran down the hallway to her dressing room. She did not need her father to remind her of their escort to the palace. Her maid, who had positioned herself outside Antonio's room, had listened to their final conversation at the door and knew how important the next hours were for Kathryn.

The maid followed closely behind the fast stepping Kathryn. Upon entering her room, Kathryn abruptly stopped in front of the dressing table, turned to the maid, and said, "I need your help."

The maid smiled, letting Kathryn know she could relax, all would be taken care of before meeting Emperor Alexis and his family—and of course ready for their escort.

Kathryn had many choices, but narrowed it down to two: "Which one do you like?" Kathryn asked the maid.

"Signorina, both of the dresses are pretty, but the one with the yellow and lavender flowers is like the light of the day and matches the beautiful necklace you are wearing." The maid asked another question which made Kathryn look intently at the lady in front of her, "Signorina Kathryn, your necklace is exquisite. Has it been a part of your family for a long time?"

Kathryn stopped moving. The maid watched a quizzical look melt over Kathryn's face and noticed that the girl's forefinger moved to touch the stone hanging from its gold chain.

"This necklace was my mother's. It is the only piece of my past that I can never be without." Kathryn wobbled over to a cushioned chair.

"Signorina," the maid asked in a concerned voice, "Are you feeling well?"

Taking her finger from the necklace, she quietly answered, "Yes, I am quite fine."

The maid moved to the dressing table. Upon it were four tiny, ornate glass containers. One was milky yellow and attached to it was a vine with yellow flowers. The maid offered the half-filled glass container to Kathryn. "Signorina, may I suggest a perfume that just arrived this morning? It is a fragrance new to the palace."

Curiously, Kathryn turned and immediately recognized the small green leaves and two pale flowers tied to the vial with a white ribbon.

She thought the glass container was familiar, but she was not sure why. Steadying the perfume bottle in the palm of her left hand, Kathryn quizzed the maid, hoping for a clue. "Who brought this?"

The maid answered quickly, "I do not know the name, Signorina. A lady presented herself to the door attendant with specific directions that the gift was to be given only to Signorina Kathryn. The doorman, uncertain of the request, brought the lady to me early this morning while you were still sleeping." In a moment of thought, the maid added, "It was odd; she acted as if she knew you. I know she was concerned that you receive the gift for your visit this afternoon."

The top of the glass vial was in the shape of delicate flowers. Kathryn lifted the top and raised it to her nose. A smile blossomed on her face.

Noticing the change in Kathryn, the maid could not help but ask, "Signorina, are you familiar with the essence?"

Kathryn did not know why she knew the scent, but with a light voice, she answered, "Honeysuckle."

Kathryn quickened her pace down the corridor once she saw her waiting father. She thought he looked remarkable dressed as a Byzantine in his new wardrobe. Kathryn now understood that this meeting would be of great importance to him—and to the Doge. She could only recall seeing him dressed so formally once before, when he prepared to visit the court of Sergius VI, the Duke of Naples. Then, as now, she believed he was one of the most striking men she had ever seen.

As she stepped to him, he took both her hands in his and held her at arm's length. "Kathryn, your timing is perfect. Our carriage has just pulled up." Antonio stood in amazement, looking at his maturing daughter. "Kathryn, you will be noticed in court today. The colors of your dress and the fragrance of your perfume are not usual to the girl who barters with merchants on the docks of Venice."

He hesitated before he next spoke. He could not believe that it was the same girl who had come to his home, learned his business, and traveled many days by his side on the Mediterranean Sea and then by caravan to Constantinople. With a beaming smile, he proudly stated, "You have become the 'Signorina Kathryn.'" Extending his hand, he said, "Signorina, shall we go? It would be in poor taste to arrive late to our visit with Emperor Alexius." As she delicately placed her hand on his, they wheeled toward the arched doorway leading to the portico.

The captain, sitting tall on his elegant black stallion, stopped the four horses that pulled Alexius' carriage to the visitor's villa. He walked his horse beside the carriage, pronouncing directions to the two men riding atop the carriage. In fluid, choreographed movements, the soldier dismounted and handed his reins to one of the coachmen, while at the same time, the other coachman jumped down from his seat to open the carriage door.

In an unsoldierly manner, more like a young boy than a captain, Stefano skipped from the street to the steps, moving in the direction of the visitors from the Adriatic Sea. Upon putting his foot on the first step of the visitor's villa, he raised his eyes, and more quickly than he supposed, he spotted Kathryn, who was watching his every move. Kathryn noticed that the soldier's cheeks reddened when their eyes met.

The soldier spoke first to Antonio and then to Kathryn. "Signore, Signorina, Alexius I extends his greeting and he is delighted to have you as guests in his palace." Staring at Kathryn he asked, "If it pleases you, allow me to ride in the carriage as your personal guard?"

Kathryn responded with a faint smile and an approving nod of her head. Kathryn shifted her focus to the coach at the bottom of the granite steps. The ornate carriage was breathtaking, the livery of the coachmen as well as that of the horses was stunning. With the carriage door open, Kathryn gave her hand to the coachman who assisted her into the royal carriage. The deep blue cushions covering the bench contrasted sharply with the white and gold-leafed designs wrapping around the interior. Antonio sat next to Kathryn, leaving the bench directly across from Kathryn for the soldier.

The coachman closed the door behind his three passengers, climbed the ladder, and snapped orders to the four magnificent chestnut horses. Simultaneously, their muscled haunches quivered, moving the carriage forward beginning the trip to meet with Alexius I.

Chapter 30

Arrival at Court

"Signorina," asked the soldier in a voice obviously anticipating approval of his inquiry, "what do you think of the city built by the great Constantine? Isn't it the most beautiful city in the world?"

Kathryn stared intently at Stefano, and responded, "The city is, as you point out, magnificent. But, I wonder if it is the most beautiful city in the world. Have you been to the cities of the East where the finest tableware and most exquisite cloths are produced? And have you been to the city of Rome? I doubt that you have been to my Venice, which will in a short time be the future of Europe's growth. Do you intend to visit Venice?"

This questioning put the soldier in an awkward position. Taking a moment to prepare a response, the soldier found his balance, and then responded as one who enjoys a scholarly contest. "Signorina Kathryn, your point is well taken. My personal knowledge of cities outside of Constantinople is limited to those within a few miles of our immediate trading ports and those I experienced while on duty alongside my Emperor." He continued with growing confidence, "I have listened to many visitors of our city. Each of them, soldiers, sailors, state emissaries, or those like you who travel the world's roads by caravan, all describe Constantinople in much the same manner. They, not me, have declared this city the '*most beautiful on earth.*'"

The soldier then directed the next question with a purpose. "Signorina, let me rephrase my inquiry. Of all the cities you have visited between your home and mine, is there another city more beautiful than the city of Constantine?"

Without hesitation, Kathryn offered her answer to the soldier with a smile, "Like the other visitors to your city, this is the most beautiful city I have seen, but I have only been here for a few hours, so my answer to your question, like my experience here, is limited. I look forward to seeing more of it." She started to speak, but the soldier interrupted in a nervous voice.

"Signorina, I have heard your home city and those on your coast are picturesque. Is it true the fruits and flowers scent the air, and food from the countryside is abundant all year?" Rushing to continue his prepared words, "I look forward to seeing your city of islands sometime in the future." Finally, coming to the end of his speech, he cleared his throat, "When that time comes, maybe you, if possible, could accompany me on a tour?" He held his shaking hands tightly not to expose his nervousness. He slowly began to feel comfortable now that the invitation he had been contemplating was presented.

Now Kathryn had to answer his obvious, yet subtle, flirtation. She hoped he could not see the hopefulness in her manner. She decided to answer quickly, hoping to be subtle in her own right. "My city has its own beauty. The streets are paved with water, not with stone like yours. My city is one of small campos—open spaces--surrounded by buildings, as are squares in other cities. We have the Adriatic Sea as you have the Bosphorus and the Golden Horn. And your city is 600 years older than mine. We both have a lot to see and learn about each other, each other's home."

It was as if Antonio was sitting on top of the carriage—his smile was not noticed.

Kathryn extended her invitation to the captain. "I can help you see the city. I would not want you to waste time wandering around strange new islands. Venice can only be appreciated by a visitor with the assistance of one who is knowledgeable concerning all the important sights."

"What would you show a first-time visitor?"

"How business is conducted at a ship's gangway and at the warehouse."

Clearly bewildered by her answer as ladies in Constantinople stayed away from the docks. "Why would that be your choice?"

Antonio decided to respond, saving Kathryn from having to explain, "My dear Captain, there is no better negotiator on the docks of Venice than the lady who sits in front of you."

"That is not ordinary in our port."

"You will come to learn, to be surprised by this lady's many talents.

All who work with her follow her lead."

Thinking Antonio is exaggerating, with a judgmental smile, quips, "All?"

Antonio's curt response quickly puts Stefano on notice. "ALL."

The Palace of Blachernae

The palace rested on the highest hill in the northwestern section of the city. From its extraordinary location, a lookout could see across the shipping lanes and see the land of Anatolia. From the carriage window, the view was breathtaking, giving Kathryn an understanding of the need for a zigzagging brick road to the palace winding around and through the many-leveled terraces. Brightly colored gardens surrounded the numerous fountains on every level. Each was cleverly manicured, using artfully sculptured rocks as frames for the carnival of floral displays.

The carriage passed a granite tower that rose to 100 feet high, which had been erected by Constantine during the founding years of the city. Deep-brown porphyry cylinders were cut and polished from the Jabal Abu Dukhan (Smoky Mountains) quarry in the rugged highlands of eastern Egypt, resting one upon the other. They were so perfectly hewn and polished, only the slightest difference in color hinted that it was not a single stone.

Most striking to Kathryn was the use of marble and granite throughout the city. The massive blocks of stone were a physical expression of the greatness of the international port city, the power of empire.

The carriage came to a stop. The visitors walked to meet Alexius I and his wife Irene Ducas. Kathryn was told by her maid thirteen-year-old Princess Anna Comnenus was looking forward to meeting the Venetian guest.

Before stepping from the carriage, Stefano took a minute to explain about the Palace of Blachernae. Initially, she did not see the greatness of the palace, but when she stepped from the carriage, and walked closer, Kathryn fully appreciated the soldier's pride; never had she beheld a more beautiful building.

Now in the palace, Kathryn, with Stefano next to her, realized she had fallen a few steps behind her father and quickened her pace.

Antonio gave her an inquisitive look as she came alongside of him, followed instantly by the now friendlier soldier. Antonio noticed a level of comfort had developed between them.

The opulence of the Palace of Blachernae, both in architecture and artwork, was of such grandeur Kathryn almost forgot to breathe. Stefano, aware of the impact the magnificent palace had upon Kathryn, attempted to break the artistic spell. He positioned himself a single pace directly in front of her. "Signorina Kathryn, we are to meet a court official to announce your arrival."

Her view of the palace momentarily blocked by her escort, she measured the uniformed Stefano: the ivory buttons on his uniform coat; the ceremonial sword at his side—and the manner in which he listened to her every word.

With a court official leading the way, Captain Stefano, Antonio, and Kathryn entered the great hall. It was as powerful as Alexius himself. The ceiling and walls of the room were covered in gold mosaics, with a floor of sparkling marble, and tables with beautifully displayed foods for all the ambassadors, guests, and members of the court to enjoy. Those in attendance knew they were invited at the will of their host, and they were ready to be in the presence of his greatness.

All the guests in the room turned to the doorway, seemingly in unison, sensing the arrival of the imperial family. Entering the room first were the two royal trumpeters, positioning themselves on each side of the marbled doorway, and without noticeable direction, the musicians began a *call to attention* with a low, quick blast of their instruments. Trumpets commanded the room to silence. A royal announcer stood off to the side of the doorway and proclaimed the arrival of the royal family.

"His Majesty, the Glorious Emperor of the Byzantine Empire Alexius the First and Queen Irene."

Emperor Alexius I Comnenus and his wife, Empress Irene Ducaena, entered the room.

The royal announcer again calls attention to the rest of the Royal Family.

"Princess Anna, Princess Marie, and Prince John the Second."

The imperial children arrive: Princesses Anna and Marie, and

Prince John II carried by a royal nurse.

Alexius wore a crown of jewels and gold. Gold threads were embroidered into his deep purple robe.

Empress Irene's long purple and green tunica was decorated with pearls and gold matching her crown, and around her waist was a long golden band of silk, which she let drape over her hand.

The princesses wore matching green silk dresses the color of limes with slippers of the same color, and lengths of twisted gold strands hung from their hair.

The banquet room was ablaze in color. The air danced from the wicks of candles each six feet high and two inches thick that stood so close to each other they formed a shimmering white picket wall. The marble ceiling absorbed the candlelight, returning from its speckled stone a rainbow of shades upon the emperor and his visitors.

Kathryn thought she had seen a wall that reflected shimmering light before but was instantly distracted by the captain.

The emperor's secretary advanced and addressed the two Venetians and their formal escort, "Signor Antonio, you and your daughter have been asked to visit with the Alexius I and his family."

Antonio asked the secretary, "Is Captain Stefano to join us?"

"Signore, as you wish."

The three followed the secretary. They walked up to the imperial family and two other guests. Just as they walked up to the royal family, the other guests departed, and the secretary performed the introductions.

After a few minutes of conversation comparing life in Venice and Constantinople, Alexius and Antonio stepped to the side, beginning a conversation of such intent, guards stood by preventing any interruptions.

Kathryn and Princess Anna, each happy to see someone of similar age, began to have a private conversation. Princess Anna asked her mother if Kathryn could visit with her the next day.

In a short time, Antonio rejoined the conversation, as did the captain who had stood to the side observing the dignitaries—keeping a watchful eye on the daughter of the Venetian dignitary.

"Father," Kathryn implored with anticipation in her voice, "when will I have a chance to scour the markets of Constantinople for the purchase of goods to take with us to Venice?" Kathryn's business sense took over. "We could find products not yet in Europe. We could become the primary dealer for articles not presently on our docks, the objects our customers don't know they want, yet. Our agent here could send a sampling of new items coming from the East, and we in turn, can push our products to new markets."

Empress Irene looked at Kathryn with concern and smiled in astonishment at the words of such a young girl. The Empress asked, "Signorina, why would a girl of your age be concerned with merchants, ships, and ports of trade? Shouldn't you care for your father's household, and consider who might be chosen as your future husband?" Looking at her daughter Princess Anna first, and then to Antonio, and then the emperor, Empress Irene continued, "Is not the work of trade to be left to men, and the work of the home to the women?"

A glance from her father signaled this was a moment to measure one's words. Kathryn understood his meaning; they often were able to communicate without speaking, which was so often necessary when deciding prices on the docks and in the warehouses in Venice. She took a shallow breath organizing her thoughts.

Before answering the empress, Kathryn quickly recalled her father's lessons dealing with those who do not share similar customs for ideas. He often spoke of how one can make a sale of any product, disarm an angry customer, and make the difficult simple using a smile, a low voice, and making the other person believe you are listening to their concern. Never let them think they are less important than you are.

In Kathryn's world of trade, she mastered the art of sales. She prepared to take her position and win the empress's approval, even though she disagreed with the ideas of specific roles for men and women. Antonio recognized Kathryn's gifts of language, math, and business and her ability to deal with customers as superior to that of any man in his employ.

"Empress, I take counsel in your words. It is inappropriate for someone of my state to ask for advice from one so worldly, but I would hope that sometime in the future I could come to you for counsel. I do know that someday my position will change, but presently, I am my father's secretary."

Changing the topic, Kathryn continued, "Empress, I would like to find in the markets of your city a few items, personal in nature, maybe some clothing or a piece of jewelry. They would be gifts for my mother and grandmother, and my friend Teresa. Could you advise me about merchants that are fair and carry quality goods?"

The empress was overwhelmed. "Signorina, I will have someone from my household take you to my personal brokers and show you the stalls filled with items for your family, but first I must get permission from your father," the empress addresses Antonio, "Signore Antonio, does the father of this precocious young lady give his permission?"

Antonio replies approvingly, but with a condition, "Empress, I must ask that Kathryn have a guard whenever she is outside the palace."

"I will make certain your fatherly request is honored."

Noticing Kathryn and Princess Anna wanting to get to know each other better, the empress asked the princess, "Anna, I think you and Signorina Kathryn should spend some time together tomorrow. Would that suit the two of you?"

They both answered at the same time, the princess in Greek, and Kathryn in Latin.

Kathryn continued after they laughed at their perfectly timed answers, "Empress, I know we will enjoy ourselves as we have thus far this evening."

At the direction of her husband, the empress and the imperial family moved on to the duties of empire.

Antonio and Kathryn went about the room, first meeting the ambassador from Alexandria, Egypt, then a merchant from Grenada, Spain, followed by a Muscovite who had just arrived by caravan from Russia. They discussed the quality of metals with a representative of the Sultan of Damascus and two other guests from Persia, marveled at a glass sculptor with the creator from Jaffa, and the many mathematicians, architects, and artists wishing to bid on the emperor's newest projects.

Kathryn listened while Antonio was in conversation with a diplomat. She began to feel uneasy. She ran her fingers over the chill bumps on her arms. Not wanting to alarm Antonio, she stepped away from him. Her eyes surveyed the entire room. The dark figure of

Abbadon moved to hide from her view, but not before Kathryn caught sight of the red tunic disappearing behind the long curtains in the back of the room.

Kathryn was exhausted by evening's end. She had held a conversation with an empress, planned a day with a princess, talked with the most interesting people of the world, and for the first time, flirted with a boy—who returned the attention—and she knew more thrills were to come.

Chapter 31

Anna and the Porphyry

Curtains of cream white silk waved to Kathryn as the morning air pushed through the windows of her palace bedroom. The door to her room was opened by a servant skillfully balancing morning delicacies and cleansing towels on a tray fashioned from a lightly buffed wood which she positioned on the dressing table. Kathryn, contemplating her night of fantastic dreams, watched as the maid prepared the washstand. Water flowed out of the spout from a jet-black clay pitcher, filling the blue and green porcelain bowl with hot water. Two towels were placed next to the bowl, one for washing, the other for drying, and a clear glass cup with steaming sweet tea was left on the tray.

Kathryn wondered how the servant knew to arrive at the same time she awoke; it must have been a coincidence. She turned her head back to the window watching as the curtains were still gently swaying, giving the soft morning air an avenue to Kathryn's room.

Kathryn turned to ask the servant a question, but she had left as quietly as she had arrived.

She fell back on her bed, looked up at the mosaic ceiling. It was as if she were looking at the night sky, but the artist wanted to show what you couldn't see during the day. Rather than the blackest skies of each month, when the moon had vanished and the sky was dotted with white specks, the ceiling above Kathryn was a sky of white tiles with an orange sun whose rays of yellow spread to the walls in the four directions of the compass. The sky was dotted by sea-blue colored stars.

She had made a friend last night. At least she thought so, otherwise, why would the princess would ask to meet today for a walk around the palace grounds. It was not often Kathryn had time to be with young people. Both girls knew they were different from others their age. The princess, like Kathryn, found that while both were so young, they had to **think older.** They both felt as if somehow, the princess in the court, and Kathryn on the docks, had been placed into adulthood by virtue of birth, or maybe by the forces of fate, to be instrumental to those around them as an actor upon life's stage. Kathryn was the youngest girl on the dock—no, she was the only girl on the dock. There were a few young boys, but they were runaways or orphans, and usually they did what they could to steal a meal, or like most, wanted to be hired as a captain's servant or a nobleman's footman.

Kathryn's day usually began early, an hour before sunrise. Teresa always had hot tea and bread prepared, and some sweet pastries to be taken to the dock. After eating, Kathryn, with one of her father's guards as an escort, would go to the main warehouse—one of the eight he now owned along the Grand Canal that also served as their primary merchant office. There, she practiced the art of trade.

Princess Anna and Kathryn were very overjoyed to have someone to talk to. They chatted the entire time they walked from the palace to the Porphyry Chamber. As they found themselves enjoying each other's company, their pace quickened.

With a smile, and holding up her hands, Kathryn interrupted Anna, "Princess, can I share a secret with you?"

The princess realized this was going to be the first time she was going to share a secret with another girl. "Kathryn, please tell! I will never let the words I hear leave my lips."

The excitement made her giggle. It was the first time her two personal guards had heard her laugh. They gave a quick look at Princess Anna, then at each other, one raising his eyebrows affirming his pleasure that the young Princess Anna was indeed more than a princess, she was a girl, like every other girl they knew—no that was impossible, she was not allowed to be anything other than a princess. The two soldiers had been chosen by the emperor himself for their loyalty and valor in war to be the princess's permanent bodyguards.

Kathryn was as excited to tell her secret as Anna was to hear it. Having spoken in Latin the entire time in Constantinople, Kathryn switched to Greek, said, "Princess, I understand your language." Kathryn continued the conversation, "I read and write in Greek. I am not as eloquent as you are. I have learned and practiced your language with my tutor and on the docks, and with my father. I find I am learning many words as I listen to everyone at the palace. If you would prefer me to speak in your language, I will happily do so."

Anna began, inquisitively, and with a sincere interest, "Why have you only spoken in Latin?

Kathryn's first concern was to let the princess know she was not being deceptive. She realized, as her father explained, all that happens in the palace is observed by spies. He had said, "Every court, in every city, at our Venetian court, as well as here, has spies who are paid by enemies, and even family members, who want to destroy a doge, a king, an emperor, or a sultan, so they can wear a crown."

"Princess, my father speaks Latin here as it is the language of trade, but I am sure he spoke with your father in Greek to discuss business in your land, but at home we speak a Venetian dialect. Languages have become a love for me. I am learning English, and I am beginning to understand the language of the Franks. My father has asked me to be his ears on the docks. There is more learned while listening than talking, especially when sailors and merchants are unaware their bragging and often secret conversations are understood by those who they think are ignorant of their conversation. Is the same true at your court?"

"Yes, my father has many servants who go about a room unnoticed, and report back to him every word spoken in every conversation." Lowering her voice, and taking Kathryn's hand, said, "Your secret is safe with me. But I must now think of a secret to tell you."

Princess Anna led Kathryn to the Porphyry, the Purple Chamber of the Byzantines of Constantinople.

The princess stopped in front of the Porphyry's ornately decorated doorway. The doors were of polished Lebanon hardwood. Not knowing where, Kathryn thought she had seen doors made of the beautiful wood.

"Kathryn, I hope you adore this building, which is really a magnificent room. In fact, this is my favorite room in all of Constantinople.

This was a special room for the princess, Kathryn could hear it in the princess's softened voice, "The Porphyry is the birthing room for children of the imperial family, for the special newborn, whose father and mother were descended from a long line of families, of noble blood, those who may someday take the seat as emperor or empress of

Constantinople. This building once stood alone on this terrace with a perfect view of the city."

Princess Anna, a lover of reading, especially history, found great satisfaction walking and talking with visitors about her beloved Constantinople, the capital of her father's Byzantine Empire.

"When we were introduced, you heard my father refer to me as Princess Porphyrogenita, the title given to those born in this royal chamber. I received the title when my mother gave birth right here in this room, on the first day of December 1083."

"I am the first born of my parents. It is expected of me to continue the Comnena Empire. My parents made sure I would have the best teachers of history, languages, and mathematics; they also want me to understand trade and politics." With excitement, "Kathryn, maybe you could be my Minister of Trade."

"Princess Anna's Minister of Trade. I really need to tell Samantha about this…" Kathryn startled herself.

"Kathryn. Who is Samantha?"

Perplexed by her own words, Kathryn remembered the dreams of her nights. She realized she did know a Samantha. She felt a strange sense of knowing all about a person who did not exist, but a person very close to her heart, a friend. Kathryn smiled.

Not getting an answer, the princess kept talking, and with a note of disappointment in her voice, "When I was born, a royal crown was made for me, but my father will most likely name my brother, John, as emperor. He is favored by my grandmother as the first-born male child. My father's mother wants the crown to stay pure. She is afraid I will marry outside the family. However, if my mother can influence my father, I will rule as the first child." With a shallow sigh over the troubled reality of royal bloodlines, she echoed the thought in her head, "But it is unlikely that I will wear the crown as Empress of the Byzantines. If my grandmother had a choice, I would be sent to a monastery to live out my life."

Deep in thought, but now her spirit thinking of the moment, almost as if reciting poetry, Anna continued. "I love coming here. It is a place I can come to be alone. It is my thinking-place. When I am here, the room's enchantment allows my mind to wander. It is a chance for me to write my thoughts, to escape the court, NOT think about my responsibilities to my family, and NOT to think about the man my parents have decided I must marry."

Anna looked at Kathryn, who she knew would ask questions about her betrothal. "We can talk about that and other matters later. It is so nice to have someone to talk to. Later, you must tell me all about Venice—about your life, your family, your future. Has a husband been chosen for you?"

"Princess, my father and mother were not promised to marry by their parents. They decided who they were to marry, because of their love for each other. I will choose my husband when I am ready, and right now, I am not ready, but—"

The princess interrupted Kathryn with an observation from the night before, "I watched you and the captain. I think he would be your choice. Kathryn, he could not stop looking at you. You, my new friend, would be his choice." Following with a big smile, and a silly laugh, she whispered, "If I could rule as empress right now, I would decree that you and Captain Stefano should wed."

Kathryn's nervous smile beamed on her blushing face, confirming what Princess Anna thought to be true as the two friends walked under the arched doorway.

The Porphyry was magnificent. As they entered the room, Kathryn inhaled with a gasp showered in the reflections of the royal chamber and its royal stone. She thought she had stepped into a magical land. Like her bedchamber and many of the other rooms she had seen while wandering in the palace, the decorating detail, especially the use of color in the granite, marble, and other stones brought a sense of wonder to each room.

This perfectly square room was built with imperial porphyry, a stone of many purples, dotted with various spots and veins of white and shining crystal. The ceiling rose from the tops of the walls to a peak, similar to the Great Pyramid at Giza in Egypt. All who walked into this special room felt the influence of traditions and the ceremony of royalty.

The chamber's every surface shone; its polished floor cast the brightness of the walls and ceiling back from where it came. The room was an architect's triumphal mix of color, space, and grandeur.

The curtains, table coverings, and wall surfaces were accessorized in royal purples, bright gold and gleaming silver.

Kathryn's eyes moved to the large white granite table positioned in the center of the room. It was as square as the room in which it stood. What made the table piece so interesting was that it had been cut from a single piece of granite. The intricacies of the legs contrasted with the perfectly flat smooth top. The size of the table fit the grandiosity of the room.

A visitor arrived with a message that Princess Anna was expected to visit with her grandmother—the two girls were instantly transformed back to princess and visitor.

Chapter 32

Anna, the Throne, Danger

The day before with Princess Anna was Kathryn's favorite day since her arrival in Constantinople. She was the guest of a real princess. In Venice, the most important port in Europe, a doge's family was treated like royalty. They were wealthy and becoming more powerful every year.

But Constantinople was ruled by an emperor and empress, who wore crowns and who sat on thrones in a throne room. They had servants and attendants filling their every wish. They had ambassadors and visitors from around the world kneeling in front of them. They also had a strong army to show their might. The walled city protected the throne of the Byzantine Empire.

Kathryn thought of Princess Anna, who carried herself as a princess who wanted to be an empress, yet a girl who had a husband chosen for her while she was still in her cradle. The princess, like Kathryn, spent many hours with her teachers studying history and mathematics, but the princess had to know about the intrigues and politics of court and empire.

"Kathryn! Kathryn! I have thought of a secret to share with you." beckoned a secretive voice entering the room. It was Princess Anna.

Kathryn jumped with surprise, excited to see the princess.

Princess Anna, standing straight and tall, her hair perfectly combed, wearing a blue and gold tunic, walked slowly across the room. As she walked in, the princess looked around the room making sure no eyes could see them, or ears could hear them, or mouths could repeat what was to be said. Princess Anna, in a voice so low it could hardly be heard, asked, "Kathryn, do you want to go on a dangerous outing today?" The princess's breathing was rapid. "Say yes, and I have a surprise for you today—a chance to do something only allowed for emperors and empresses. We will sneak into the throne room and sit on the cedar throne chairs of Alexius and Irene!" More nervous than when she first arrived, the princess, for the second time, searched the room for spies. Believing they were safe, Princess Anna, excitedly informed Kathryn, "We could be put in jail if caught, or possibly lose our lives. It must be hard for you to understand, but Alexius is my emperor first, my father second."

"Kathryn, are you ready for the adventure?"

Kathryn could not understand the full impact of what was offered, or the reason Princess Anna wanted to include her in this perilous escapade, and why any emperor would put his daughter in jail, or have her killed, just for sitting in a chair. Could any chair be that important?

Kathryn's face warmed with danger. The idea of doing something against custom, a dangerous mission, so unthinkable and risky, a crime punishable with jail, and so threatening, that the princess was concerned about their lives caused Kathryn's heart to pound—her father would not be able to protect her if she was caught.

"Yes!" She was unable to control her anticipation of the unknown.

When the princess let out a shrill giggle, Kathryn become aware the princess was behaving like any other girl her age would behave.

"Kathryn, my father is inspecting his newest warship today and not expected to return until this afternoon. When he is gone, no one will be in the throne room. This is our chance to be alone there."

"How do you know we will not be seen? Aren't soldiers guarding the room?" Kathryn was beginning to lose some of her bravado. "What do we say if someone sees us?"

"In this palace, everyone is a spy. There are no secrets from the emperor. If he found that someone kept a secret from him, they would lose all."

"Princess, why are we doing this?" Kathryn asked with a broken voice.

"I have had no friends my age, no girls, other than my younger sister. I never play, and never have an adventure."

The answer did not make Kathryn feel any better. She did feel sorry the princess did not have a friend. But then, Kathryn didn't have any friends either, only the men on the docks and her father's servants, but at least she had Teresa to confide in and Corrado with whom she could share her thoughts. But the princess was different than adult friends, more like a real friend. Kathryn said, "Princess, let's sit on the thrones!"

Princess Anna grabbed Kathryn's hand leading her down the hallway. They ducked behind a stone statue of Zeus, the Greek god of thunder and lightning. The princess covered her mouth with her hand letting Kathryn know not to speak. Seconds later, one of the palace guards walking patrol, marched past them. They looked at each other, exchanging worried faces.

The princess stepped out, searched for others in the hallway, and waved to Kathryn. "Let's go."

The next doorway was the entrance to the throne room. "Kathryn, when we get in front of the doorway, we will slowly walk in just to make sure no one is there, and then we'll run straight to the thrones. You know, I need practice sitting on my future seat, so this is a great time to start. Mine will be the one with the pillow on it. You can sit on the chair of the empress."

They were now in front of the doorway. It was open. Kathryn's heart was pounding so hard she could hear it echoing in her ears.

Kathryn went forward when two hands pushed her into the throne room. As the princess ran past Kathryn, she pronounced, "Empress Kathryn, follow me to our thrones!"

Sitting motionless on the chair, Kathryn did not know if she should talk or act like an empress. She watched the princess wave her arms as she commanded her army. Kathryn proclaimed a festival in honor of the visitors from Venice.

As quickly as they had become empress and minister of trade, they knew they were in trouble.

Both girls looked up the instant the sound of men's voices echoed from the hallway.

"Run, follow me, be quiet!" Upon command, Kathryn followed the princess to the far side of the room. They hid behind two giant flowerpots. Frightened, not moving a muscle, they stared at each other.

Two palace guards walked into the room. The girls could not understand what the guards were saying but were sure they must have heard them ruling their empire.

The guards glanced around the room, and after a few moments, not finding anyone in the room, marched out. When the room was empty, the girls breathed again, but still, they did not move. Kathryn watched Anna. After she was sure no guards were near the room, the princess waved her hand, pointing to a tapestry of Emperor Constantine winning the Battle of Milvian Bridge.

The princess put up her hand, wiggling her fingers. Kathryn understood. The princess counted down. When her last finger dropped, they both ran, Princess Anna sliding under the bottom edge of the wall-hanging with Kathryn close behind.

On the other side of the tapestry was a secret passage. It took them to the next room. The princess looked through a hole in the stone, seeing it empty, she led her friend through the room and back to the hallway. They were out of trouble—no jail, no execution. They began to laugh very loud.

When Kathryn walked into her dressing room, the maid was waiting.

Handing Kathryn a package, the maid said, "Signora, just after you left this morning, a package came for you. It is from Princess Anna." The package had a note folded in half on top. It read:

I have been told that tomorrow is your birthday. So, I had this gift delivered while we were on our adventure. Sleep well tonight. Keep this day in your dreams, so you can visit it forever.

Your friend,

Anna.

Kathryn quickly tore back the wrapping. She pulled out a set of beautiful silk pajamas. The cloth was so light to the touch, it was almost weightless. It had thin threads of green vines with delicate yellow and white flowers throughout the garment. Kathryn smiled and thought, "I have a friend."

Throughout the day, Kathryn met many people while she strolled around the palace, and the princess was busy with her family—unlike Kathryn who was adored by Signora Moretti, Princess Anna and her grandmother did not get along.

At sunset, Kathryn and Antonio met for a light snack, and then with a trip to the main marketplace of Constantinople planned for the next day, she went back to her room and readied herself for bed. That night she dreamt of a building with a bakery, and a fence with a walkway, and saw the face of a girl named Samantha. And as usual, the places and people in her dreams were familiar, comforting, yet could never be explained—she often went to bed hoping to return to the land of her dreams.

Chapter 33

The Last Day in Constantinople

Kathryn wanted her last day at the palace to be special. Everything had been packed for their sailing except for what she would purchase today. She knew this day's shopping would be one of exploration and wonder—a day unlike any other.

Her father had a final meeting with Emperor Alexius. He had two envelopes, both with special instructions of utmost importance. One was a signed trade agreement between the Emperor of Constantinople and the Doge of Venice. The other was equally important. Antonio and Kathryn would not be returning to Venice as originally planned. Before returning to Venice, they would go directly to visit with Urban II in Clermont, France. Antonio would tell Kathryn he could not divulge the details of their secret mission until they were aboard ship.

Not waiting for her father to return, and with the help of her maid, who had prepared her clothing, she dressed quickly. On her breakfast table were bowls of dates and fruit marmalades, rice pudding mixed with honey and pistachios, fire roasted flat bread, sweetened juices, and tea.

As promised by the empress, the palace escorts stood outside her door, waiting to take Kathryn shopping. After a description of the day's plan, they went to the waiting carriage.

The marketplace of Constantinople was a spectacle of travelers who had arrived on ships and wagons from every corner of the map. It was a circus without seats. The performers were citizens of the world selling their wares. There was fine porcelain from Cathay. Others had brought intricately designed statues from Baghdad. Tables were covered with brass platters and cooking pots from Persia and hanging from tall poles were flowing laces and colorful linens and hides from Kashmir. She observed tropical birds and animals from foreign jungles. Captivated by the rhythm of the market, she observed men covered in tattoos, snake charmers, acrobats, and musicians added to the din.

All around her were sellers of clothes entreating her to purchase the fashions woven from unusual threads and bright dyes of yellow, orange, indigo, and green. There were hundreds of jewelers selling vast arrays of braided chains, and gems to be placed in intricate settings for rings and necklaces, bracelets, and crowns.

The more she saw, the more Kathryn wanted to move in every direction at the same time. She found herself in the world Corrado had tried to paint with words, but now that she was in Constantinople, Kathryn understood no language could fully describe its character.

Constantinople was a sea of colors, a city of all languages, a city of aromas foreign to the docks of Venice, where cooking oils heated pans and pots filled with warming spices infusing meats, fish, and vegetables to feed the wealthy and the poor.

Once Kathryn began to move with the multitude, she added her beat to the pace of the city. She had become just another member of the throng of travelers buying and questioning peddlers in front of their kiosks and behind wagons. She followed no special pattern; at times she swayed left and next to her right, letting the vendors pull her attention to their stands.

The activity of the morning's walk through the city's many streets caused Kathryn's stomach to growl. The smell of Mediterranean spices painted on roasting vegetables and lamb came from a small wagon in front of her. Kathryn's meal was skewered on a stick over hot coals by a husband and wife from Tarsus.

Often an item would catch her attention, initiating the negotiation of price between dealer and buyer. Kathryn moved to her every whim, both as a bargain hunter and a purchaser of goods. She stopped at a table displaying a varied array of silver jewelry. The seller stood to engage the shopper. "Any item of special interest to such a fine lady?"

"Tell me, sir, what do you know about this braided chain."

Thinking he will make a day's profit with this inexperienced visitor, he flatters and informs, "You have good taste. This delicate piece just arrived from Alexandria this morning."

Kathryn responds, "The price?"

"Like you it is exquisite. Is it a gift or for you? Tell me my price and it is yours."

"The worth of this silver necklace is dependent on want and ability to pay."

Enjoying the bartering, he proposes, "Your clothes tell me you are able to pay what I ask, so, now you must decide your want."

Kathryn reaches into her purse, pulls out coins. As she lays each coin on the table, she reads the seller's face. Three coin are on the linen tablecloth.

"If I had a barrel of coins, I would only give you what you see on your table."

The seller realizes he has met his match. He is happy with the profit and does not want to lose the sale. "You are a shrewd young lady. I will take what you offer. The prize is yours."

Kathryn stepped back to ask her two companions—the guard and translator—if they would like something to eat. She turned in a complete circle. They were nowhere to be seen, and instantly she realized she had not talked to them for quite some time.

The merchant notices. "Are you looking for someone?"

"Yes, my escorts."

"I did not see anyone with you while we talked."

Kathryn decided to go back to the corner where she last remembered being with them. After a few minutes, she knew she was lost in the maze of alleys and streets, and now she became concerned for her safety. Kathryn was aware she must push back the sense of panic rising inside her, but she felt her shoulders tighten and her stomach roll as she continued to find her guards. Beads of sweat appeared on her brow. She quickly looked back and forth, eyes wide, searching for familiar faces, or at least a familiar location.

Suddenly, a wave of relief washed over Kathryn. She took a deep breath relieved of the fright of being alone and unprotected.

The street market where she had purchased a scarf earlier was now in sight. Her eyes franticly searched for familiar faces, and in the distance, not more than fifty yards away, she spotted the red feather atop her guards' helmets.

She saw them nervously turning in circles looking for her, seeking to make contact.

She relaxed and the nervous twitching of panic began to subside. Her stomach eased, but from her fear, she could taste the biting acid which moments earlier had burned in her throat, its bitter taste remained on her now dry tongue. She wanted to scream for her companions, but it was tempered by her knowledge that she should not bring attention to her alarm. The sun, now acting as a guide, was positioned directly over her guards standing on the upper steps of a city church. She took a moment to think and to plan her route to reach them.

Kathryn began moving in the direction of her guards, but the path was not going to be a straight one. The many carts, shoppers and merchants moved at different tempos, intersecting each other causing her to bump into or to go around groups of people. She still had to cross the long distance to the safety of her escort. Walking quickly, Kathryn maneuvered through the labyrinth, determined to stay on course by keeping visual contact with the church's steeple. Kathryn's vision was obscured intermittently as she tried to keep sight of her companions.

Kathryn stepped sharply to her right to go around a crowd yelling at a driver of a donkey cart carrying hides who had stopped in the middle of the street.

The next instant was a blur. One never really knows the length of an instant. Is it a portion of a second? A single second? Or two? Or three? Or maybe, the moment of an event so consumes the individual, that time cannot be measured—so it was for Kathryn.

Her guard directly in front of her seemed like a giant when he moved between Kathryn and the sun. His size was such that he turned the bright day into a dark shadow, as the moon eclipses the sun allowing only a glow of light to trim its edges. The hands pinned her arms to the sides of her body with their overwhelming strength.

The kidnapper's tightening fingers pushed through her tunic and pressed her flesh against her bones. She fought. Yelled, "LET ME GO! LET ME GO!" Her fist against the abductor caught him by surprise, momentarily lessening his grip. She broke free but sees Abbadon coming toward her.

She spins, changing direction, collides with the second guard. He pins her arms to her side. Kathryn pushes her hand under her blouse grasping her pendant, pulls hard breaking the chain, cutting her neck. Another set of hands bound her with cord.

When she opened her mouth to scream again, a hand grabbed her throat, while another pounded a cloth ball against her mouth, mashing Kathryn's lips against her teeth. The attacker forced the knotted wad into her mouth, widening her jaw so she could not bite, and stopping her from emitting a scream. It prevented her from sending a single sound of distress, and then the taste of blood mixed with the vinegary taste from the herbal knot now buried into her mouth dizzied her thinking. Then her nose was covered by a wet cloth saturated with the same compound that burned her throat.

In that terrifying instant, Kathryn became confused. Though dizzy, Kathryn thought she heard the clatter of horses' hooves on stone and men shouting. Kathryn lost consciousness and fell into darkness when she was thrown onto a rug and rolled into a cocoon. She was quickly heaved into a cart, and a large skin was tossed over the human package. She was hidden from sight.

Just after Kathryn and her escorts left for the market that morning, an unknown woman, wearing the purple of royalty, somehow made her way past the office guards and stood before the desk of Captain Stefano. She informed him of a rumor how a visitor from Venice, a young girl, would be kidnapped that morning.

Hearing about the girl, who could only be Kathryn, he quickly walked out of the room to call for the guards. When he returned to question the mysterious lady, who was probably part of the plot to collect ransom, or had hoped to be paid for her information, was gone.

Captain Stefano did not hesitate. He had a guard run to Kathryn's room. The guard returned within minutes, "Captain, the room servant said Signorina Kathryn and her escorts left for the market over two hours ago."

Stefano rushed to notify Alexius. He ran into the throne room without asking for permission to speak. When Stefano informed Alexius of the strange encounter, Antonio was summoned. Antonio was told of the situation and what was to take place. Emperor Alexius, talking as a father not a ruler, asked, "Other than my soldiers who are ready to leave to find your Kathryn, is there anything you want of me?"

Antonio said, "I must go along with your soldiers."

Emperor Alexius ordered, "Captain, whatever Antonio wants, you will do. His request is my order to you. Now, time is of the essence. Captain, Antonio, find the Signorina!"

Captain Stefano had four platoons of cavalry quickly move to the location he had been given by the woman informant. Each line of horsemen moved in from different directions, and one hundred foot soldiers surrounded the marketplace to block off all exits.

When Captain Stefano and Antonio arrived in the square, along with the other riders, the wagon Kathryn had been tossed into was pulling away.

Once the soldiers arrived, the market transformed to mayhem. Shoppers and merchants were yelling when the soldiers overturned kiosks, spilled carts of their goods, and shoved shoppers and merchants trying to find the Venetian girl. Many people ran to hide, while others moved their stalls, wagons, and goods to stay out of the way of the horses and newly arriving formations of soldiers.

But above it all, a small woman in purple, standing atop a wall, called Stefano's name. Her voice cut through the clamor, getting his attention. Stefano realized it was the same woman who had been in the palace minutes ago. Antonio, watching the exchange between Stefano and the lady, followed her hand as she pointed in the direction of a moving wagon. She called, "Captain, the girl is in the wagon! Look in the wagon! Quickly, it will be lost in the crowd. She is in danger!"

Both Stefano and Antonio turned their horses toward the wagon that had almost disappeared in the chaos.

Stefano broke into a gallop and brought his horse alongside the wagon and with a hack of his sword cut the reins, stopping the wagon's escape. Stefano slid off his horse onto the wagon. The driver raised a sword to Stefano, but a soldier's spear thrusts into the driver.

Antonio followed Stefano, and jumped from his horse to the cart, and clashes with Abbadon. The force of their desperate collision sent them off the cart and onto the ground. Abbadon is quick to his knife fighting Antonio, whose sleeve has turned red from Abbadon's blade. Stefano's soldiers pile onto Abbadon knocking him off Antonio. Abbadon on the ground, a spear at his throat.

Antonio rose swiftly to his feet and went to the cart. He yanked the hide covering Kathryn and then with help from Stefano, they lifted her from the wagon onto the stone street. Kathryn was freed from her wrapping, and the gags were removed from her mouth and nose.

Kathryn began to stir once she was able to breathe fresh air. She looks past Antonio, eyes wide with fear. Antonio and Stefano follow her eyes. She cries, "ABBADON!"

Stefano reacts first to the human growl coming from his side. He tries to stop Abbadon, who has jumped across Antonio reaching for Kathryn's hand. Abbadon rips the chain and pendant from her hand, shouting a demand of the ring. She fights back to get the ring. Abbadon strikes first:

"Give me your strength. I will have your power. Stop all who oppose me."

Antonio and Stefano are rendered helpless. Kathryn seizes the moment cast upon her. She wraps both her hands around Abbadon's. They face each other, eyes locked in combat.

Abbadon's yellow eyes glow, his smile wide. "It is mine, now. I demand to be pharaoh."

An ancient voice from centuries ago wells up from Kathryn.

"I am the ring. ONLY I can command thee!"

A light begins to glow from within their gripped hands. Abbadon's face senses what is to come. His eyes brighten then begin to darken, his pupils fade to brown. Kathryn's voice beseeches, reaching into the past.

"I COMMAND IN THE NAME OF MY QUEEN, CLEOPATRA, ABBADON BE NEVERMORE!"

Abbadon collapses in a heap, explodes to dust.

Kathryn physically exhausted.

Antonio and Stefano come out of their stupor.

She opened her eyes to find herself in the arms of her father. Kathryn's head ached. Her nose and throat were sore. Her lips split from the gag. Her neck red from the chain.

Kneeling in front of her was Captain Stefano. He held both her hands in his. She looked at him, and then down at a broken gold chain dangling from her tightly held fist.

Their eyes met again when Stefano raised her hands to meet his lips.

The palace doctor placed wet compresses on Kathryn's scored neck and split lips, and cooling salves were applied to her multiple bruises.

Pouring the hot contents of the pot in front of Kathryn, the maid inquired, "Signorina, would a cup of tea be to your liking?"

Smelling the sweet tea's bouquet, Kathryn said, "Thank you, I would. What kind of tea do I smell?"

Serving the tea, without answering Kathryn's question, the maid spoke in a comforting voice, "Signorina, you will need to rest after such a frightful day. I will do your hair. A cup of tea will help you relax."

Before combing Kathryn's hair, the maid filled the teacup.

There was a voice at the door of Kathryn's room. In response, the maid went to inquire. Kathryn could hear a man's voice in conversation with the maid. When the maid returned, she said, "Signorina, a soldier, a Captain Stefano, would like to speak with you. Should I send him away?"

"No. Please tell the captain that I will meet him in one hour under the portico."

When the maid returned, she noticed Kathryn's teacup was almost empty, and filled it. While continuing to comb Kathryn's hair, the maid softly said in a voice the sleepy Kathryn warmly recognized, "The answer to your earlier question about the tea, dear, is **Grandmother's tea.**"

Kathryn began to relax, her eyes beginning to tire, she fell into a deep sleep.

Part Five

The Haglady

Chapter 34

Pajamas, Thirteen, the Neighbor

Samantha's voice traveled up the staircase and down the hall, awakening thirteen-year-old Kathryn and causing Chubby to stir.

Opening her eyes, Kathryn was not sure if her dream seemed real, or if she was in the dream. She wondered if a dreamer's dream is as true as life itself. Or can a dreamer be the dream?

What puzzled her most about her nighttime fantasies was how her dreams flowed like chapters in a book, where the main character moved from place to place, event to event. Kathryn had many nights when she was lost in time and other lands. There were exciting experiences, foreign cities, and fascinating people. The dreams included an extraordinary uncle, and the always-present lady in purple, who appeared at special moments and then vanished without a word, but who kept her safe.

Kathryn often lived a different life when she fell asleep. Many times, just as her head touched the pillow, she eagerly anticipated the journey her slumber might provide. She never heard anyone explain dreams the way she experienced them—she marveled how the ancient lands, wonders, and adventures seemed so real.

As she pushed the covers to the bottom of the bed with her feet, she lay still, thinking over the dream from the night before. Looking up at the ceiling, then closing her eyes, she recalled a moment in her other world. She closed her eyes and could see a large marbled room with curious ceiling tiles made to look like the evening sky.

Samantha's voice bellowed, "Kathryn, get down here, get down here right away. I have the best surprise for you. You will not believe it!"

She sat up quickly and looked around the room to be sure of where she was. Kathryn realized it must be Sunday morning. Samantha's usual "wake-up" call signaled breakfast was waiting for her. But Samantha's voice had a special excitement today.

Samantha's voice, along with the smell of rye toast, Canadian bacon, and freshly brewed coffee told her she was not dreaming. The growling in her stomach let her know she needed breakfast, and her grandfather was the master of the kitchen. Kathryn skipped her usual morning stretch. Coach Gepp told the team that stretching prevented injuries and a good breakfast was the foundation of a healthy soccer body. The coach must have been right; Kathryn had not missed a game from injury or sickness and had recorded perfect school attendance for the past three years.

The light of the early June sun squeezed though the curtains, warming her bed. As the summer rays washed over her extended limbs and twisting back, the tips of her hands touched the edges of the headboard while her toes reached the cool metal footboard. How odd that she could not recall ever extending and touching that far in all directions at the same time.

Ready for breakfast, Kathryn swung her legs over her head, carrying her body off the bed and to the bathroom. She grabbed her toothbrush, pushed down on the peppermint paste to cover the white bristles, and briskly gave her teeth their morning workout. Next, she dowsed her face in cold water before moving in the direction of the stairs.

Kathryn grabbed her hairbrush, started to run it through her thick mane, looked in the mirror, and for the second time that morning, she became puzzled. Why did she feel different, and how could she look different than she had the day before? Can the mirror lie?

First to greet her when she entered the kitchen was Samantha.

"Kathryn, you won't believe it, you just can't believe it. The best-ever cooking day in my life happened. Your fantastic, wonderful, smart, best pancake maker grandfather just shared his recipe with me. But before he did, I had to promise him I would never, ever, share the ingredients with anyone and he said, "Samantha it is our secret, you can't even share it with Kathryn!"

Samantha continued without a breath, "Well as you might have guessed, I promised. Let me make you a couple of MY pancakes."

Grandpa Hastings was all smiles. "I think I have a fan club. Only one member, but still, I have a fan club."

Samantha gave Kathryn a quizzical look, "Kathryn, you look different!"

"Good morning, Kathryn," was the welcome by her always cheerful grandfather. "Is that a new set of pajamas? They are the fanciest pajamas I have ever seen. Did you get them for your birthday?" He looked to Grandma Hastings saying, "Our Kathryn looks older today, in fact, she looks quite a bit different today. Did we feed her special vitamins yesterday?"

Standing up from the table, Grandpa Hastings announced he was off to the garage. He said to Kathryn, "You are now in the hands of the new breakfast chef." He picked up his mug of coffee—always one sugar and extra cream—gave Grandma Hastings a kiss and walked over to give his granddaughter a hug as he did every morning since moving into Kathryn's house.

Just as Kathryn sat down, Grandpa's eyebrows lifted as he observed some change. "Kathryn, now I know what is different, your hair color is lighter. It must be summer. I swear you do look different to me. How old are you? And Kathryn, when did you lose the green in your eyes?"

Grandma Hastings quickly responded, "She is thirteen and I am convinced she is quite a different person today than she was yesterday. My dear, do you agree?"

Kathryn answered her grandfather, "Grandpa, of course I am different. As has already been noted, I was thirteen years old yesterday. Your new, best buddy, Samantha the Chef, says we are now adults and should be treated as such. Samantha, is that correct?"

All Samantha could muster was a nod of her head. She was too engrossed in following the recipe, and she barely heard the conversation.

Both Grandpa and Grandma Hastings stared at Kathryn. Grandpa Hastings asked, "Kathryn, you somehow went from being a kid yesterday to a young lady today." He laughed and walked out of the kitchen to shine the real love of his life, his 1957 two-door yellow and white Chevy Bel Air which had been a part of his Sunday ritual for as long as Kathryn could remember. Samantha followed Grandpa Hastings to ask about an ingredient in his recipe with which she was unfamiliar.

Kathryn began to wonder about the odd "you look different to me" comments from Samantha and her grandfather.

Grandma Hastings continued to look at Kathryn, and then inquired about her sleep the night before.

Jerking her head up, "Why do you ask?" inquired Kathryn.

While asking the question of Grandma, Kathryn got up to get some napkins. Reaching into the pantry, she looked at the full-length mirror covering the inside of the pantry door.

She was shocked! The figure in the mirror looking back at Kathryn was not exactly the one she expected to see. Grandpa was right. First, Kathryn did not own the pajamas she was wearing, but she was sure she had worn them before. She blinked and saw a figure flash in her head. Somehow, she remembered them as a gift to her from a girl who wore a long fancy dress.

And her grandfather was right. Her hair was quite longer than it had been the day before, in fact, her hair was at least two shades lighter, as if bleached by a desert sun, and extended down her back, in contrast to the "just above the shoulder" length she had always worn. But the biggest change of all jumped out at her when Grandma Hastings walked up to her.

Kathryn, again with some surprise, exclaimed, "Grandma, I'm taller than you."

They both stood quietly as the two sets of eyes surveyed the pajama-clad figure in the pantry door mirror.

Grandma Hastings broke the silence, "Well dear, I do believe your grandfather was correct. Those must be new pajamas, and I just don't know when you grew taller than me in such a short period of time. When did you begin sporting a new hair-do?"

Grandma Hastings watched as Kathryn ran her finger along a thin scar between her shoulder and elbow. She continued, "My dear, I do believe you are a changed person."

She stared at her grandmother with a sense of disbelief at her words. Kathryn stared. And stared.

Grandma Hastings's eyes moved to the fingers on Kathryn's right hand. "Kathryn, how was the journey?"

Again, Grandma Hastings broke the silence, "Kathryn, we have much to talk about."

Taking a moment to assess the situation, Kathryn realized that her grandmother surely must know something about the morning's odd conversations, and certainly would not dismiss her dreams as those of a silly young girl. She considered what it was she proposed to say, wondering why anyone would take her seriously.

Kathryn's quizzical trance ended, and she spoke, "Grandma, I had the most unbelievable dream. It was so real; I feel like I have lived another life."

"Did you?" Grandma's asked with a hint of a smile, continued, "Would you like a cup of tea, dear? I will brew our favorite tea. Take a seat in the living room. I'll meet you there in a few moments."

Kathryn was almost always able to read her grandmother's face, a skill Kathryn had been able to depend on, but in this instance, it failed her. Grandma Hastings somehow had detected, rather, knew what Kathryn was going to tell her, as if she had been prepared for the moment at hand.

Kathryn felt relieved that her grandmother was willing to listen, and it was apparent Grandma Hastings was almost eager to begin the conversation. The suggestion of tea indicated the upcoming conversation was to be remarkable.

Grandmother Hastings always had tea before important events, and since the "tea in the living room" decision followed immediately after Kathryn's perplexed inquiry, maybe a family secret was to be unearthed.

Kathryn went into the living room and sat in her grandfather's favorite chair next to the big picture window. Grandma and Grandpa Hastings had positioned two chairs and a small oblong antique table from their bakery there "to observe the change of seasons."

Kathryn was puzzled. She was now taller than her grandmother, her eye color had changed, her hair was longer and a different shade than it had been a day earlier, and the silken pajamas she was wearing were as unfamiliar to her as they were to her grandparents—maybe.

She did not know if she should scream or cry.

Grandma Hastings walked to the table with a white tea kettle filled with her special tea. The aroma of honeysuckle filled the room. As Grandma Hastings filled the teacups, Kathryn noticed the ring on her grandmother's hand. She remembered a dream of a small cottage of remarkable colors and another place where cookies came from a special brick oven, and a bedroom of marble, all were places that served tea.

Grandma Hastings was smiling, "Kathryn, did you enjoy your adventure?"

With a gasp, Kathryn asked, "Was it real? How could you know?"

Taking a giant breath, Kathryn's words excitedly burst from her, "Oh Grandma, it was wonderful. I am not sure I understand all that happened, but I know that you can help me understand the special people in my life."

"Kathryn," Grandma Hastings directed, "have a sip of tea and I will explain most of what happened over the past two years."

With a gasp, Kathryn giddily asked, "Grandma, have I really been gone from you and Grandpa for two years?"

"My dear, you and I must go to the jeweler's this afternoon." Grandma Hastings looked at the pouch hanging from Kathryn's pajamas.

Kathryn looked down to see a small pouch tied to the cord of her pajamas. She untied the bag and pulled out an opal pendant with a broken gold chain.

Kathryn picked up her teacup and stood. She felt as if she were being pulled, positioned by some force to the middle of the living room's big picture window. She took a sip of tea, thinking how much she loved honeysuckle. She lifted her head and saw a familiar face framed by the sun standing in front of her house.

The Haglady was wearing a purple dress with yellow trim and a matching hat that had feathers sticking out of the band, and she was walking—no, floating—in front of the house, and in her hand was a vine of green leaves with yellow and white flowers.

The lady in purple hesitated for a moment, looked directly at Kathryn, and they exchanged smiles.

Kathryn looked down at the pendant dangling from her hand, and then at the Minnie Mouse watch on her wrist.

Kathryn, eyes filled with tears, looked up to see the lady.

But, the Haglady was no longer in sight.

Grandma Hastings walked in front of Kathryn and pulled her close.

Kathryn, content with what she now understood about her family, was also saddened she could not go to see the visitor of her dreams. Grandma Hastings answered Kathryn's questioning gaze, "Kathryn, let's talk."

Now in a lighthearted voice and stepping back, Grandma Hastings continued, "But first, before I answer all the questions you must have, I ran into Coach Gepp at the bank late yesterday. With him was a student who just arrived from Europe who will be attending your school."

Kathryn's eyes brightened. Her face blushed as if her hand had been kissed by a first love. With knowing anticipation filling her heart Kathryn asked Grandma Hastings, **"Is it true?"**

Grandma Hastings nodded, saying, "Yes my dear, his name is Stefano!" They both began to smile.

Thinking out loud Kathryn blurted, "I have got to talk to Samantha!"

But in a far-off land, and a distant time, ancient rumblings abound.

The abandoned donkey cart used by Abbadon and his kidnappers rests outside of Byzantium's Grand Bazar.

Grains of red sand covering the cart begin to quiver, coming together forming a red tunic. A faint heinous laugh vibrates from under the cloth.

***

Stories of Kathryn and the Haglady

Be sure to look for Kathryn as ***Enchantments*** take her to the Port of Alexandria. She will stand on the front paw of the Great Sphinx, climb the Great Pyramid at Giza, and visit with Cleopatra in the Pharaoh's Royal Quarter.

She will also travel to Florence, Italy and the "Eternal City" of Rome during the Renaissance, crossing paths with Leonardo de Vince, the Medici family, and other notables in AD 1500.

As Samantha always says:

"If your mind is open to what can be, anything can happen!"